She was solidly buil
like they'd been s
back very tightly and held in place with a long brown needle that I suspected doubled as an emergency stake. Her face was round, her skin was cocoa colored, her lips not too wide, and actually looked capable of smiling every now and then, which wasn't the case for a lot of female Body Men. They can be a pretty damned grim bunch.

As it happened, though, she wasn't smiling at that moment

She had me squarely targeted with the crossbow, and she was holding a gold inlaid wooden crucifix in her left hand. The thing was huge. In the 19th century they could have used it to drive railroad spikes.

I moved right, then left. The crossbow never lost its track of me, and then I saw a small laser target device mounted atop it. I looked down at my chest and sure enough, a little red dot was squarely over my heart. This was just getting better and better.

She still hadn't spoken. "Look, sister," I said, trying to seem more annoyed than anything, even as I felt barely controlled panic welling up within me. "You want to point that thing somewhere else? We're on the same side."

"Are we?" Her voice was light and sounded almost musical, which didn't exactly fit the moment.

"Yeah."

The crossbow sight staying fixed on me, she crossed the room quickly, came right up to me, and brought the crucifix forward. And unlike my mother, who just waved it at me to see if I would recoil while hissing angrily, this girl shoved the thing right up against my face.

I screamed.

Crazy Eight Press is an imprint of Second Age, Inc.

Cover illustration by Glenn Hauman
Design by Aaron Rosenberg
ISBN 978-0-9836877-3-3

First edition

Pulling Up Stakes

A Tale of Relenting Horror

Peter David

CRAZY 8 PRESS

One

My Dumb Ass Situation With My Mother

"Wake up. It's time to go out and kill something."

I moaned softly and pulled my blanket over my head.

"Vincent!" said my mother, Dina Hammond, and this time she reached down and shook me so violently that I was sure my teeth were rattling. "Vince, for God's sake! You haven't got all night!"

My head poked out from underneath the blanket like a turtle from its shell and I looked at her with bleary eyes. "I'm actually pretty sure that I do."

"Oh good. You're alive." My mother frowned in concern. "You've been sleeping through a lot of days lately."

"Well, I've been working nights."

"Let me check."

"Oh, Mom, for God's sake—"

"Let me. Check." There was no waffling in Mom's tone; nothing that indicated that there was going to be any wiggle room in the discussion or any possible negotiating of terms. You'd think I was fourteen instead of twenty-four. Although admittedly my room hadn't changed much since my teen years, with the same rock music posters clinging to the wall even though the bands had either broken up or gotten totally ass. There wasn't much clutter because Mom tended to be a like a python on a titmouse about such things, although I was lousy about remembering to hang up my weapons or secure my guns. They lay on the shelves, out and open and loaded. But it wasn't like we had kids in the house, unless you counted me.

"Go. Away." I retreated back under the black, scratchy blanket.

"Vince, damn it, I'm not screwing around any..." Her voice trailed off. Then, very coolly, she said, "Okay. Do what you want. Stay in bed. Waste your nights the way you waste your days. That's perfectly fine by me."

"Excellent," I said.

I remained where I was, hoping against hope that that would be the end of it. It was less than a minute later that I realized I should have known better.

That was how long it took for Mom to creep back into my bedroom, yank my blanket off my prostrate form, and shove a crucifix at my face, holding it an inch or so away.

I stared up at the large religious icon with a dead Jew immortalized in silver. I knew it all too well. It was my mother's, and had been her mother's before her, and before her, and so on and so on going back five, six, or seven generations. It was hard to be sure; my mother's story kept changing, depending on the point she was trying to make and how much she had had to drink. "Hey, look. I found Jesus."

Mom said nothing; her lower lip simply curled more intently as she waited to see if there would be some reaction from her son other than my being a smart ass.

"Seriously," I said, "the guy's been found more than Waldo. You know what Jesus needs? A Lojack. Then finding him would be way easier." When she didn't so much as crack a smile, I tapped the crucifix with my finger like a dying comedian. "Is this thing on?"

"All right, all right," said Mom, withdrawing the crucifix.

"Or maybe Jesus could use a GPS so he wouldn't keep getting lost in the first place and everyone wouldn't have to keep looking for him."

"You win, all right?" said Mom. "You're not turning. You're just a bum. Happy?"

"Ecstatic." But I knew that going back to sleep wasn't really an option, especially since Mom was continuing to stand there, glowering at me. Bowing to the inevitable, I sat up and set my stocking feet onto the floor.

"Since when do you wear pajamas?" said my mother.

"Since you started coming into my room and waking me up all the damned time....ow!"

That last exclamation came as a result of my mother's having grabbed a fistful of my shaggy black hair and pulled back on it. "*Ow*! Mom, what the hell!?"

"Just double checking." She studied my neck with expertise born of years of practice, checking with a mirror for extra certainty. She did it so casually that she might have been a concerned mother inspecting her son's head for signs of a tick, instead of my throat for twin puncture marks.

"Waving Jesus in my face wasn't enough?"

"I'm also trying to prove a point."

"What point? That you're a paranoid nut job?"

"That long hair can be your enemy." She released her hold and I rubbed the back of my head. "That's how that blonde stake-slinger bought it. One of those bastards grabbed her from behind, yanked hard, ripped her head off, and that was that for her."

A stake slinger was the derisive term Body Men used to describe anyone who did what we did but wasn't part of the proud order of the Chevaliers de Sang. The Knights of the Blood.

"Thanks, Mom. That was exactly the mental image I needed to kick off the day...night," I corrected myself.

"I'm just trying to keep you alive. I wouldn't be doing my job if I weren't trying that." She gently prodded me with the end of her cane. "Get the point?"

"I get it, I get it. Happy?"

"Never." The depressing thing was, she said that with all seriousness and meant it. "Now get dressed. I've gotten reports of a possible nest."

"Aw God." I moaned. "Another one?"

"They're like cockroaches."

"Yeah, well, scientists say cockroaches could survive nuclear holocaust, so I'm not loving our odds."

She slapped me on the shoulder. "Get dressed, come downstairs, and I'll go over the map."

My mother turned away from me then and headed out the door. As always, it took her a while to get there. The metal prosthetic that extended from out her right trouser leg afforded her balance, but not speed. I listened until the "clack-clack" of my mother's slow, measured step had receded and then I got out of bed.

I went into my bathroom and threw water on my face. After that I took a fast shower and then layered on the anti-perspirant, brushed my teeth assiduously and practically chugged the mouthwash.

I pulled on a pair of black cargo pants with plenty of pockets because that was what my line of work demanded, and a black t-shirt over my head that stuck to my still-wet chest. I emerged from the room and the smell of hamburgers grilling wafted up the stairs to me. I managed to steady myself after a minute, forced a smile, and trotted down the stairs.

Mom had just removed the burger from the grill. "I ate already, if that's okay with you," she said.

I shrugged. "Whatever," I said indifferently.

Mom tossed the burger carelessly onto a roll and placed it in front of me with a handful of potato chips piled on next to it. For Mom, that was a gourmet meal. The truth was, she was an indifferent cook. Dad was the gourmet in the family. Damn, I missed him.

I ate the burger resolutely, almost stoically. My mother looked at me askance. "Something wrong with it?"

"No, it's great," I lied.

"So," and Mom pulled a large black binder down from an overhead shelf. "The nest."

"Right, right. The nest." I put the remains of the burger aside. "What've we got?"

Mom sat down opposite me and flipped open the notebook. There was a copious list of dates, times, suspected movements. All of it was courtesy of an extended network called "questers." They were one step down from actual "cavaliers," which was technically the rank that Mom and I held. (Or at least it was the rank that Mom held before the accident that had rendered it impossible for her to go out into the field.)

But no one actually used the term "cavaliers" anymore. A more vernacular term had sprung up and been embraced by most of the newer generation: "Body Men," because when the bodies start piling up, we're the ones who come in to deal with it. Our elders had resisted the term at first and still refuse to acknowledge it officially, but they use it now, too.

Mom ran her fingers down the list of spottings and said, "Here. In the general vicinity of Broadway and Austin, between 10th and 30th. A body was found there, with the marks. A young girl. Tracy Manor. Five eight, brown hair, about a hundred twenty pounds. And if there's one," she said darkly, "there are sure to be more."

"Mom, that's..." I pulled out a map and unfolded it on the table. "That's a forty block radius."

"Give or take."

"And most of those buildings are pretty run down. A lot of them are abandoned."

"Exactly!" said Mom triumphantly. "The precise sort of place where vampires would be holding up."

"Still, that's a lot of territory to cover—"

"You can bring some questers with you. Have them help narrow the search..."

"No, no, it's okay," I said quickly. "They've done their job. Now I have to do mine." I shrugged in a resigned way. "That's just, y'know...what we do. What we *did*. What *I* do."

"Vince...it's okay." She rested a hand on mine. "I'm not oversensitive about the leg. I mean, yes, it was horrible when it happened, but I know my stalking days are over now. You're out there for the both of us. And when it's your turn to bring a child into the world, you'll train him or her in our line of work. These things go in cycles. It's your turn now and I don't resent that. I cherish it."

"Me too, Mom," I said tiredly. Somehow it just didn't seem worth worrying about or, at the very least, discussing. Then I looked at her kind of sideways and said, "The body they found. She was drained?"

She checked her notes. "No," and she sounded a little surprised. "Funny that they'd waste food like that."

"Yeah. Hysterical."

I suited up for the gig. Mom smiled as I strapped on the night vision goggles; she was a big fan of those. Under my black leather jacket I had my twin .45s, my preferred firearms because I'd grown up on the Shadow and the Phantom and shit like that and so I just felt like having twin .45s strapped across my chest was about as cool as it got. Silver bullets, of course. I had a cell phone fully charged in case I got into trouble, with a direct number I could call that would ring at the central headquarters for the Garrison.

I had my special stake securely tucked into its sheathe and made sure to hold it up so Mom could see it right before I headed into the garage. My cycle was waiting for me, an antique Harley, made back in the days when men were men, vamps were vamps, and cycles were cycles. I tapped the garage door opener and once the door slid up with its usual normal rattle, I roared out into the night. The night air blew my hair around like a son of a bitch, which was fine because there was nothing especially cool about wearing a helmet and I tried to avoid it whenever possible. Plus it's not as if I really needed it.

You might think that Body Men would operate together in one vast pack since we were all tight with each other. But the members of our particular division of the Chevaliers, Garrison Thirteen, (lucky number, I know) tended to operate as loners or in small groups at most. Getting a group of Body Men to agree on the best method of attack was typically like herding cats. I'd heard that some Garrisons managed it, and they could mount astoundingly devastating raiding parties. For the most part, though, the Body Men in our local Garrison tended to do our own thing, share up information as needed, and call for help if we suddenly found ourselves in over our heads. Of course, on those occasions that we *were* in over our heads, chances were that we'd be dead before there was an opportunity for backup to arrive. In any event there was no reason to start dragging questers into tonight's festivities.

It wasn't as if I didn't know where to go.

I made it over to the target area in short order, turned onto Broadway, and glided up the street until I reached 37th, then hung a right. Within minutes I had parked the Harley in an alleyway, locked it down, and set the alarm. Then I made my way down the alley, having no trouble seeing in the dark. I stepped over a random bum who looked up at me with bloodshot eyes and seemed too far-gone even to ask me for some money.

There was another, though, who had a bit more life to him. "Hey, fella," he said, and he held out his hand for money without even bothering to say what it was he wanted. It was pretty obvious. I tried to step around him but he actually had the nerve to grab at my leg.

I turned and drew back my lips, displaying my fangs while growling low in my throat. I sounded like an angry panther, or at least to my own mind I did. In real life I probably sounded more like a Volkswagen that needed a tune-up. For good measure I let my eyes go red, which hurts like a son of a bitch when you do it, but is good for effect if you want to really creep somebody out. It worked great in this case as the guy fell back, yanking his hands free from me and sputtering something that I couldn't make out and certainly didn't care enough to worry about.

Without giving him any more thought, I walked toward a solid metal door in the middle of the alleyway. The door and the wall were covered with graffiti, but if you listened, you could hear the steady throb of music coming from the other side. I rapped on the door three times.

A small window situated in the upper section of the door slid open. I saw a pair of gleaming red eyes peering through.

"Joss sent me," I said.

"You're hilarious," came an annoyed voice from the other side. "Name?"

"Vince."

"Vince who?"

"Vince I'm Gonna Kick Your Ass if You Don't Open This Door."

The guy on the other side sounded less than impressed. "Your name ain't on the list."

I closed my eyes and sighed softly to myself. "Tell Duncan that I'm here."

"That you're here."

"Yeah."

"And your name?

"*Vince, dickweed!*"

The little window slid shut again. I was tempted at that point to just rip the door off the hinges. Certainly I had the strength to do it. But this was Duncan's nest and I didn't see any reason to be a jerk about it, even if I was trying to do them a solid and they were busy acting like assholes.

A couple of minutes passed like an hour. I felt a wave of nausea seizing me that I couldn't resist, so maybe it was better that the guy at the door was being kind of a dick. I walked to the other side of the alley, allowed my stomach to do its business, and a few seconds later Mom's burger was decorating the floor of the alley. My mouth felt dry and I licked my lips. Then I looked down. A rat ran over my foot. I grabbed it, sucked it dry before it even had a chance to squeal, and then tossed it aside. It made me feel a little better, helping to cleanse my pallet, as it were.

The things we do to avoid upsetting our mothers.

Two

My Visit To Moveable Feast Gets Totally FUBARed

I heard the bolt being shot at the door and it swung open. The bruiser at the door stood there with his shoulders hunched and a face that looked like soggy Gouda, both in color and consistency. "Enter freely and of your own will," he said which is, y'know, what we typically say.

There's a myth, by the way (God knows there's so many of them) that we can't enter places if we're not invited. It's bullshit. Vampires used to be gentlemen, you see. Landed gentlemen, and frequently titled as well. An elite club of bloodsuckers. And they were polite, okay? It's really no more involved than that. If you've a shred of decency, training and class, you don't enter someone's house without being invited because, well, it's rude. That's all. Just fucking rude. They were vampires, not monsters. So they would wait to be invited in. Which isn't to say they couldn't kick down your door and stomp in if you told them to go screw themselves, but they wouldn't, because they were gentlemen. Bram Stoker got a ton of stuff wrong, and it may be kind of hard for modern audiences to wrap themselves around why women thought Bela Lugosi was swoon-worthy, but what he nailed was the elegance, charm and old world sensibility that once was common place, but now not so much.

People used to be classier, is all I'm saying. And vampires were the classiest.

Anyway, I walked in at cheese face's invitation. "Thanks loads," I said to him as he pulled the door shut.

He stared at me levelly and then held up a box of Tic-Tacs.

I looked at them suspiciously. "You got rat on your breath," he said.

Yes, we have breath, in case you were wondering. I don't get how people can think on the one hand that vampires don't breathe, and then on the other hand, they watch them on TV or in movies smoking a cigarette, or talking for that matter since you need air to produce sounds. It's not that we can't expel air; we just don't *have* to breathe. We just do it because we're used to it. Just like our hearts, which beat because we're accustomed to it. Most of the rest of our internal organs tend to atrophy pretty quickly, though. When was the last time you felt your spleen working? Or your liver? See what I'm saying?

I was tempted to tell cheese face to go screw himself and his mints, but, well, I *had* just sucked down rat. So reluctantly I gave a nod of thanks, took two breath mints and popped them in my mouth.

The music was pounding and bodies were gyrating on the dance floor as I made my way toward the back room, the DJ bouncing around like a lunatic at the far side of the room. The large room was almost blacked out, with stray red spotlights strobing through the place for atmosphere. It was a heavy metal beat and it took me a few moments to recognize the band. It was Slayer. The DJ had one sick sense of humor.

Cheese face guided me to a room in the back and there was Duncan, looking as laid back and reserved as he ever did.

Duncan had a shock of gray hair and a face like a hawk in flight, which seemed even more so because he typically leaned forward, although now that I think about it that just made him look like a gargoyle. His office was cramped, but what there was of it was decked out with velvet curtains and creepy antique furniture, like there'd been an explosion at Dracula's warehouse.

"Hey there, Vince Dickweed," said Duncan.

"What?"

"That's what Harvey said your name was," and he waved lazily toward cheese face. "But I figured out who he meant."

And your name? Vince, dickweed!

I gave cheese face, nee Harvey, my best glare. He managed to hide the fact that he was no doubt thoroughly intimidated.

Instead he smirked and walked away.

"Welcome," said Duncan, "to Moveable Feast."

"Is that what you're calling it now? Not Garden of Bleedin' or Bleedin' Eden anymore?"

"Yeah, that was too on-the-nose. Moveable Feast has more shadings. Plus I'm a Hemingway fan. You like it?"

I actually really did, but I just shrugged.

There were all kinds of rumors about Duncan. It was said he'd died a few times and kept coming back somehow. Some people said that he used to sleep in alleyways, zipped up inside a sleeping bag filled with dirt from his native soil.

Most modern day vampires used as role models various televisions shows or maybe *Lost Boys* (although no one aped *Twilight*. Sparklepires? Come on. Real vampires considered those books to be such a loose flow of unmitigated crap that they were typically referred to as Vampirrhea.)

Not Duncan. He wanted to be Dracula in the worst way, and most of the time, he was.

He was seated in what he probably thought was an ornate throne, but instead looked like something that was left over from a community theater production of "Camelot." He was wearing a blue velvet jacket, black pleated pants, and a ruffled white shirt. It was the kind of thing that you wanted to laugh at, except Duncan was a pretty decent guy and offered a huge support system for vamps. Sure, he had his eccentricities, but really, who didn't?

I glanced toward the curtained off area in the back and saw a gleaming black box. "New coffin?"

"You like? Custom made. Moveable Feast is paying major dividends."

"Coffins." I chuckled. "You really are old school."

He was wary. "Old school. But *not* Old Country. We both know that, don't we, my friend?"

"Sure we do."

His face twisted with disgust and I knew a rant was coming on. "Goddamn O.C.'s. You can have a perfectly good thing going, and then the O.C's show up with their attitude and their sense of entitlement, and suddenly the villagers are storming your castle with pitchforks and torches, you know what I'm saying?"

"Absolutely."

"Assholes." He shook his body like a dog tossing off water or maybe fleas and then turned his attention back to me. "So what brings you around, amigo?"

"A girl. Her body turned up with marks. Terry something..."

"You mean Tracy?"

"Yeah, yeah, that's it."

He shook his head and made a clucking sound, like a disappointed chicken. "Too bad about her."

"You knew her?"

He smiled like he was somebody's best uncle, or maybe Santa Claus balancing you on his lap while you told him what would float your boat for Christmas. "I know all the kids. Memory's still razor sharp, my friend. Tracy, she was your typical Wanna V."

I probably need to clarify here. Most people's idea of a vampire nest is bodies littering the place, or maybe terrified human beings trapped in cells, sobbing and screaming for release. And yeah, such places do exist. They're run by the O.C.'s and, like Duncan said, they're the kind of joints that bring the torch and pitchfork brigade down on your head.

But most of the nests of the Nu V movement, which was the popular vampire philosophy since around the 1960s or so, weren't like that. It used to be called the "True Blood" movement until Charlaine Harris cribbed the name for the drink in her books, which led to the TV series, and so to avoid any confusion they started calling themselves Nu Vs. And the Wanna Vs are an intrinsic part of the Nu V movement. (Speaking of Harris, you have no idea how many Wanna Vs have claimed that they were the basis for Sookie Stackhouse. It's gotten to be such a clichéd chat-up line that it's become a joke that all the vamps play along with. "*You're* the basis for *Sookie?* Really? Tell me more!")

Anyway, as the name implies, basically they wanna be vampires, and so they hang out at places like Moveable Feast and make themselves available, hoping that eventually someone will sire them or, to use the Nu V term, "sponsor" them. And the vampires feed on them. They don't drain them, you understand. That would be not only stupid but also gauche. You don't go to buffet and clean out the entire container of chicken wings. They drink enough to sate their appetites—a little Chinese, a little German, whatever they're in the mood for—and the Wanna Vs get a buzz and feel cool, and they're served orange juice and Fig Newtons and everyone has a good time. Vamps called it "grazing." I think it's a stupid term, but if people feel comfortable comparing themselves to cows then, you know, whatever.

And that's what this girl was, apparently. A Wanna V.

"Except she's dead," I said.

"Yes, I know," said Duncan. "Too bad. Arnold was just totally broken up about it. He thought she was the sweetest thing. He was even thinking of sponsoring her."

I didn't know Arnold, but at the moment I wasn't that interested. "Then what—?"

"It was just her time."

"I still don't—"

"It was one of those things, Vince," said Duncan, spreading his hands in a *What can you do* manner. "Arnold was grazing on her and everything was going fine, and suddenly Tracy cried out and grabbed at her chest and said she couldn't breathe and couldn't see anything, and then she just collapsed. Poor girl had a heart attack or a stroke."

"They're two totally different things, Duncan. Which was it?"

"Do I look like Ben Casey to you?"

"I don't know. Who's Ben Casey?"

"Never mind," he said with obvious annoyance. "All I know was, down she went like a box of rocks. Arnold knew she was a goner and was trying to sponsor her. He made the cut, he dripped blood into her mouth, but it didn't matter. She was already gone. And dead is dead."

That might sound kind of weird coming from a vampire, but I totally knew what he meant. People think we're walking dead guys, and we're not. We exist in a sort of between state. Not dead, not alive. You know on medical shows how you see people die and then they're brought back with electric paddles on crash carts? Being turned or sponsored or whatever you want to call it…it's just nature's version of a crash cart, except we don't quite come all the way back and we need constant jolts to keep going, but jolts of blood instead of electricity.

And it's just as easy to lose a convert as to create him. There aren't that many vamps who are one hundred percent reliable at turning. You know the axiom "One good turn deserves another?" Comes from vampires, from the old days where turning someone was seen as a good thing, a way of cheating death. So the person who'd been turned then had the responsibility to spread the good word and turn another.

This was back before the French Revolution, which was the first real vampire purge, cloaked as a social uprising. So many of the nobility were vampires that the citizens just decided to kill 'em all to play it safe. That's where the order of the Chevaliers first came from. They defined *sang froid* for generations to come.

"So it was accidental, is what you're saying."

"Completely," said Duncan, and I had no reason to disbelieve him. "Probably a pre-existing condition. Poor girl could have gone at any time. Just our bad luck that it happened on our turf. Where'd the body turn up? Bronx? Queens? Jersey?"

"Ten blocks away."

That was the first time in the conversation that the full weight of the problem dawned on Duncan. He'd been sitting with his feet propped up, but now he slowly lowered them, first the left, then the right, each with a thud. "Ten blocks away?"

"Yeah."

"From *here?"*

"You're starting to see the situation…"

"Son of a bitch!" roared Duncan, and he tossed aside the whole sunny uncle bit like it was a tattered blanket. "I'll kill him! I'll—*Raul!"*

You had to love the names of the guys who worked for Duncan.

There was a pattering of feet and a tall, angular dark-skinned vamp burst in. He was sloe of eye and slow of wit. "Yeah?"

"The girl. Terry…"

"Tracy?" I said.

He fired me an annoyed look and said, "Now you've got me

doing it. Yes, Tracy. The girl who died the other day, Raul."

"The one you told me to get rid of?" said Raul slowly.

"Yeah. Her. What did you do with her?"

"I got rid of her."

"Where?"

"Where?"

"What am I, talking to myself?" said Duncan with mounting annoyance. "Yes, where? Where did you dump the body?"

He scrunched his face as if trying to mentally reconstruct the entire evening. "Like…in an alley, I think."

"Nearby here?"

"Not…*right* nearby."

"*Jesus Christ!*" Duncan practically exploded. "What were you thinking? *Were* you thinking?"

"I dunno. I was heading out, and there was this really cute girl, and she was all, y'know, 'Hurry back,' and I didn't think she'd be here if I didn't hurry, so…I hurried," he finished lamely.

"Why didn't you just bring the cute girl with you on the job?" I asked.

He frowned. "Oh. Yeah, that would'a worked, I guess."

"So you…what? Tossed her in the trunk of the car, drove ten blocks, dumped her in an alley, and came back?" said Duncan.

"Yeah, pretty much."

Duncan moved pretty fast for an older guy. He came around the desk, grabbed Raul by the front of his shirt and slammed him up against the wall. "*You should have gotten her the hell away from here!*"

"You didn't tell me to!" Raul's tone was so whiny that I was tempted to just rip his throat out with my fangs myself.

"I shouldn't have to! What's the first rule of vampirism, Raul? What's the first rule?" And when Raul seemed too petrified to speak in the face of Duncan's ire, Duncan turned to me and said, "Vince? The first rule?"

"We don't shit where we eat."

"*We don't* shit *where we* eat," and he banged Raul against the wall on the two words he was emphasizing for good measure. "Even the O.C.'s know that, and they're dumb as mud. We don't leave a lot of bodies behind us, but if we do, we leave them *way* behind. Even Vince knows that and he's a newborn next to you."

Raul was trembling, and Duncan released him in obvious disgust. Raul cowered there, unsure of what he was supposed to do now, and Duncan said, "Let everyone know we're going to have to start packing up. Tomorrow's moving day. *Dammit,*" he added as Raul scurried out. "We *just* got this place the way we wanted it." He looked at me wearily. "Thanks for giving me the heads up on this, kid."

"Look, Duncan, maybe it's not as bad as all that. Maybe you don't have to take off. I mean, I'm the only one who's investigating this right now. I can take a few days, then go back and tell my mom that there's no sign of you guys. That you must have relocated."

He gave me a pitying look. "I'd like to go with that, Vince. I really would. But if the first rule of vampirism is not to shit where you eat, the second is that if your shit's scent gets caught, you're next. I can't take the chance. I owe it my people, and to my own neck, which I've come to care for a lot. Don't worry about us, we'll be fine."

"But where you gonna go?"

He looked amused that I sounded concerned. "Don't worry, kid. There's an abandoned hotel in Astoria I've had my eye on for a while. We can easily—"

That was when three things, none of them good, happened all at the same time.

First came the explosion that erupted from the general area of the front door. Something had blown the thing clear off its hinges. Even from where I was, it shook me to my fangs and caused some of the knickknacks that Duncan had around the place to tumble off their shelves.

Second came a series of small, rapid blasts, as if the entire place had been dropped into the middle of a gigantic popcorn popper. This was followed by a massive illumination of light.

Third came the howls of agony.

Vampires are nocturnal by nature. Despite what you may have heard, we can walk abroad in the sunlight. But we burn pretty easily. We're like redheads with fangs.

And our eyes are light sensitive. *Very* light sensitive. And we have extremely keen hearing as well.

Which is why when Body Men enter a nest, oftentimes the first thing they do is throw in flashbangs.

The flashbang, or stun grenade, was first developed in Great Britain in the 1960s and it has become an indispensible tool for Body Men. Basically a flashbang does exactly what the name makes you think it does. It generates a big flash of light accompanied by a very loud noise. The light flash overloads the receptors in the eyes and the noise disorients you, and if you're a human being you stand there or more likely fall down and flop around like a freshly landed carp for about five, maybe ten seconds. Which is all the cops need to slap the cuffs on you.

When you're a vampire, it's like being hit in the crotch with a sack of bricks that's been fired out of a cannon. You're not blinded for ten seconds. Your retinas are good and fried for a minute or two at the least, and your head is ringing for even longer. Not only that, but it makes your eyes go crimson and typically instinct kicks in and your fangs snap out. That makes it easy for Body Men to distinguish vampires from humans in case we're grouped closely together.

It was all happening incredibly quickly as screams were being cut short by squishing sounds, like mallets slamming into watermelons. I knew that particular noise all too well. It was coming from the dance floor that was now flooded with intense floodlights, courtesy of the raiding party, keeping the already blinded vampires off balance. Stakes were being driven into the chests of the denizens of Moveable Feast.

Yes, wooden stakes kill us.

I swear to God, I don't know why. Like I said, beating hearts are just old habits that many of us refuse to drop. Maybe it's because it's so hardwired into us that stakes can take us down that something in us just gives up. Some people claim it deflates us or something, although that doesn't answer why the heart is any better a target than any place else. Really, your guess is as good as mine, but long story short, if a stake gets slammed into a vampire's heart, it's game over.

I heard feet pounding up the stairs toward the office, turned to Duncan and said, "Out the window! Quick!"

"It has bars over it on the outside!"

"Well *that's* just lousy planning! Break 'em!"

"There's no time!" But even as he said it he ran to the window, smashed through the glass. There was no point in being subtle; whoever was coming up the stairs was moving pretty damned fast and was going to be in there in a second, maybe two.

I ran to Duncan's side and together we slammed our fists into the crossbars. The bars remained firm, but fortunately the mounting that held them in the windows gave way. The whole thing flew from the casement and just as Duncan was hauling himself out, a figure appeared at the door. I only had enough time to note that it was a woman and she was armed with a crossbow. If she saw me there helping a vampire escape, I was cooked. The room was too small. Quick as I was, I'd still never be able to avoid the shot. Not of a trained Body Man (women are called Body Men too, in case you were wondering.)

I took the only course open to me. The split second she filled the doorway, I had my stake already in my hand. It had just enough time to register on Duncan, and then I slammed the stake down with all my strength on Duncan's back, right above where the heart was. If the stake is long enough, you can nail a vampire from behind, and mine most certainly was.

Duncan screeched, his voice going higher and higher, almost sounding like a bat. I yanked the stake clear and Duncan tumbled forward, out the window, screaming all the way down before the sound of his body hitting heavily on the ground reached our ears.

I turned and faced the Body Man with as triumphant and non-fangy a smile as I could manage.

"I had it covered," I said.

I had no idea who she was. She wasn't local, that was for sure, nor was she alone, which—as I mentioned earlier—probably indicated that she and her people weren't from around here. It wasn't uncommon for out of town clans to show up on wide-ranging hunts. Garrisons weren't especially territorial. But it was usually considered good form to give the locals a heads up, kind of like registering a flight plan, so that no one crosses anyone up. I had literally gotten no memo about newcomers, and I wasn't thrilled.

She was solidly built, wearing tight black clothes that looked like they'd been spray-painted onto her. Her hair was tied back very tightly and held in place with a long brown needle that I suspected doubled as an emergency stake. Her face was round, her skin was cocoa colored, her lips not too wide, and actually looked capable of smiling every now and then, which wasn't the case for a lot of female Body Men. They can be a pretty damned grim bunch.

As it happened, though, she wasn't smiling at that moment.

She had me squarely targeted with the crossbow, and she was holding a gold inlaid wooden crucifix in her left hand. The thing was huge. In the 19th century they could have used it to drive railroad spikes.

I moved right, then left. The crossbow never lost its track of me, and then I saw a small laser target device mounted atop it. I looked down at my chest and sure enough, a little red dot was squarely over my heart. This was just getting better and better.

She still hadn't spoken. "Look, sister," I said, trying to seem more annoyed than anything, even as I felt barely controlled panic welling up within me. "You want to point that thing somewhere else? We're on the same side."

"Are we?" Her voice was light and sounded almost musical, which didn't exactly fit the moment.

"Yeah."

The crossbow sight staying fixed on me, she crossed the room quickly, came right up to me, and brought the crucifix forward. And unlike my mother, who just waved it at me to see if I would recoil while hissing angrily, this girl shoved the thing right up against my face.

I screamed.

Three

My Learning About the Major Thing Nobody Bothered to Tell Me About

And what I screamed was, "Get off my foot, you asshole!"

She looked down and saw that she was indeed crushing my toes with her black, steel-toed combat boots.

"Sorry," she said, and stepped back, but she still kept the crucifix against my face, really mashing it in there.

I sounded nasal because she was kind of shoving my nose to one side as I stared at her from either side of the tiny figure of the executed Jew. "Do you have *any* idea," I said with great forced calm, "how stupid you look?"

Okay…let's get the whole cross and crucifix thing out of the way right now.

A lot of vamps remain pissed off with Bram Stoker to this day about letting people know about stakes and beheading. But as far as I was concerned, Stoker more than made up for that by all of the misinformation he unwittingly spread. Crosses don't do shit. Neither do crucifixes, rosary beads, stars of David, or whatever other apotropaics (go look it up) you want to wave at us. Nor does garlic have any effect, although it does tend to put me in the mood for bruschetta. But if you're expecting that waving religious icons or cloves are going to repulse a vampire, you're going to be fatally disappointed.

For us, though, these stupid myths are of tremendous benefit, particularly in situations such as these. We've made damned sure throughout the decades to milk Stoker's bullshit for all it's worth. It lures Body Men or stake slingers into a false sense of security; they think they're protected and they fatally learn otherwise. It also means we can defy detection, which was exactly what was happening now. This girl could wait for me to flinch or shriek or start burning from now until sun-up and nothing was going to happen. Which meant that, as far as she was concerned, I couldn't possibly be a vampire.

Were I murderous, I would then simply wait for her to lower her guard, apologize for suspecting me, and then when she turned around, snap her neck like a twig.

Luckily for her I wasn't so inclined.

It was the weirdest thing, though. Someone else would have lowered the crucifix by that point, and muttered a sort of chagrined apology. Not this girl. Her eyes narrowed, and she continued to keep the cross pushed up against me, as if trying to will it to do something.

And then she said something that absolutely chilled me to the bone:

"Maybe crosses don't work against vampires."

There was a screech of panic in my head. The last thing any of us wanted Body Men to find out was that their defense of choice was in fact useless, because it was something that had given us an advantage any number of times. I certainly didn't want to be the one who blew the bit. If that happened, then there would be one of two results. Either this girl was going to succeed in killing me and live to spread the word to her pals. Or possibly—and I would prefer to think more likely—I would have no choice but to kill her in order to protect the others like me. I really didn't want to do that, because I hadn't actually killed a human being, ever. I was what the O.C.'s referred to as a virgin, and if that sounds as if they were being contemptuous, well, they were.

In order to try and hide my burgeoning anxiety, I adopted what I hoped looked like a casual pose and said, "Okay, fine. Test your theory."

"Test it?"

"Yeah. Kill me. You've got the crossbow. You've got me targeted. And if you're right, and I'm a vampire and crosses don't work against me, then I'll turn into some desiccated corpse and you can carve another notch in your stake. On the other hand, if hundreds of years of vampire lore turn out to be right and you're wrong, then you get to explain to your Garrison heads why you decided to murder a guy in cold blood who was just standing here."

And slowly, very slowly—I'm telling you, there were glaciers that moved faster than this girl—she lowered her crossbow, although she seemed prepared to bring it to bear in a split second. She was smart to be so cautious; even though I wasn't a threat to her, there were plenty of my kind who would have been. "You're one of us?" she said.

"Sure. What did you think?"

"Could have been a stake slinger. Can I see yours—?"

"My stake? I'd…rather not," I said and patted the hip holster into which I'd slid it. "It was my dad's and it's…well, it's kind of personal. I don't like other people to touch it."

"Fair enough," she said, which was generous of her considering that it sounded like total bullshit to me. "Your father was a Body Man?"

"Dad, Mom. Uncle. Cousins. My brothers and sisters would be if I had any." I stuck out my hand. "Vince Hammond."

Her eyes widened as if she were incredibly startled, and then she laughed. "You're Vinnie Hammond?"

"I kind of prefer Vince, but I'll pretty much answer to anything, and what's so funny? Does my reputation precede me and it's a really lame-ass reputation?"

"No, no, not at all. I've heard you do good work," she said quickly. "It's just…well…this is kind of bizarre…"

"I like bizarre."

"I'm…" She tapped her own chest and seemed as if she was on the verge of making the greatest joke in the history of humanity. "I'm Amber."

"Okay."

"Amber Singer."

"Okay," I said again, not having come up with anything particularly clever to add since the last time I'd said "Okay."

She seemed confused that I wasn't reacting in the way that she obviously thought I was supposed to. "You don't understand…"

"Yeah, but it's not your fault. Not understanding is kind of my default response."

"I'm *Amber Singer,*" she said, clearly thinking that the name was supposed to mean something to me. I was starting to feel a little paranoid. How could I possibly not know who she was when she so obviously thought that I should. One of us had to be completely wrong, and if history was any indicator, it was probably me. She went on, "Your father...I heard about when he was killed, and I'm so sorry. But surely he must have told you before it happened."

"Told me what?"

"Uhm...okay," and she put up her hands, palm out, in a cautioning manner. "Promise not to laugh."

"No problem."

"I'm..." She hesitated, took a deep breath, and then as she exhaled the words she'd been struggling with came out: "I'm your Bond Mate. Your fiancée."

I laughed. I knew I had promised that I wouldn't, but it just seemed so funny to me that I couldn't help myself. But then I saw the look on her face and I stopped laughing. "You're serious."

"Yeah."

"You're *serious?*"

"Well, my folks are, that's for sure. I know the whole thing may sound ridiculous, but..."

"No!" I jumped in quickly. "There's no 'but' after that. It's ridiculous, and that's where it ends."

"Except it's *not* going to end that easily, Vince!" said Amber. "My parents are really old fashioned when it comes to these kinds of customs. And they figured your dad was the same way when he agreed to the marriage..."

"He *agreed* to it!?" I felt like my head was swimming, as if the entire world had stopped making sense. "No way. No freaking way. Where the hell does he get off, thinking he can just unilaterally stick me with some...some..."

The line of her jaw hardened and there was an unmistakable undertone of danger in her voice. "You'd better think long and pretty damned hard before you complete that sentence, Vinnie."

Realizing that I had overstepped myself, and reminding

myself that I was just giving her even more incentive to discover I was a vampire and drive a stake through my heart, I mentally tossed aside the word I'd actually been about to use, and just as quickly dumped the second, third and fourth words as well. "'Stranger' is what I was going to say, Amber." I saw an ever-so-slight relaxation of her shoulders, but she still looked distrustful and on edge. "That's what we are, you and me. Strangers. How can anyone expect two strangers to get married because their parents cut a deal?" It was madness. I kept expecting someone to start singing "Sunrise, Sunset."

"First of all," said Amber, "it's how *my* parents wound up together, and that turned out all right. And they just wanted me to honor the traditions that worked for them, and their parents before them. It's how our Garrison has been operating for generations."

"Yeah, I know that, but this is the 21st Century. You're a modern woman. How can you be cool with this?"

"Modern women don't all think with the same mind, *Vinnie,*" and she stressed the name enough to make it clear that now she was calling me that to piss me off. "Some of us have respect for traditions."

"Amber—"

She put her finger to my mouth to shush me. The very tips of my fangs were protruding and I withdrew them as fast as I could. She didn't notice them, thank God. "Look...no one's going to force me to marry anybody I don't want to marry. And I have no intention of insisting that you honor agreements your father made, especially considering he apparently didn't tell you about them. That's your 21st century woman for you."

"I appreciate that."

"But," she continued, "I also have enough respect for my parents that I'm not just going to tell them to go to hell. They're two of the bravest, most dedicated people I've ever known. They've certainly earned my at least giving their opinions a chance when it comes to something as important as this."

Part of me wanted to think that she was making sense. The other part of me felt like she was getting on my nerves. Who the hell has that kind of relationship with her parents? I sure didn't.

Even when they were both living and things were at their best, my parents frequently got on my nerves.

Figuring that this wasn't exactly the best time to make an argument out of it, I shrugged and said, "Okay, well…whatever." I was trying to sound cool about it. She gave me one more brief, uncertain look and then turned and headed out. Not seeing any other choice, I followed her.

It was mind-numbing to witness the aftermath of the chaos that had been unleashed on Moveable Feast. There looked to be about half a dozen Body Men in addition to Amber. They had found a central light switch and now all the overhead lights were on. There were nine, maybe ten Wanna Vs milling around, mostly girls and one or two guys, clustering together for imagined security, whining and simpering and some of them moaning the names of vamps that had fallen. And there were plenty who were fallen, all right. There was cheese face from the door, with several gaping wounds on his torso; apparently he had gone down fighting and one stab hadn't gotten the job done. But Raul, he was good and gone, lying there with a rictus of permanent confusion etched on his face. And many other vampires were lying around as well. I was certain, though, that there were fewer bodies scattered around than had been there when I first arrived, which led me to believe that some had escaped.

I felt like my mind was splitting right down the middle. Not all that long ago, I would have been one of those killers who was moving through the room with the swaggering pride of sportsmen who had just brought down a ten point buck. Yet now all I could do was feel sorry for the poor blood-sucking bastards who had been minding their own business, grazing upon donors who had been all too willing.

It was those donors, the Wanna Vs, who were now the main point of interest for the man who looked to be the leader of this bunch. He was tall, powerfully built with pale skin and blonde crew cut, like an oversized G.I. Joe come to life. But when he spoke he had a faint Austrian accent, giving him a definite Arnold Schwarzenegger vibe. "I never understand you sick bastards," he said, circling the cowering Wanna Vs who still looked in shock over all that they had witnessed. "What kind of spell do the demons cast over you? Why do you enable them? Why are you willing to just stand there and let them suck you dry?"

One of the guys rallied in the face of this total stranger who was throwing around attitude as if he had cornered the market on it. The pimply faced, gangly loser said, "You don't understand, you...you murderers! You don't understand how they make us feel!"

"You're the ones who don't understand," said the Body Man. "We saved your lives. And if you had a lick of sense and an ounce of gratitude, you'd be thanking us for what we did instead of defending those things."

"*They're* not things! *You're* the things! Unfeeling, uncaring—!"

Suddenly he stopped talking, which was understandable considering that the large Body Man had clamped one of his oversized hands on the kid's throat. The guy gurgled and his face looked like curdled yogurt.

"You," he said in a gravelly voice, "don't know what you're talking about. I've been doing this since before you were born and, if you're not careful, will still be doing it long after you're dead. Now what other nests do you know about?"

The guy he was questioning wasn't exactly in a position to respond considering his air was being choked off, and one of the girls cried out, "We don't know about any other nests!"

"How did you find this one?"

"Word gets around."

"How?"

The girl didn't answer. The Body Man didn't let up his grip on the guy but turned his attention to the girl. Her legs were starting to tremble and she looked like she couldn't decide whether to pass out or upchuck.

My nose was sharp enough to perceive what the Body Man didn't yet realize; the girl was so terrified that she had just wet herself.

The hell with it. Right then I didn't care if my own neck was on the line or not.

"They get it off the Internet," I called out.

The Body Man noticed me for the first time. He released his

grip on the guy, who sagged backwards and would have collapsed if several of his pals hadn't clustered together to stop him from falling. "Who are you?"

And that was when Amber said four words to this utter bad ass that confirmed all my worst fears: "Dad, this is Vinnie." That four word death sentence was followed by, "Vinnie, this is my dad, Lawrence Singer."

Terrific. My planned future father-in-law had Helter-Skelter eyes and the personal charm of a rabid tiger.

"Pleasure," I said with a joviality I did not remotely feel.

"You? You're—" He cut himself off. A thorough professional, he wasn't about to let this rather odd introduction to his daughter's intended distract him from the business at hand. "The Internet?"

"Of course." I sauntered in leisurely fashion down the short stairs that led to what had once been the main dance floor and was now instead a killing field with disco lights. "It's not like they have to run from door to door, handing out notes. They have a website somewhere that can only be viewed by members. One of the members is the Alpha vamp who runs the nest. He puts out word where their new place is and they come running."

"How do you know?"

"Because one of our people found one about three years ago. The site keeps moving but we keep finding it. Right now it's MIA, but we'll turn it up again."

Lawrence shifted his gaze to the terrified Wanna Vs. "Which means these pathetic creatures know where the current one is."

"We don't know anything!" said one of the girls.

"We'll find out about that," he said.

"Dad, come on," said Amber. The motley crew of other Body Men remained stone faced, but Amber was obviously becoming increasingly uncomfortable.

"These people are potential leads, Amber."

And now I had taken all that I was going to take. Perhaps my strength came from knowing that—if push came to shove—I could gut this guy before he knew what was happening. It would naturally blow my secret to everyone else standing there. On the other hand, disemboweling him in front of his daughter would certainly solve the whole engagement problem. So it would be a wash.

I covered the remaining distance between us and stood less than a foot away from him. He was a head taller than I was, and I tried to look as commanding as I could, considering I was craning my neck to look him in the eyes. "These people are private citizens who have committed exactly no crimes. And you're not a cop even if you had caught them doing something wrong. Being a Body Man doesn't give you any legal or moral authority or the right to be a bully, and it certainly doesn't give you the right to torture somebody..."

"Who said anything about torture?" he said sharply.

"Unless you're planning to pry information out of her over dinner and a show," and I indicated Miss Pee in her Pants with a tilt of my head, "that's obviously what we're talking about here. I don't know how it works where you come from, but in our little corner of the world, we don't go around beating information out of humans."

"They're accomplices."

I didn't shift my gaze from Lawrence Singer but I was addressing the Wanna Vs, as I said, "Leave. The lot of you. Leave right now. And so help me, Larry," I kept talking before Amber's dad could say anything, "if you have your people block the door, then we're going to have a situation. And that's not exactly the way to make your introduction to Garrison Thirteen. Because they'll back me on this and you won't like how the hearing goes down."

He stared at me with a level gaze that seemed to be dissecting me. He was wearing a loose fitting black coat, and he suddenly reached into the inside pocket. I braced myself, certain that he was pulling a weapon, uncertain to what use he was about to put it. Just how far gone was this guy, anyway?

He withdrew a small stack of business cards. Then he turned back to the Wanna Vs and his entire tone and body language shifted. Instead of being towering, threatening, a presence more terrifying than the supposedly monstrous vampires had ever been for these kids, he transformed into a calm, rational sounding individual, a guidance counselor only concerned about their best interests.

"At some point," he said gently as he handed cards out to each of the Wanna Vs, "you may reach the realization of just how close you came to walking a horrific path to damnation. Don't believe what you've read. A tendency toward vampirism is not something that is ingrained into you from birth. It is a lifestyle choice, and not a choice that you should be making. There's a phone number on there for counseling services that we provide. I strongly, *strongly* suggest you take advantage of it. Thank you for your patience and my people will see you out. Pray that we do not meet again under circumstances that I assure you will prove fatal for you if you make the wrong decisions with your lives."

I let out a sigh of relief. I'd been concerned that Lawrence had embraced the Hitler Youth philosophy. No, not *that* Hitler Youth. The Hitler Youth was one of the more radical schools of thought in the Garrison. You know the old philosophical conundrum about, if you had the opportunity to kill Hitler as a child and possibly avert World War II, whether you should do it? The Hitler Youth movement for the Body Men who embraced that philosophy was that Wanna Vs were all youthful Hitlers. They weren't in a position to hurt or kill anyone yet, but given time and a turn, they would be. So the smart thing was simply to kill them while they were still humans and so avoid the problem down the line.

This had been a hot topic for debate. The local Garrison to which I belonged didn't embrace that philosophy. We were a Modernist Garrison, officially. Modernists were sort of middle of the road, striking a balance between the radical reform beliefs of the Avant Guard (yes, that's how they spell it) and the stuck-in the-18th-century philosophies of the Old Guard (which is why the A.G.s spell it "Guard" instead of "Garde." It's a sort of response movement to the Old Guard.)

I could tell that Singer and his people were definitely Old Guard, and that made them extremely dangerous. They couldn't be reasoned or bargained with. Vampires were absolute evil and the Body Men were absolute good, and all the old ways were to be followed without question.

It was in the Old Guard movement that the Hitler Youths resided, but apparently Larry here wasn't a student of that particular school of thought. Or if he was, he wasn't about to indulge in it in front of me.

His cards distributed, Lawrence's people were guiding the shell-shocked Wanna Vs out of a place that many had come to regard as a second home. Pulsing with life and joy only minutes earlier, it was now nothing but a house of death, filled with the semi-mummified corpses that the deceased vampires left behind.

"Clean up crew, you're up," called Lawrence, and in walked several guys with flamethrowers and fire extinguishers and wearing gas masks. I had to admit, his crew was efficient. Wearing rubber gloves, they pulled the various corpses together to create a pyre, but it was going to be a controlled burn so that the building didn't go up in flames. Clean up crews were informally referred to as ghost toasties. I don't know why. It's just something we do as Modernists. Or maybe it's just something I do because I like to screw around. Hard to say.

"Mr. Hammond," he said, and stuck out his hand. I shook it. I was strong enough to crush his hand, and yet it seemed like he was in fact capable of pulping mine. He radiated the sort of confidence that only someone absolutely convinced he was morally superior to just about everyone could muster. Even when not threatening other people, his voice was deep and resonant. "We have much to discuss. A tragedy about your father. He was a good man."

"Thanks."

"And it is only to the son of such a man," and he draped his arm around Amber, "that I would trust my little girl."

"Daaaaad," and Amber rolled her eyes in that universal manner that only the patiently mortified daughter can.

"I'm sure that Mr. Hammond here understands what I'm talking about."

"Honest to God, Mr. Singer, I have no freaking clue at all what you're talking about. No offense intended, but my father never said a thing to me about a fiancée and—again, no offense—I'm not especially sure I'm ready to get married."

"That's because you haven't gotten to know Amber. Trust me, once you do, you'll—"

"Captain," said one of the guys with the flamethrowers. "We're about ready for you."

Lawrence was holding a gas mask in one hand and extending another to Amber, who took it from him. "Do you perform rites?" he asked.

"Rites? You mean, like, may their souls rest or be welcomed into the kingdom of heaven?"

He stared at me with undisguised bewilderment, and then his voice dropped even lower than it had been as he said, "You have a sharp sense of humor, Mr. Hammond. Vampires have no souls. Everyone knows that."

Inwardly I bristled at the off-hand dismissal. Despite the dire nature of the situation—I was still vastly outnumbered, surrounded by Body Men who functioned with military precision, thus making the odds nothing that I was especially wild about—I wanted to tell him that he had no idea what the hell he was talking about. That it was this exact kind of backward thinking that made it impossible for us to live together, and allowed the extremist thinking of the O.C.'s to determine the nature of vampire/human relationship. But there was no point in my making an issue out of it, because I didn't need them wondering why I was suddenly so defensive about vampires in general. These were not people that you wanted to have suspicious of you, especially when you had as much to hide as I did.

Taking my silence for acknowledgment of my hilarious comedy instincts, he continued by way of explanation, ""We perform specific rituals while their bodies burn that ensure these demons never find their way back out of hell and into new hosts."

What I wanted to say was, *My God, what a big steaming pile of Old Guard bullshit.* What I actually did say was, "That's...a good idea."

"We find it more effective than simply cutting off their heads."

"I would think so."

Amber explained, "It has to be done while they're burning. Smoke inhalation's a real danger."

"I bet," I said, and nodded, and remained where I was, and then remembered that I was supposed to be concerned about the prospect of my lungs collapsing. "Okay, so I better get outside. Maybe give my mom a call and tell her that her future in-laws are in town."

"Excellent idea," said Lawrence Singer, who then expectantly looked down at his daughter. "Amber?"

Amber paused only an instant and then she went to me, pulled my head toward her so that I was closer, and kissed me chastely on the cheek. It was actually kind of sweet. She smelled good, like a homicidal baby seal. Then she slid her gas mask into place.

I headed toward the door, tilting my head slightly to the ghost toasties as I exited, and went out into the alleyway. I considered calling the police so they could show up and demand explanations for what the hell they had just stumbled upon, but I decided not to be a total creep about it.

As I backed away from the scene of the crime, I looked down the alleyway carefully, trying to see some sign of movement. Then, from behind me, I heard a voice croak, "You! You're a monster!" I whirled and saw the old man, the derelict I'd flashed my fangs at without considering the possibility that a squad of vampire killers were going to pop by for an evening's entertainment. He was pointing at me, his finger quivering. "Those guys who went in there…they kill your kind!"

"Look," I started to say, "I'm sorry if I scared you, but—"

He wasn't listening. Instead he cupped his hands to either side of his mouth and began to shout, "*Get out here! You missed one! There's another monster, standing right here!*"

And suddenly someone grabbed him from behind, one hand clamping over his mouth, the other holding his shoulders firmly. There was a sharp twist and a loud crack, and the old man went down without another sound. His words had not been heard from within, because they were too busy wasting their time in pointless rituals.

He had that same, stupid look on his face that I've always seen on people when they die unexpectedly. Kind of, "Now? It's now? Now is when I die? Well, that sucks." Like if they had managed to live just one more day, that would have been the day that made all the difference and given their empty lives some kind of meaning and purpose and made sense of it all.

The old man, who would become no older, slid to the ground, and standing behind him was Duncan. He looked down at the old man with annoyance and then to me. "Were you just going to stand there and let him blow the whistle on you? What the hell is going through your head?" Then he reached down, picked up the old man and chucked him into the shadowy recesses of an open dumpster.

"What was going through my head is that I didn't just want to kill the guy in cold blood."

"Then you've got to get your head out of your ass and start prioritizing. First of all, when it comes to either you or him, you vote for you. Second, how can you not have smelled that he was dying anyway?"

"Huh—?"

"Cancer. Rectal, by the stink of it. He had a couple of months of agonizing pain to look forward before he wound up in digs not much better than this." He walked over, closed the dumpster's lid, and then said, "Let's go before they come out."

He started walking and I quickly fell into step next to him. "I can't. They're from out of town and they know me and if I suddenly vanish, it's going to raise all kinds of questions..."

"Jesus, Vince, when are you going to realize it's not your life anymore? When are you going to cut ties with it? Tell your mother..."

"Tell her what? That I converted? You know what'll happen then."

"Living a lie isn't living at all."

"I'm undead. I'm not doing much in the way of living anyway."

We stopped at the far end of the alley and Duncan turned to face me. "Come with me, Vince. You'd be invaluable to Moveable Feast, and to vampires everywhere. You know all the inside workings of the Chevaliers. More than that, you're someone who's got vision. You're able to plan, to anticipate. You knew enough to start packing that special stake for exactly these kinds of emergencies."

"What, Mister Shaft?" I said. I had pulled out the stake and was pushing the pointed end against my palm. It retracted into the inner recesses of the hollow shaft on the spring-loaded mechanism I'd devised. It didn't do so automatically; I needed to be pressing in on the carefully camouflaged trigger hidden in the top. That way it could pass casual inspection and still seem like a normal, vamp-slaying stake.

"Exactly. If you teamed up with me, you could employ all your expertise, all your experience, and improve and extend and save the lives of your people. Your *real* people, Vincent," and he rested a hand on my shoulder. "If you're smart enough to anticipate needing a trick stake to carry around, then you're smart enough to know that you're not going to be able to keep this up forever. Sooner or later your mother is going to realize what you are. You think there haven't been millions of guys in a position similar to yours about any number of things?"

"I'm not stupid, Duncan. I get the metaphor. But..."

"You know what?" and he put up his hands. "There's no point discussing this with you now, I see that. Just keep this in mind: I know you for what you are and accept both sides of you, even though I think you're totally delusional thinking that you can keep it going. But those people—your mother, those murderers in there—they wouldn't exactly be so understanding now, would they."

I didn't say anything. I didn't have to.

"There's going to come a time," said Duncan, "when you have to realize who your friends are, who your enemies are, and who your real family is. You try to have it all, and you're going to wind up with nothing."

"That's deep," I said, trying to sound sarcastic, but he was right and I knew he was right and, worse yet, he knew that I knew it.

He didn't even have to say any more. He just shook his head, turned on his heel and walked away.

No, we don't turn into bats either. Believe me, though, if I could have transformed into some small, flapping rodent and disappeared into the night sky, I would have done it in a heartbeat.

Four

My "Origin," Such as it is

My earliest memory of my father, Boris Hammond, was when he was sitting there looking straight at me, and I was in my high chair, I think, and he said, "Just remember: Everyone in the world is ignorant except you."

I had no idea what he was talking about. But in my defense, again: high chair. When you're talking about someone whose feet don't touch the ground while he's sitting, I think that someone is entitled to a little slack.

He didn't mean that I was smarter than he was, or Mom, or anyone else in our Garrison of the Chevaliers. By "you" what he meant was me in my capacity as a young Body Man in training. And when I say "in training," I'm not just kidding around. What I didn't mention was that when I was sitting in that high chair, I wasn't waving around a kiddie knife or spoon. I had a little plastic stake and Dad was in the process of showing me the proper way to thrust it. He was drilling the muscle memory into me literally as far back as I can recall.

I never went to public school. None of the kids in our Garrison did. We lived a very insular, very isolated life. When I was growing up there were about thirty families in our Garrison, and we were as tightly knit a group as you could possibly imagine. We didn't live in a compound, although some Garrisons did. Instead all of us resided within a five-block radius of each other down in the Village, in apartments that had been owned by the Garrison for close to sixty years.

Social services didn't know what to make of us. All of us

were home schooled, and they would have had an easier time understanding us if we'd been, say, Chassidic Jews or something. They couldn't quite make out what our deal was, but they had no basis upon which to lay claim that our parents weren't doing a top-notch job with us. Our respective families excelled in giving us a well-rounded education, although it wasn't as if any of us were college bound. And naturally we were all in terrific athletic condition. We had to be on the top of our game physically if we were going to be able to hold our own against beings that were far stronger than we were.

The Garrison managed to support itself through a variety of means. First of all, let's just say that there were some rather wealthy, highly placed individuals in the city who were aware of what we were up to. These were alliances going back many years, formed out of gratitude when our people came in and rescued family members of the rich and famous from the "evil clutches" of vampires while the police stood around helplessly and declared that such things couldn't possibly exist.

Also we managed to filter word through the underground that if every day, street level folks found themselves facing situations that were beyond normal understanding—the kind of thing they'd be too embarrassed to bring to anyone else—that Garrison Thirteen was willing to help them out. Every so often we'd get an undercover cop trying to draw us out, but we'd gotten pretty good at sniffing out those types and so we'd play dumb until such plants went away.

And finally, we'd roll the bodies of any vamps we killed, which would help with day-to-day petty cash type considerations. Why not? You can't take it with you. Trust me, I know, because I've seen plenty of people depart empty handed.

All the money the various families earned, along with the generous financial support from our sponsors, was put into the Garrison's central fund and stipends were then generated. I suppose some people might scream that it was socialism or communism, but when the chief "ism" that occupies your life is vampirism, you don't really give much of a shit about all the others.

My best friend growing up was a guy named Scotty Daniels. Scotty was five years older than I was which, at that age, can be a vast gulf. But Scotty was an only child like me, and he treated me like the kid brother that he never had. If for some reason Dad didn't have the time to work with me, then Scotty took charge of my training. If Dad and Mom were out on a job, Scotty would keep an eye on me until they returned.

Funny. It never occurred to me that there might be a job from which Mom and Dad might not come back. Or that Scotty, with that swaggering walk and utterly confident air, might ever not be there.

The Scotty incident happened when I was fourteen. It started innocently enough: Scotty was out on a job and he was overdue returning. This in and of itself wasn't necessarily anything to be alarmed about. Vampire hunting wasn't an exact science and a job could extend to a week or more depending upon what's involved. But when Scotty went missing for two weeks, word began to rumble through our little community. I heard all about it, of course, but I was still positive that everything was going to turn out just fine.

Not so much, as it happened.

I would love to tell you that I never saw Scotty again. But that was not the case.

We have a place of worship that we refer to as the chapel. The Chevaliers de Sang have no official denomination. We endeavor to be inclusive, and so we have what is simply called Sunday Gathering, which runs about an hour and is almost more like AA meetings than services. "I'm Bob, and I killed two vampires last week and am pleased that my God gave me the strength to accomplish it." "Hi, Bob!" That kind of thing.

A full month after Scotty disappeared, we were informed there would be a Friday Gathering. That was never a good sign; a Friday Gathering meant that something really, really bad had happened in our community.

We came together as we were supposed to. The Garrison President was, and is, a guy named Jeremiah Salk. He's British, so how he wound up with us is anybody's guess. He's kind of round, with a face that looks like it was mashed with a frying pan, and a bulbous nose and a voice like a foghorn.

Salk made no attempt to explain to us why we'd come

together or prepare us in any way for what we were about to see, although the adults sure looked like they'd been prepped. They spoke to each other in low voices, whispers, that none of us could overhear no matter how much we strained to.

Then a door opened at the far side of the chapel and a coffin was brought in. It was a simple pine box, carried on the shoulders of several pallbearers. And by now you'd be thinking, Oh, it's a funeral, except the occupant of the box was banging around inside and hurling profanities and promising all manner of vengeance.

And my heart sank, because I knew that voice. I'd been hearing it my entire life. It was Scotty.

The coffin was set upright at an angle so that we could all see it, and the lid slowly removed. There was Scotty, tied up practically head to toe except for an area right across his chest that was exposed. He was struggling furiously to break the ropes, but they were far too thick and securely fastened around him. His eyes were wide and wild, and as he howled his fury, the glistening fangs protruding from his lips were visible to everyone.

All of us kids cried out in shock and horror at what had happened to him, but the adults remained deathly silent. With everything I've seen before and since, that remains the single eeriest moment of my life.

Then Scotty seemed to gain control, like he was noticing us for the first time. The fangs retracted and suddenly there he was, back with us, like this was all some big practical joke.

"Listen to me," he started to say desperately.

But Jeremiah Salk stepped forward and spoke in that arch, stentorian voice, "Behold the face of the enemy. He may look like our friend, talk like our friend—"

"*Will you shut up*!?" Scotty shouted at him.

"—but he is not our friend," continued Salk, unperturbed, as if Scotty hadn't even spoken. "He is the result of a moment of carelessness upon our friend's part. Or worse, a weakness of spirit that caused him to drink of the forbidden fruit..."

Scotty gave him a look of disgusted disbelief. "Oh my God, could your metaphors be *any* more mixed? I always thought you were an idiot, Jerry, but thanks for removing any doubt."

This actually prompted a few snickers and guffaws from some of the kids, but they quickly silenced themselves when Jeremiah Salk gave them an angry glare. "This is the fate," and he waved toward Scotty, "of anyone of you who is careless enough to get sloppy, or fascinated enough by the sinful allure of that which we battle. Do not let yourself be drawn into this deviant lifestyle."

"You have no idea of the lifestyle, Jerry," said Scotty, and there was a desperate pleading in his voice, trying to get across to all of us his point of view and knowing—he *must* have known—that it was a lost cause even as he spoke. "There's so much you can't begin to understand. You think we're these demonic killing machines, but we're not, I swear to you, I swear to God—"

Salk slapped him across the face as hard as he could. "Do not mention the Lord's name! It is blasphemous from your lips!"

"Then let Him strike me down. He has that right. Not you."

"He *is* striking you down by using the strength in our arms and our spirits." Then Jeremiah gestured for someone to approach. Scotty's parents responded, shambling forward as if their feet were encased in lead. Scott's father's face was set and determined; his mom looked like she was holding herself together with spit and bailing wire. His father was holding a stake.

Scotty saw them coming, and he started pleading with them to keep back, to not do what they were clearly intending to do. "It's our responsibility," his dad said as if he was talking from beyond the grave. "We failed to train you and prepare you sufficiently, and now we must attend to our mistake."

"You trained me fine! You did great! You can't help that everything you taught me was wrong! It's all wrong! You have to listen to the Avant Guard! They have the right idea! They know what's going on—!"

"You will not mention those demon lovers here!" Jeremiah informed him.

All while I was growing up, I had been terrified of Jeremiah Salk. He was humorless, single-minded, and considered himself the definitive Body Man. Yet suddenly I was on my feet and I heard my own voice saying, "Let him speak! He deserves to speak!"

Salk looked stunned that I had spoken up. Then he turned to Scott's parents and said angrily, "You see? He is threatening to corrupt an entire generation!"

"Well, *you're* the one who brought me here, dumbass," Scotty said.

"Let him speak!" I said again.

Scotty looked at me, and there was such gratitude on his face like you couldn't believe. And he said, "Thanks, Vince. I really mean that, more than you can possibly—"

"Do your duty to the Garrison!" Salk shouted at Scott's parents, and it was as if his voice was an electric jolt to them.

Even as Scotty screamed "No!" his father's arm was whipping around, acting purely on reflex, and he slammed the stake into his son's chest, without even thinking about what he was doing, because if he had been thinking about it, he would have stopped himself. At least that's what I'd like to believe.

Scotty's body spasmed uncontrollably as he let out a high-pitched screech, and people young and old cried out in response. My parents had always been tight with Scott's, and even as Scott's parents fell back, unable to look upon their son's suffering or deal with their own sense of guilt, my dad put his arm around the shoulders of Scott's dad while my mother embraced Scott's mom, who was unable to contain her grief any longer and started sobbing onto my mom's blouse.

And then Scotty's head slumped to one side.

My boyhood friend was gone and I think, in many senses, he took my boyhood with him.

Incredibly, no parents took issue with the way that Salk had handled things. To me it was a pointless, needless exercise in cruelty, and had anyone asked me my opinion, that's what I would have said. But nobody did.

I never did find out what they did with Scotty's body. Maybe they had it buried; more likely it was cremated. We were ushered out of the chapel and, except for us kids whispering to each other about what we had seen, there was no further discussion of it. Certainly none of our parents seemed to want to talk about it. I don't know whether that was at Salk's orders or if they just felt that he had done them a disservice but were reluctant to say anything about it.

Now do you see why I stay with my mother, even though I've been turned? Why running away isn't an option? If I ran, then my Garrison, my former friends and coworkers, would hunt me down, and haul me to my very own Friday Gathering, and my mother would be forced to stab her son to death. Obviously I don't want to put her through that. With everything she's been through, she deserves better than that.

Besides, Sun-tzu—in whose teachings I am thoroughly schooled, let me assure you—always talked about keeping your friends close and your enemies closer. What better way to make sure that the Body Men didn't come gunning for me than by staying as part of their ranks? That makes sense, right?

Right?

Screw it. Maybe I just have a death wish. It's not like I was all that enamored of life in the first place, especially after Dad died and Mom nearly did.

Dad always said that Mom was the best partner we'd ever had, and even though most of our Garrison was big on the loner thing, Mom and Dad were inseparable out in the field. He said they acted so smoothly, so automatically with each other that it was like they were one person with four arms, four eyes, and so on, and that that gave them a big advantage in dangerous situations. "She's the brains of the outfit," he would say. "She's the one who's in charge. I wouldn't know what to do without her."

So maybe it somehow figures that they didn't know they were going to be in a dangerous situation. It figures that the only way something bad would happen to them was that they would wander into the middle of something without the slightest clue that it could all go to hell in an instant.

A real estate investment. Of all things, that was what Dad said he wanted to check out. There was this run down building in Soho that had signs up all over it about it being for sale, and Dad, he was this "man of vision." That's how Mom always described him, at any rate. He said that he thought he could turn it into something. Some sort of new work out or training facility for the Garrison. "Something really state of the art," is how he described it, and Mom could totally see his point. The training facilities we had, the ones overseen by Jeremiah, were practically ancient in comparison. He and Jeremiah Salk had gone head to head any number of times over training practices for our Garrison. Salk swore by techniques that were centuries old, but Dad wanted to produce tricked out obstacle courses augmented by virtual reality. Salk didn't trust any of that stuff, and said that the Echelon—the highest levels of the Chevaliers, our ruling council—was opposed to deviating from traditional practices. But Dad was adamant that something like what he was envisioning—a sort of "Laser Tag" set-up but geared toward the particular needs of the Body Men—was the way of the future. Finally he wore down Salk to the point where Salk said, "We don't have the space here. If you can find somewhere that could possibly work, I will consider supporting it."

And so one bright day, Mom and Dad headed off to check out this real estate opportunity that Dad was sure would wind up benefiting our Garrison. "This could be the beginning of our whole future," he told me right before he headed out. I was twenty years old. It was the last time I saw him before the funeral.

They wandered into a nest. Right into a damned nest, and they had no heads up, no warning, nothing. From Mom's description of the place, it definitely sounded like an Old Country-style nest. Hell, if it had been a Nu V nest, I can pretty much guarantee that Dad would be alive, Mom would have two good legs, and I wouldn't be chowing down on rodents or small animals instead of Mom's cooking whenever I had the opportunity (although to be fair, again, Mom's lack of mastery of cooking is such that, even when I was normal, a rat might have been more edible than Mom's Thanksgiving turkey.)

Mom and Dad were packing because they were always packing. That was just standard procedure. So the result was a running firefight, with Mom and Dad trying to get out and the vampires managing to cut off all their exits. They wound up being driven to the last place that you want to be if vampires are chasing you down: the basement. The windows were boarded over and there was no way out.

But Dad was nothing if not resourceful. Mom said that Dad

was determined that if they were going down, they were going to "take the whole stinking nest with us." Dad found some old cleaning supplies down in the basement that he was able to rig into explosives, and just as the vampires came crashing down the stairs after them, he blew the place. The place, as it turned out, was apparently held together mostly through the efforts of bunches of mice lined up within the walls joining hands. When they scattered, down came the building.

I have no idea if the vampires managed to get out and get to safety. All I knew was that by the time the emergency crews were on the scene, Dad was already dead, having been killed almost instantly by the explosion. Mom had been blown backwards and lay buried beneath rubble for several hours before they finally managed to reach her. Her right leg was crushed, unsalvageable; it was nothing short of a miracle that the rest of her was intact. As it was it still required nearly a year of physical therapy to get her back up on her feet…well, foot.

As for me, I went a little nuts.

I stood over my mom's bed in our infirmary. Our Garrison had its own private clinic and Mom was transferred there as soon as it was permissible to move her. They were keeping her so doped up on painkillers that I wasn't sure if she even knew whether she herself was alive or dead. I looked down at her and she had tubes sticking out from just about everyplace, and it was like my entire life was collapsing down to that moment. There was Scotty in my head with the image of what they had turned him into, and Dad was dead and Mom was only a few steps above dead, and every muscle in my body was trembling with fury.

And then Mom's eyes slowly flickered open. Her gaze wandered and then focused on me.

"Mom?"

Her lips started to move. Then she licked them and spoke again, and her voice was little more than a croak, but it was still understandable.

"Find them," she said, "and put their balls into a nutcracker and squeeze."

Ladies and gentlemen: My mom.

I armored up and fled into the night, determined to clean my city out of every damned bloodsucker that was out there.

I tore through every lead I could scrounge up, every hang out, every low dive where one of the patrons might have spotted something that could be of use to me. But everything I found was a dead end.

That was when Tyler came through for me. Tyler was about three years younger than me, and field material he most definitely wasn't. But he was a computer researcher that nobody else could touch, and he'd been poking around on the Internet. Remember that whole Wanna V website I mentioned to Lawrence Singer? Tyler, he of the skinny build and overlarge forehead, was the one who turned me onto it. He managed to impersonate one of the other long-time regulars and turn up, through "casual" questions, what the current location for Bleedin' Eden (as it was then called) was.

I showed up outside the Bleedin' Eden and there's every chance that, had I gone in there guns blazing, I would have gotten myself good and killed.

And that's when *she* entered the scene.

The shadows were long in the alley just outside the Eden's then-location, and there was this young woman who came up right behind me just as I was casing the joint. I heard her footsteps and turned and fired my Super Soaker at point blank range.

Yeah, I forgot to mention that. Salk hated it because he said it wasn't dignified, but the younger Body Men absolutely loved the notion that I came up with: loading up Super Soakers with Holy Water. The idea was that it would be like throwing battery acid at the vampires from fifteen yards away.

So I sprayed the young woman and she let out an annoyed yelp as I soaked her face. Other than prompting her to voice confused outrage, it didn't have any impact on her.

"*What the hell—!*" she cried out.

Realizing that she was human, I said in a low voice, "Look, you'd better get out of here. I'm pretty sure there's a nest of vampires in there."

"Are you *shitting* me?"

"I wish." My dad's words came back to me from so many

years ago. About how everyone was ignorant compared to me, because I knew the truth of the world while everyone else, all the so-called normal people, were just freaking clueless. "I know it sounds insane. I know *I* sound insane. But these things are real. They killed my father, they brought my mother to the edge of death. These things are demons that can't be allowed to exist. They just…they just can't. I have to do everything I can to make sure that nobody else suffers because of them…"

"You mean suffers like you did?" When I didn't answer, she spoke again, and actually sounded understanding. "So much pain in you. Poor, poor kid."

"I'll be fine," I said, which was bullshit because I was about as far away from "fine" as anybody could be. "Now please, just… get out of here, before it's too late."

She turned and walked away, taking my word for it, and I shifted my attention back to the outside of the building I was preparing to storm singlehandedly, and wondering if maybe I should indeed call for back-up before I was in over my head.

And suddenly she was right there, and she struck me from behind. I went down, the world spinning around me, and I was lying on my back, trying to pull myself together, and the next thing I knew my hands were cuffed behind my back.

She's a cop? I thought.

Then her hands were at my belt, undoing it, undoing the top of my pants, and she was pulling them down around my ankles.

Okay, she's a prostitute. Or a really aggressive nymphomaniac.

"Look, I…I think you've got the wrong idea," I stammered out.

Her hair was long and black and hanging down around her face, but she tilted her chin back just enough for me to see the fangs.

I was paralyzed.

Without a word she sunk her teeth into my inner thigh. I tried to struggle but it was amazing how quickly she was able to draw the blood from my body. It only took seconds for me to become so lightheaded that, had I been able to see my hands, I wouldn't have been entirely sure how many fingers were on them.

She was smart, of course. It's easy to spot twin bite marks on the neck, but who checks the upper thigh?

And as I lay there, dazed, confused, my head swirling around me, I felt more at peace than I ever had. I was certain that I was about to join my dad, and maybe somehow Scotty would have caught a break on the other side and been given a free pass upstairs. Maybe it wouldn't be as bad as all that.

Then she was lying atop me, and she had made a small incision with her fingernail just above her right breast. Alcohol from her breath washed over me. I didn't know that vampires drank alcohol. It didn't make sense. Nothing about it made sense. "The Holy Water...why didn't it..." I managed to say.

And she cooed to me, "Poor, poor thing. You'll understand soon." She raised my head to her breast like I was her infant, and the blood dribbled into my mouth. I tried to spit some of it out, but more of it went down my throat, and when it did, it was as if some sort of switch had been flipped in the innermost parts of my head. Suddenly I wanted more; I couldn't get enough.

She held my head against her breast and her laughter filled my ears, and then everything went black.

When I came to, I looked around and saw that I was in a darkened room, lying on a futon. My head was pounding and my mouth, my throat, were bone dry. Slowly I sat up, putting my hand to my throbbing head, and that was the point at which I realized that I was no longer handcuffed.

"Look who woke up."

I saw Duncan, although obviously I didn't know that was his name, standing a few feet away. "Evening, sleepy head," he said as he'd wandered in from a Tennessee Williams play. "It's a cliché, but...welcome to the first day of the rest of your life."

I leaped at him.

In my defense, that's what I'd been trained to do when I saw a vampire.

What I wasn't prepared for was the greater strength and speed that my new status gave me. Duncan tilted slightly backwards and I flew right past him, out of control, and slammed into the far wall. I sank to the floor and stared at my hands.

"Why do the newbies always stare at their hands, like they

just grew them or something?" said Duncan. He leaned on the edge of the futon. "I don't understand that, I really don't."

"What did you do to me?"

"What did *I* do? Nothing. Except give you a place to sleep off the change."

"The...the change?" I reached up, touched my face, my mouth, and pricked the tip of my finger on one of my fangs. "Oh my God. *Oh my God!"* I scrambled to my feet and ran to a mirror hanging on the wall. I checked out the fangs and howled, *"Oh my God! My mother's going to kill me! They're all going to kill me! I—"* Then I stopped, confused. "Why can I see myself in the mirror? What's up with that?"

Duncan was shaking his head and he looked amused. "The things you people accept as givens. Come on. We don't reflect in mirrors? Seriously? How would the physics of that work?"

"It's...it's not about physics," I said, my mind still trying to grasp what had happened. "It's because you don't have a soul."

"Then by that logic, if you hold up a mirror to a corpse, the corpse wouldn't reflect either. Go to a mortuary, see how that works out for you."

"But..."

"Do you feel like you don't have a soul?"

"I..." I hesitated. For some reason I put my hand to my chest and was surprised to feel my heart still beating. "I...I don't know."

"Exactly. So why assume you don't have a soul when there's no reason to?"

"But vampires are evil—"

"How do you know?"

"You kill people—"

"So do humans. As a race, humans have killed far more people than vampires as a race could ever hope to." He laughed. "Compared to humans, vampires are pikers. Does that mean humans are soulless creatures, slated for damnation?"

"I..." I hesitated. "Maybe, I guess—"

"Look," he said, and he regarded me sympathetically, "I know it's a lot for you to take in. Your head feels like a firecracker just exploded in it and blew everything you previously thought all to hell. But I want you—if you can—to put aside all your beliefs, all your concepts, everything that you've been taught. Turn yourself into a tabula rasa..."

"Tabula rasa?"

"A blank slate." I was still on the floor and he knelt opposite me and rested his hand on my forearm. "Close your mind's eye for a minute, and then very slowly open it. And I want you to give yourself and me an honest answer to the following very simple question: How do you feel?"

"How do I—?"

"Feel, yes. How do you *feel?*"

"I feel..." And I did what he had instructed, because it wasn't as if I hadn't had training in meditation and other techniques designed to keep you calm in a stress situation. For nearly a minute I let everything else wash out of my mind. Every fear, every preconception, everything that I had ever known, I just compartmentalized it. Tucked it into a box and closed that box and put it aside, and finally when I did answer his question I was surprised to hear the words coming out of my mouth. "I feel... *alive.* Like...I'm seeing the world clearly for the first time."

"Exactly."

"Who did this to me?" I said.

"That's a good question," said Duncan who now stood up and extended a hand to me, pulling me to my feet. "Her name's Dominique. She's not one of my regulars. I see her every once in a while. Not sure if she's an O.C. or a Nu V or what her deal is. She blows into our neck of the woods sometimes, stirs up some trouble, blows out again. She's a wanderer. Yeah, the wanderer. She roams around, around aroun—"

"Yeah, I get it. I know the song." I wasn't exactly in the mood for cutesy cultural references. "Why did she do it?"

"I dunno. You'd have to ask her, if she ever turns up again. She brought you in here, asked me to keep an eye on you until you were turned, and then lit out. No telling when she'll come by again."

There was just so much going on, so much to try and understand. But there was one thing that I knew all too well, knew deep in my heart, which was still beating, and my soul, which I guessed was still hanging around, maybe out of morbid curiosity to see what was going to happen next. "There's no going back, is there," I said.

"No, but why would you want to?"

"I have a life, a family. My mom...she..." I felt despair welling up within me. "Vampires killed my father. How am I supposed to tell my mother I'm one of them now. One of you?"

"Kid...I'm really sorry about that," and he certainly did sound regretful. "I don't know what the deal is that brought about whatever happened to your dad, but it wasn't anyone in my crew. We're not killers. We don't have to be. We have way too many volunteers."

"My mom's not going to know or care about that. Neither will anyone else in my family."

"Yeah, well, who's your family? A bunch of vampire hunters?" He laughed at that and then he saw my face and the laughter died in his throat. "Wait...seriously?"

"Seriously. I'm a Body Man with the Chevaliers. Garrison Thirteen."

"Oh my God."

"You couldn't tell from the weapons I had on me?" I patted myself down, suddenly realizing. "Where are my weapons?"

"Dominique must have disarmed you before she brought you in here so that you wouldn't start trying to kill everything you saw when you came to. This is," and he scratched his head thoughtfully, "...okay, this is a whole new thing now. I mean, it doesn't change the basics. You can't go back..."

"I have to."

"You *can't* go *back.*"

"If I don't," I said, "then they'll come here, wherever here is. They will come here and they will find it and they will wipe out you and your crew down to the last one."

Duncan stared at me. "Okay, fine, go back if you have to. At least for a little while. And..." He shrugged. "Maybe it'll work out. This could maybe be the start of thawing relationships between your Garrison and my people. I mean, don't get me wrong. I'm going to relocate this place now that you know where it is, just in case the Chevaliers try to beat the location out of you before they kill you..."

"That's smart," I said, not feeling terribly enthused about the idea.

"But still, if you do decide to tell them what happened… maybe it'll work out. Maybe your mother will surprise you."

"You don't know my mother," I said.

Five

My Mother's Reaction to the Whole Amber Thing

If I wanted a preview of what my mother's face would look like if she found out that I was a vampire, I didn't need to look much beyond her reaction upon discovering that her little boy was engaged, or more accurately, that he'd been betrothed by his late father.

We lived in a brownstone that was populated entirely by Garrison families. We used to have the top apartment, but after Mom's mishap, the family on the ground floor generously agreed to switch with us out of respect for Mom's damaged leg. There was an attached garage, which was nice, because parking in the city wasn't always the easiest of endeavors, and that's where I stored my motorcycle.

I got back home before any of Lawrence's Body Men and went straight to the apartment, only to discover that Mom had company. They were sitting in the kitchen, downing mimosas, which was Mom's preferred drink, and they were laughing like two old friends catching up over the years, but I had no idea who she was. As it turned out, neither did Mom.

"Oh, Vinnie!" she said when I walked in. "How did it go? Did you find anything?"

"Uh...yeah," I said, studying the woman. She was a black woman with Amber's general features but darker skin and curlier hair. I was struck by her eyes, which were quite large and seemed surprisingly warm. I say surprisingly because the eyes of most female Body Men are by nature cold and calculating. As are the men's, I suppose, but somehow it just seems more noticeable in a woman. At least it does to me. "Yeah, I did. It was, uh... who's this?"

"This is Amanda Singer. Amanda, this is my son, Vince."

Singer. Perfect.

"She's been telling me all about you," said Amanda. Her voice had the same lilt to it that Amber's did. She got up from the chair, came to me and shook my hand firmly. She had a strong grip, and she seemed to be sizing me up. I couldn't tell if it was in a "Is he good enough for my little girl?" sense or a "I wonder how he is in a fight?" sense.

"Yeah, well, it's all lies," I said, a joke that sounded weak even to my ears.

"Yes, I'm afraid I've been dominating the conversation telling her how wonderful you are," said Mom, trying to sound apologetic and failing miserably. It was nice that she boasted about me to other people. I guess in her mind it made up for the fact that, face to face, she pretty much focused on all the shit she felt I was doing wrong. "Amanda just arrived from out of town and came by here to introduce herself. She's with Garrison Ninety Nine out in San Diego."

"Really." Although I was talking to my mom, I was watching Amanda for reactions. "And did she get a chance to tell you *why* she came by to see you, specifically?"

"Her husband was a friend of your father's, apparently," said Mom.

Amanda and I exchanged looks, and we both knew at that moment that we were on the same page and Mom wasn't even in the same book. "Actually—" Amanda began to say.

I jumped in before she could get it out because, really, how often do you get to drop this kind of bomb on your unsuspecting mother? "It turns out I'm engaged to their daughter. 'Bonded' I think is how she put it it."

In modern day we used the regular words like "engaged" and "fiancée," but "bonded" was the word that went back to the oldest days of the Garrison when arranged marriages seemed the best means of ensuring that the blood line of the Chevaliers would remain unsullied. It took a certain type of individual to be a Body Man and the reasoning was that the best way to ensure that more of the same were made was to cross-pollinate already existing Body Men.

Mom stared at me blankly as if I'd just suddenly started speaking in Urdu. "What?"

"Yeah. First I'd heard of it. Dad set it up a while ago. He didn't mention it to you?"

"What?" It was the same word, but it was flat, lifeless. If it had been her heartbeat, they would have called the time of death. Before I could reply, she shifted her gaze to Amanda and said for the third time, *"What?"*

"I'm...a little surprised you don't seem to know," Amanda said. "Parental Bonding is an honored Chevalier tradition.

When overwhelmed with a notion that she was still having trouble wrapping herself around, Mom switched into her default response. She looked back to me in an accusing way and demanded, "Did you know about this?"

"Do I *sound* like I fuc—like I knew about it?" I said in exasperation.

"Look, you...you two obviously need to discuss this matter," said Amanda, gathering up her purse. "Maybe I should get my coat—"

"Sit," said Mom, talking to Amanda in a way that I hadn't heard her address anyone except for me. It was an order, and God knew what she would have done if it had been disobeyed. I suppose Amanda could have taken offense at being talked to in that way. Instead she automatically dropped right back down into her chair and then seemed belatedly surprised at her instant obedience. She glanced at me and I shrugged, looking at her in my most sympathetic and understanding manner. Welcome to my world, lady. *"We two* need to discuss this matter?" Mom continued. "You're the mother of a girl who is being presented as my future daughter-in-law. I think you have a stake, pardon my language," which is what she always said reflexively whenever she used the word "stake" in anything other than a vampire-killing context, "in what's going on here. First thing's first: Why now?"

That wouldn't have been my first thing, but Mom was running the show right then and I wasn't about to interrupt.

"Well, Amber just turned twenty-one," said Amanda, finding

her voice. "Some Garrisons said the marriageable age for the girl is sixteen, but when Boris and Lawrence made the arrangement, they mutually decided that twenty-one was the better age. You're more mature, have a clearer idea of who and what you are once you're twenty-one."

"I don't know if I agree with that," said Mom. "Vinnie is several years older than twenty-one, and there are days I don't think he knows who and what he is."

So much for her focusing on me being wonderful. Actually, I knew exactly who and what I was. It was my mother who didn't, and I intended to try and keep it that way for as long as possible. But I decided the best course of action at that moment was to keep my mouth shut.

"And when did our respective husbands make this arrangement?"

"Twelve years ago, during the Great Stake-Out."

The Great Stake-Out, as it had come to be known, had been a legendary time in recent Chevalier History. I was a kid back then and only had a vague understanding of what was happening. The race of vampires whom I would later learn were referred to within vampiric ranks as the O.C.'s, the Old Countries, embarked on some sort of major power play, actually trying to plant O.C.-controlled agents in pivotal roles in the government, for some purpose at which we could only guess. The Chevaliers caught wind of it and went after the ruling O.C. cartel that was behind it. It was the vampiric/Chevaliers equivalent of a world war, except it was fought entirely in underground channels and the mundane world never knew a thing about it. It briefly united at least thirty Garrisons across the country. Mom stayed home with me because I was so young and to this day talked about how much she regretted missing out on it. Dad was gone for three months, the longest he'd ever been away, and there were days I was sure I was never going to see him again. And when he did finally return, he didn't talk all that much about the stuff that had gone on during that time. At least he didn't talk to me about it.

Apparently there were things he didn't talk to Mom about as well.

"I just...I'm having trouble understanding this. No offense," said Mom, "but Boris never mentioned Lawrence to me."

"That's odd, because..." She stopped.

"What? What were you going to say?"

Amanda shifted uncomfortably in her chair. "I don't want to make it seem as if my husband was somehow 'better' or more forthcoming in the way he conducted himself. I wouldn't want you to take offense..."

"Well, I don't know about 'better,'" said Mom, keeping her voice surprisingly even and in control, "but it's becoming pretty obvious that he was more forthcoming. So say what you want, because I'm not someone who gets upset about the truth."

I made a mental note of that comment just in case Mom ever found out the truth about her son.

"I was just going to say," said Amanda, "that Lawrence spoke rather glowingly of your husband. They were in some rather serious life-and-death situations together and pulled each other's fat out of the virtual—perhaps even literal—fire several times. And I guess they felt that by promising our children to each other as Bond Mates, that they would be solidifying that union."

"That's all very well and good," said Mom, "but—"

"And certainly Lawrence trusted him that Vincent would be a good match for Amber."

"Yes, I'm sure—"

"Otherwise I doubt he would have paid the rather significant dowry."

That was when my mother found herself something that she typically wasn't: speechless. I shouldn't say "typically," in fact. I'd never heard her completely at a loss for being able to say anything at all. But that's what was happening in this case. Her mouth was moving but no sound was emerging except for a weird combination of a squeak and a croak.

Fortunately I was able to jump in, because suddenly it was all starting to make more sense to me. "Dowry?"

"Yes. We have a different set-up in our Garrison from what I understand yours does," said Amanda. "We believe in individual wealth, and Lawrence, well, he comes from a very old, very renowned family with very old investments. We're quite wealthy, actually. And Lawrence was so taken with Boris that, to show his confidence in him, he was willing to pay Boris a sizable sum at the time of the agreement without waiting for the actual wedding."

"How much of a sum?"

"I believe it was one hundred thousand dollars."

Mom's croak changed into a slight gurgle. I wasn't sure how to react at all. "I...guess I should be flattered," I finally managed to say.

"Well, Lawrence was very anxious to make the deal. I suppose part of that came from what he'd recently found out about our older daughter..."

"Amber has a sister?" I said.

"Oh yes. Hannah. A bright girl, very smart, excellent Body Man, but not exactly what you'd call marriage material."

"Why not?" In discussing someone else's marriageability, Mom had finally managed to find her voice.

I, however, was already ahead of her in this instance. "Let me guess," I said although it wasn't really a guess. "Men aren't exactly her thing."

"That's pretty much it," said Amanda.

Mom looked at the both of us. "You mean she's..."

"You got it, Mom."

"...a feminist?"

"Aaaand I spoke too soon."

I had to credit Amanda that, under the circumstances, she was able to smile at that. She tried not to do so openly but the edges of her mouth were undeniably twitching. "She's a lesbian, Dina."

"Oh," said my mother. "I'm...so sorry."

"It's not like she died, Dina. It's just...it's who she is. You have to accept your child for who and what they are."

"I could not agree more," said my mother.

That was the second comment in as many minutes from her that I made a mental note to file away, in anticipation of her singing a very different tune at some point in the hopefully-very-distant future.

"Look," said Amanda, "I know this is a lot to take in. I think that I should leave you and Vince to discuss this." She had removed a pad and pen from her bag and was scribbling down an address. "Here's where we're staying. A hotel over on the East Side."

She tore it off and handed it to Mom, who looked at the name with a raised eyebrow. "I know this place. It's nice. Expensive."

"Thank you. We co-own it, so obviously we're not all that worried about room rates."

"Obviously," Mom echoed faintly.

"Why not come by for dinner tomorrow? We can all get acquainted in a proper manner."

"That sounds like a good idea," said Mom, although I wasn't sure if she was in a state of mind to recognize a good idea if it came up and punched her in the face.

Amanda gathered her things, said her good-byes, and just as she was heading to the door, a thought occurred to me. "Excuse me, Mrs. Singer, I was just wondering," I began.

"Please. Amanda."

"Okay, Amanda," I said gamely. "I was wondering...if, for some reason, Amber and I don't get married...what happens with the dowry?"

"Oh. Well," and she shrugged, "Lawrence would want it back. I doubt that he'd demand interest, but certainly it would seem only right that the money be returned. Doesn't it?"

"Absolutely," I said.

"And I imagine he'd be very, very upset if it weren't returned. So let's all hope it doesn't come to that."

She smiled, nodded, and moments later I heard the sound of her high heels heading off down the sidewalk outside.

Mom and I sat there in dead silence for a few minutes.

"Mom," I finally said. "What did Dad do with the one hundred grand?"

As if she were answering from somewhere within *The Twilight Zone,* Mom said, "I haven't the faintest idea."

So to summarize: I was a secret vampire engaged to the human daughter of a family of vampire hunters, and if I broke off the engagement I would owe him more money than I'd ever seen in my life.

I tried to think if there had been anyone in the last hundred years who had been more profoundly fucked in so many ways that didn't involve a sinking ocean liner or Nazis, and nothing was coming to mind.

Six

My Unexpected Phone Call From the Morgue

You probably think that, when you've got guys like us—"us" meaning Body Men, not us meaning vampires—who operate primarily in the shadows and fringes of humanity, that we're isolated and more or less on our own in our day-to-day, night-to-night operations.

Not the case. At all.

I mean, it's not like the police commissioner has a Batphone in his office sitting inside of one of those clear plastic cake display stands (I never knew what was up with that) that he'd use to give the Garrison a call whenever vampire activity was suspected. Although I have to admit, that would be pretty cool.

But we have people on the inside in key places. We didn't recruit them. Instead they sort of fell in with us, usually because we helped them out of some difficult situation. Maybe one of the Body Men wound up saving them from a vampire who tried to prey on them. There are some rogues around that don't subscribe to any particular vampire belief system, but just go around doing whatever the hell they want to whomever they want. They're kind of the Libertarians of vampires, except they won't talk your ear off for hours on end. They'll just bite it off. And when we encounter one of those rogues, we'll put 'em in the ground pretty quickly. Even I'll do that, without hesitation. They're bad for business. Everybody's business.

Or maybe they were people who heard the rumors about us and sought us out because weird stuff came to their attention and they needed someone to step in and handle it. And from that point on, they'd be there to do anything they could to help us in return.

One of those guys was Teddy Olshefsky.

Teddy was a big, gangling guy who had a real sweet face and disposition, and always seemed cheerful and perky. When you asked him what he did for a living, you'd figure that maybe he was a clown or one of those DJs you hired for Bar Mitzvahs and such. So you'd be pretty much gobsmacked when he would then tell you that he was a police M.E. working at the city morgue, because you figured that guys who work in morgues would be like ghouls or something, no matter how many times you see them on television crime procedurals as good-looking young Hollywood actors. Or maybe they'd be hardened and dour because of having to work with stiffs every single day, many of which had died from some kind of violent encounter.

Not Teddy. He was what he was, and he had a perfectly fine attitude about it.

I crossed paths with Teddy purely by accident. I was supposed to be out hunting vampires and instead was hanging out in a bar, which I wound up doing more often than I should have. I tried not to make myself a regular at any of them. Endeavoring not to be noticed was simple force of habit. While I was there, though, I spotted Teddy being chatted up by this one young woman who I picked up was a vampire almost immediately. She didn't spot me, though, since her attentions were entirely on him. I could see the bloodlust in her eyes, although Teddy obviously mistook it for something else. She guided him out into the alley and I followed, and found her on top of him and not in a good way. He was trying to scream and not succeeding because she had her hand clamped over his mouth even as she set about burying her teeth in his neck.

I have my trick stake for show, but I always make sure to keep a real one secured inside my boot for just such an occasion. I slammed it into her heart from the back, which might not have seemed sporting, but when you're killing someone then you've pretty much tossed aside the whole Marquise of Queensbury rules thing. The female, whose name I never got, shriveled away and Teddy gaped at her remains. I'll never forget what he said.

"Vampires are real?" And when I affirmed that, yeah, they were, his response was, *"Awesome!"*

Which may seem a damned strange thing to say, but the way that Teddy explained it to me, all he meant was that the existence of vampires opened up an entire world of possibilities where all kinds of things, from UFOs to leprechauns, might exist. That made life more exciting to him somehow. Me, I wasn't entirely sure that I followed his logic, but it seemed to be good enough for him, so who was I to disagree?

It was Teddy who volunteered, right there on the spot, to feed me news about anything odd that came across his table, and he also urged me to use him as a source if there was anything I wanted to check out. I assured him at the time that it wasn't necessary, but that was just me being polite. I welcomed the help.

So naturally when Tracy Manor's body turned up on his slab, and he started checking her over, he saw the bite marks on her neck. The moment he did, he rang up the Garrison to let us know about it. That's how Mom knew about it in the first place.

Now, though, I was sitting at home in my room, staring out through the window at the rising sun. I was wearing sunglasses in order to make the brightness a bit more bearable. Then I nearly jumped through the ceiling when my cell phone rang. It just wasn't what I was expecting at that particular moment. I fumbled with it before finally snapping it open.

"Yo, Boss," came Teddy's voice. "This a bad time?" He always called me "Boss." I have no idea why. I guess he figured it was a sign of respect. The first few times I'd just told him to call me "Vince," and he would just say, "Sure thing, Boss," so I gave up.

"It's barely dawn," I said. "I don't know whether you're calling insanely late or incredibly early. What kind of hours they got you working there?"

"Man, you got no idea. Look, I figured I'd call you directly on this one 'cause I didn't want to roust your mom in case she was sleeping."

I'd known Teddy for about two years; he was pretty much up to speed on our current situation, although naturally I hadn't bothered to let him know about my personal undead status. "Yeah, okay, smart thinking. What'cha got?"

"I got the autopsy results back on that girl, the vampire victim."

"Tracy Manor?"

"Yeah."

"Okay, well...don't keep me in suspense."

He decided to keep me in suspense anyway. "You'll never guess, Boss," he said with what he figured was a dramatic flair. "You get three tries."

I, of course, knew already, but decided for the sake of discretion to pretend I didn't. "I figured we knew already. Vampire attack."

"Nope." He sounded pleased to be one step ahead of the Great Vampire Hunter.

I acted surprised. Ever since I'd been recruited, I'd become one hell of an actor, just out of a sense of survival. "Really? No kidding. Are you sure?"

"Positive."

"Okay, then how did she die?"

"Two more guesses."

I rolled my eyes as I sagged back onto my bed. It had been a hell of a night and I was feeling totally wasted. The last thing I needed was to engage in an extended guessing game over something that I already knew. Still fully dressed, too tired even to remove my clothes, I said, "Okay, uhm...stroke."

"Nope. Try again."

"Heart attack."

"Nuh-uh."

"Not...stroke or heart attack?" That was puzzling. From what Duncan had told me, I would have said for sure it was one or the other. "Okay, well...what then?"

"Sure you don't want three more guesses?"

"I'm hanging up, Teddy."

"Okay, okay. She was poisoned."

I'd been fighting to keep my eyes open and not to give into exhaustion, but when he said that, fatigue was no longer an issue. I snapped back awake immediately and sat right up. "Poisoned?"

"Yup."

"But I thought—" I caught myself before I said anything that would be stupidly incriminating. "I mean…that doesn't make any sense."

"Why doesn't it make sense?"

"Well, because…when vampires are involved, you just figure…I mean, who would want to poison her?"

"That question's above my pay grade, Boss. I just say how they were chopped; I don't have the name of the butcher."

"Yeah, okay." My mind was racing. "So…what kind of poison? How did it get into her?"

"That's the weird thing…"

"You're telling me she has vampire bites on her but died of someone poisoning her, and asking what kind is the weird thing?"

"Actually: yeah. Because this poison doesn't exist."

"Teddy, what the hell are you talking about?"

"The nearest thing I can liken it to is digitalis. Basically, in this instance, it shut down the electrical system of her heart, causing heart block. But it's not digitalis. Or if it is, at the very least it's digitalis cut with something else that I've never run into."

"But why? Why cut it?"

"Because digitalis is fairly fast acting, with a lot of pretty obvious symptoms. Nausea, vomiting, delusions. All that good stuff. That didn't happen with this girl. It was in her system for almost a day before its toxicity was unleashed. I wasn't with her, obviously, but my guess is that she was pretty much functioning as per normal during that time. If it had been a slow build, the symptoms would have sent her to an ER. This girl, judging by her clothing and her blood alcohol level, was out partying. Then the toxins kicked in all at once and down she went. And rather than calling an ambulance, whoever she was partying with decided to just dump her in an alley. Nice, huh?"

"Yeah. Nice," I echoed tonelessly. "You didn't tell me: How'd it get into her? Did she eat something—?"

"Nope. Injected directly into her. I found a single puncture wound on her left upper arm."

"Vampire puncture?"

"Nope. Way too small, and only a single one. So either it was from a baby vampire who only had one baby fang grown in, or—more likely—it was from a needle of some sort."

"So someone," I said, trying to process it by speaking aloud, "decided to poison this girl, for no reason that we know, by injecting her with some sort of toxin that's unfamiliar, so that she would drop dead after a long while. That just makes a whole lot of sense."

I could almost hear Teddy shrugging over the phone. "Provides an alibi, I guess. Especially if she was injected someplace public. Someone poisons her, she keels right over, the first person they're gonna start questioning is the one who was standing right next to her when it happened. Might lead to questions they don't want, especially if it turns out they had a motive for wanting her dead."

"Or it could be some random guy who just did it for kicks."

"A serial killer?" Teddy whistled. "But there's no multiple bodies."

"A journey of a thousand bodies starts with a single corpse."

"You should be a freaking philosopher there, Boss."

"Thanks." I wasn't entirely sure it was a compliment. "The cops on this?"

"Yeah, of course. I mean, it's ruled a homicide. Why wouldn't they be? Do you want the case number...?"

"No, no, that's okay." It wasn't as if I was going to stroll into police headquarters and try to compare notes with the detective in charge. The first thing he'd do is ask me what my interest in the case was, and the conversation wouldn't lead anyplace good, at least as far as my interests were concerned. "Uhm...just out of curiosity...in your report, did you mention—?"

"The fang marks? I kinda had to; they were right there on her neck. But I attributed it to aggressive sex play. It didn't have anything to do with her death, so why dwell on it? I mean, I don't wanna be the guy who goes around shouting, '*Vampires!*', y'know? How would that look?"

"I totally get it." Of course I did. Teddy was in the know, but most of the world still considered vampires creatures of myth and legend, and that was fine with us. No cop wanted to see "vampire killing" as a cause of death on his caseload. If nothing else, you just know the press is going to pick up on it, and suddenly the whole city is up in arms about it, and the police are being asked a ton of questions that they simply don't have the answers for.

"So, uh..." Teddy hesitated and then asked, "are you gonna look into this, Boss?"

"Why would I?" I said, and it seemed a reasonable question. "I mean, yeah, obviously vampires were involved. But if they didn't have anything to do with her death, then it's out of my bailiwick. I figure, y'know, let the cops handle it."

"Yeah. Yeah, you're right."

There was something in his voice that didn't sound right. "What, you don't approve?"

"Well...look, Boss...it's not for me to say or anything, but... we're talking about a girl who was involved with vampires, which are bad news to begin with, and then on top of that, she was poisoned with something way off the beaten path? I mean...that's just a hell of a coincidence, don't you think?"

It actually hadn't occurred to me. The likely reason for that was that I regarded vampires differently from Teddy, for obvious reasons. To him, it was straightforward. Vampires equal evil. Poisoning equals evil. Therefore, vampires were likely responsible for the poison. For someone like me who naturally had a bit more nuanced view of vampires and their place in the world of morality, I wasn't drawing that immediate straight line linking the two. Now that he was saying it, though, regardless of the inherent evilness of vampires or lack thereof, I had to admit that if it was a coincidence, it sure as hell was a pretty big one.

"Yeah. Yeah, I guess it would be," I said, trying not to sound reluctant in acknowledging it. "Okay...maybe I will stick my toe in this one. But just a little bit. Just enough to see what it is we're dealing with before I jump straight into it."

"Makes sense to me, Boss."

I signed off and then sat on my bed, mulling it over. I knew I should get some sleep. The irritation from the rays of the now rising sun was sending me a not-so-gentle reminder that this wasn't my time of day.

But I couldn't sleep, because I couldn't get the notion out of my mind. Duncan had explained to me how the whole thing was just some unfortunate happenstance of nature. That it had been Tracy's time. How the hell was it your time if someone pumped poison into you?

So okay, the cops were looking into it. But if Tracy was like your typical Wanna V, she would have covered her tracks in her personal life. The Wanna Vs did everything they could to protect the vampire lifestyle from prying eyes, so I suspected that when the cops invariably went poking into her life, there wasn't going to be anything that would lead them into the circles I ran with.

However, I had a bit of a leg up on the cops, because I knew where to start looking.

I fired up my computer and moments later had made my way to the chat board. That is to say, *the* chat board. It was called Grave Site (cutesy, I know, but go argue with the Internet) and it was a private chatroom where all the Wanna Vs hung out. The Garrison didn't know about it. In fact, to the best of my knowledge, no one in the entirety of the Chevaliers were aware of it. The only people who knew were the Wanna Vs themselves, and vampires. It wasn't like, once you were recruited, you got a little book filled with FAQs that provided the location of Grave Site. It was just one of those things that, eventually, you found out about.

The Grave Site served a vital purpose to the Wanna Vs. It was where they shared up information, such as the names of vampires who might be more inclined towards turning them. And there were indeed some like that. Guys who just ran around converting Wanna Vs, just for the hell of it or to prove that they could. Wanna Vs called them Studs, which seemed appropriate, I guess. Studs were contrasted to the more cautious vampires who didn't just go around reproducing indiscriminately. They practiced what the Wanna Vs referred to as—wait for it—Safe Sucks.

The other main use for the Grave Site, when they weren't nattering on about whether the actors in vampire movies were really vampires because no human actors could possibly be that hot, was that they shared up information as to where Movable Feast was currently situated. Whenever Duncan was established at a new location, he always fed it into Grave Site and the network would take it from there, so that both vampires and Wanna Vs would know where to go.

I logged onto Grave Site and found a number of the usual suspects in the midst of some discussion about how there was just too much damned vampire literature on the market. They all went by fake names, which was typical, but I was pretty sure that some of them corresponded separately or even hung out together in real life. I just wish I knew what name Tracy had gone under.

There were six of them at that moment. I typed in, *Anybody here know Tracy Manor? It's kind of important.*

My message popped up, next to the name I'd adopted for the purposes of the chat board: *Renfield.*

They knew me as a regular there, so they wouldn't hesitate to respond the way they would if it were a newcomer on line. There was, however, a pause, because I had dropped the question into the middle of another conversation.

One girl calling herself "Darla" typed back, *Who is she?*

I almost typed *One of you* before correcting it to, *One of us.*

What does she go by here? That question came from another girl, "Drusilla." At least I assume it was a girl. It's the Internet; you never know.

No idea. But I thought one of you might know her from real life.

This got me a chorus of "nopes" and "don't know her." Then one of them asked the million dollar question: *Why are you asking?*

There was no point in being coy about it. *She's dead.*

Good for her! That was the immediate response, of course, promptly echoed by others, because they're, well, idiots.

I restrained myself from informing them of their idiocy and instead typed as quickly as I could, *Not vampire dead. Dead dead. Murdered.*

This prompted a flurry of OMGs and WTFs. Someone asked how it had happened. I decided not to go into too much detail. That way if someone did come to me with genuine information, I'd be able to tell if they were the real deal.

Not sure, I lied. *Information still sketchy. But...* I hesitated and then decided to lie some more. *She was a friend, and if there's any way I can help the police get leads, then that's what I'll do.*

Tracy's dead? Holy shit.

My fingers froze. It was from some girl calling herself

"Sookie42." Naturally.

Sookie42 had just logged on moments before and had apparently read the list of comments back and forth.

I flexed my fingers and typed quickly. *Let's chat,* I wrote. I arrowed directly atop her name and clicked on it, creating an invitation for her to speak to me privately. Then I waited, fingers crossed, hoping that she would take me up on it.

She did so immediately. *I can't believe it. My God. Where do you know her from?*

I was now in uncertain territory. If I really tried to pass myself off as a friend, Sookie42 might start asking questions that would reveal the lie. I switched tactics, veering closer to the truth. *That was for public consumption. Actually, I'm a private detective, hired by the family. They don't trust the cops to get the job done.*

I don't blame them. Cops suck.

That was a relief. She'd probably been busted for some minor transgressions. Or major. Who cared? All that mattered was that she and I be on the same wavelength.

No argument there. Look, I'd like to be able to talk to you. Find out what you know.

Why not just do it now?

I didn't want to say that, if we were face to face, I'd be able to tell immediately if she was lying about something or trying to cover things up. *It's just better to do these things in person. Plus I have some pictures of some likely suspects I want to show you, and my scanner's broken.* More bullshit, but plausible bullshit. *We can meet somewhere public, in case you're concerned.*

Okay, she said. *How about midnight at the new location for Moveable Feast?*

I wasn't sure where that was. Quickly I jumped over to the FAQ section and yes, sure enough, it had been updated with an address in Astoria. I wrote back to her, *That works for me. How will I know you?*

Tight-fitting red dress, black shawl.

How festive. Going for charm, I wrote back, *Don't own either. How about if I wear my blue chiffon and combat boots?*

LOL, she wrote back.

A friend of hers was dead, but at least she could laugh out loud.

Seven

My Incredibly Uncomfortable Dinner

That evening, the taxicab dropped off Mom and me outside an extremely upscale hotel called the Plaza 25, which came from, I assume, the number of stories tall it appeared to be. It was ritzy, even by New York standards, with long-coated guys standing outside waving for cabs for the patrons. Because apparently when you're rich, you're so fragile that just gesturing for a taxi might blow out your rotator cuff.

As we stepped out, I spotted Amber waiting just inside the door. She was looking around nervously and when her gaze fell upon us, she seemed to relax. Then she saw Mom and she was apprehensive again, apparently being reminded that she was about to meet a prospective in-law. For some reason I found that endearing. Here was a young woman who was completely at ease in life and death situations, facing off against (what she fancied to be) monsters and displaying nothing but aplomb and rigid professionalism. But the act of meeting her fiancé's mom was enough to throw her off her game.

"Mrs. Hammond. I'm Amber," she said, putting her hand out.

Mom promptly went into full Mom mode. "A hand? A hand you're giving me? Come here," she said, throwing her arms wide as if greeting a long-lost relative. Amber looked a bit startled as Mom embraced her with a ferocious hug. "I've always wanted a daughter. Always."

"Gee, thanks," I muttered. She didn't hear me, or at least pretended not to.

Mom not only hugged, but she even did one of those things where you swivel at the hip a few times, as if she were about to wrestle her to the sidewalk and try to pin her. Then she stepped and said, "Let me look at you."

"So you can see how much she's grown?" I said.

She made a dismissive noise and said to Amber, "Ignore him. He doesn't even know how to talk to his mother."

"I've tried using English but it just doesn't seem to take."

Following her own advice, she ignored me. "Now," and she patted Amber on the shoulders as if she were fluffing her. "You have a mother, so I'm not sure you want to be calling me 'Mom' because God forbid she should think I'm trying to horn in on her. But please, none of this 'Mrs. Hammond' business. Call me 'Dina.'"

"But never call me late for Dina," I said, making a joke that sounded way better in my head than when I actually opened my mouth and said it. They both gave me the exact same pitying look, at which point I knew I was pretty much screwed.

Mom continued ignoring me. She had gotten really good at that. "So what are you out here for? Shouldn't you be inside?"

"I just figured I'd welcome you. You know. See a friendly face outside waiting for you."

"As opposed to the unfriendly faces waiting inside?" I said.

"Vincent!" Mom snapped at me.

But Amber quickly interceded. "Actually, it's just..." She cleared her throat. "There's...well, there's kind of a lot of pressure in there..."

"Pressure?" I wasn't wild about the sound of that.

"It's, uh..." Amber was clearly trying to find the best way to express it and nothing useful was presenting itself. "It's less like a family get together and more like a U.N. meeting. I mean, I *thought* it was just gonna be, y'know, us. The parents and us. But then the head of your garrison showed up..."

"Salk is here?!" I couldn't believe it. "What the hell is Salk doing here?"

"Dad invited him."

I winced. Fantastic.

"Plus then Dad decided to invite his crew along because he

said they were in a strange city and deserved to join in the celebration. So now there's a whole bunch of people there for something that should have been just an intimate get-together. At least we've got a private room off the main dining room, so that's something."

It sure was. That way if everyone wanted to have a complete meltdown, it could be done in relative privacy. I didn't see that as necessarily being a good thing. There are certain societal constraints that you feel on you if you're out in public. Voices stay lowered and you generally keep a tighter hold on your horses. Once privacy rears its ugly head, then pretty much anything can happen, and typically did.

I forced a smile as we headed in. Mom seemed oblivious to the potential disaster that was waiting for us. Instead she was enjoying chatting it up with the daughter she always wanted, undeterred by the notion that, if Amber was her daughter, I'd be marrying my sister. Mom was never what you'd call a big picture lady.

Amber brought us into the private room, and sure enough, there were the Singers. Amber's mom, Amanda, came forward and she and my mom did that air kiss thing, and then Amanda turned and introduced Mom to Amber's dad.

He bowed slightly, took her hand and kissed her knuckle with a real old world type style. "Boris spoke of you so often, I feel like I know you," he said with that low rumble of a voice.

"Really?" Mom looked at him sideways. "He never mentioned you to me at all."

She didn't sound at all nasty about it, and yet an expression of annoyance flickered over Lawrence Singer's face. He covered it quick, though, I'll give him that. He was obviously someone who liked to keep his emotions in check. "Obviously Boris was someone who liked to play things close to the vest," said Lawrence. "I suppose we all have our secrets."

All I could think was, *Man, you have* no *idea.*

Lawrence then introduced us to the guys in his crew. I nodded, shook each of their hands, and then promptly forgot all their names. I wasn't sure where any of this was going, and I didn't feel like wasting brain cells on committing a bunch of guys to memory who I probably wasn't going to be seeing again after this.

One of them, though, stuck in my mind for two reasons. He was a muscular guy with a pale blonde crew cut and a chin that could have been used to open cans. The first reason he made an impression was that he studied me with the kind of cool, sullen hatred one doesn't typically get off a relative stranger. The second was his name, which was Kubrick. First or last name, I wasn't sure, but I said cheerfully as he shook my hand, "I loved all your movies." He obviously didn't think it was funny, and in fairness, he promptly was kind of sick of hearing it. He did, however, proceed to grip onto my hand so fiercely that, if I didn't have vampiric strength, he would have crushed my knuckles. As it was, I saw mild disappointment in his eyes that I wasn't gasping under the pressure of his grip. He didn't realize, of course, that I was holding back. I could have broken his hand off at the wrist, but that would hardly have been a convivial way to kick off the evening.

Salk was also there, just as Amber had said, and apparently he'd been keeping the bartender busy. He wasn't shit-faced or anything, but he was way more relaxed than I'd seen him before, which was reasonable considering that usually he had a big old stick up his ass.

There was a very long table that had been set up, and the lot of us made innocuous small talk as two waiters came by and took orders and kept the food coming. Lawrence made it clear early on that this entire evening was at the expense of his own garrison and that our money was simply no good here. That was lucky, because I certainly wasn't in a position to whip out an Amex and absorb the entire cost.

You'd think that a table full of vampire hunters would be talking shop, but such was not the case. That, I have to admit, was something of a pleasant surprise. Amanda seemed interested in knowing what Broadway shows we would recommend, and when I jokingly said, "So, how about them Jets, huh?" Lawrence immediately lit up like a Christmas tree and started talking football. Which caught me off guard because, honestly, I didn't give much of a crap about the game, but suddenly the other members of his crew and Lawrence and I were all talking about the Oakland Raiders (their team of choice) and how they were going to dominate this year. Meanwhile Mom, Amanda and Amber started bonding over that endless array of fashion shows on Bravo about being a model or a designer or some other damned thing having to do with clothes. I didn't think it was possible to not care about something less than I did about football, but clothes were it. Most guys really don't give a damn. Clothes were the things that, if you were a guy, you wore to keep warm, and that a girl wore so that you wouldn't see her naked, and what guy is in favor of that?

All things considered, matters were going about as well as they possibly could have, and that was because no one was bothering to address the elephant in the room: namely, two strangers were being brought together and being told that they were expected to get married. The larger elephant, of course, was the one that I was being forced to carry on my own, that being that one of the members of the lucky couple happened to be a vampire. Every single person at the table, up to and including my own mother, would instantly try to kill me if that little factoid happened to surface, as it inevitably would if we engaged in domestic bliss.

Don't get me wrong. I was still fully operational down south. My junk put the "un" in "undead." But Amber wasn't stupid. Sooner or later, she was going to figure it out. If nothing else, she'd want to go hunting together, and then what? We burst into a nest and the guys all go, "Hey, Vince. Long time no see. Who's your friend?" Yeah, that was going to work out well. I could have moved out west with Amber, joined her garrison, but being surrounded by her family 24/7 wasn't an attractive notion. And in our lifestyle, just pulling up stakes and starting fresh somewhere completely new really wasn't an option since other garrisons tended to ask a lot of questions of newcomers. Ultimately, I had no real workable explanation as to why we couldn't continue to live with either of our garrisons. Not one that would fly with Amber, and certainly not with anyone else.

Not to mention that, as interested parents eagerly awaited the arrival of grandchildren, they were going to become increasingly disappointed. Plus I could just see it if Amber wanted to seek additional medical aid in conceiving. The first thing they'd want is a sperm sample. Low motility? Try no motility. The gun worked fine but the ammo was blank. By the time that report came back, I'd be on the run.

I excused myself at one point and headed to the bathroom. There I vomited up the nice meal we'd been having. When I emerged from the stall, I froze. Kubrick was standing there, glaring at me.

"Hey there," I said. I approached the large mirror to wipe bits of sickness off the edge of my mouth. "Something disagreed going down, I guess."

"Sure you didn't cause yourself to upchuck?" He was studying my reflection suspiciously.

"Yeah, that's exactly right, 'cause in my day job, I'm an anorexic supermodel." I noticed the way that tall, light and Aryan was looking at me in the mirror. "Problem?"

"Reflex," he said. "Always looking to make sure people have reflections. 'Cause if they don't, then I get to kill them."

"Good for you. Nice to see someone getting job satisfaction."

I ran water over my hands and slapped some onto my face, and suddenly he was shoving my head against the mirror, banging it so hard against it that it was a miracle the glass didn't shatter. "Dude! What the hell—!"

He leaned in close and practically snarled in my ear. "If you got some kind of eating disorder, then get it straightened out fast. Understand, 'Dude?' 'Cause if you hurt Amber in any way, you are dead. Got that? They won't be able to identify your body from dental records."

Considering I had fangs, I was kind of betting they would have been able to, but obviously I didn't say that. What I did feel, however, was a pounding fury starting to build. The vampire within me, at its primal core, was a beast. A predator beast. And this bozo was in serious danger of unleashing that beast in a manner that I might well not be able to control. Were that the case, I would easily break free of his hold on me and snap his neck, stopping only to suck him dry faster than a sports fan chugging a beer during a playoff game.

That, unfortunately, would lead to all kinds of questions, starting with, "Hey, where the hell did Kubrick go?" and spiraling downhill from there.

I gritted my teeth, fighting to prevent my fangs from extending, like an erection, in the face of the lust for blood pounding in me. "You," I growled, "really need to let go of me."

Both to my relief and my disappointment, Kubrick did so. I managed to pull myself together, pushing down the bloodlust and bottling the beast, at least for the time being. I turned to face Kubrick but he was already out the door, banging it behind him.

"That was festive," I said to no one.

I made my way back to the table and slid into place next to Amber. She looked at me with concern. "You okay? Kubrick said he was going to go in and check on you..."

"Yeah, he, uh..." I saw him glowering at me from the other end of the table. "He was really concerned. Is there, uh...is there something going on between the two of you I should know about?"

She laughed. Terrific. The guy tried to make me a permanent part of the men's room's interior decoration and she was laughing. "There is in Kubrick's own mind, I suppose. He's always had a thing for me. He says stuff like that he'd kill anyone who tried to take me away from him, like he ever had me in the first place. But that's just him spouting off. Nothing to worry about."

Fantastic.

Interestingly, it was Salk who decided to fire on the aforementioned elephant in the room. Toward the end of the dinner, he got to his feet, lurching slightly while doing so, and he raised his glass and started tapping it with his spoon to get attention. This he managed to do pretty quickly and in short order all eyes were on him. He raised his glass and automatically everyone else around the table did so as well, even though some of them were empty. I considered that to be appropriately symbolic.

"On behalf of Garrison Thirteen," he began, "I wish to welcome the renowned Singer family to our fair city. Your accomplishments, and those of your garrison, are well known to all Chevaliers. And how even more serendipitous that your arrival is tied to such a festive, even momentous occasion: the announcement, Lawrence, of your daughter's bonding with one of our most promising, most upstanding Body Men, Vincent Hammond."

Promising? Upstanding? Salk couldn't stand me, nor I am. His ability to spout complete and total bullshit was simply unparalleled in our little community. And yet everyone was smiling and nodding as if this was the most truthful sentence ever uttered in the history of, I don't know, sentences.

"Furthermore," Salk went on, "you may be impressed to know that the Echelon itself has taken notice of his union and has asked me to extend, on their behalf, the heartiest of congratulations. They believe that this alliance is long in coming and promises a great future for our order."

This prompted some low "ooohs" and "aaaahs," and I suppose it was understandable. It simply didn't get higher up than the Echelon. If you were Catholic, it was like finding out that your upcoming marriage had flipped a switch at the Vatican and the Pope was sending along personal greetings and a free ring to kiss stuck in a box of Cracker Jack.

The whole "alliance" thing was straight out of the oldest days of the Chevaliers, harkening back to a time when marriage was less about love and more about brokering and commodities and creating blood ties between powerful houses. That sort of thinking had long ago faded into the pages of history with a Modernist garrison such as ours, but the Singer's garrison was clearly as Old Guard as it got. As for Salk, even though he oversaw a Modernist garrison, I was pretty sure that he had always been a closet Old Guard, and that was just getting more and more obvious as the evening progressed.

"And so a toast," Salk nattered on, "to the happy couple, and to a union between your forces and ours. And may the result be the final elimination of every vampire from the face of the Earth."

"Hear, hear!" came echoes from all around the table.

Which was when I made the mistake of muttering under my breath, "Well, not *every* vampire."

Ever have one of those moments where you say something

really quietly, just for your own amusement, but at the exact moment the words come out of your mouth, there's this total silence and what you said carries way more than you were expecting it to?

That's what happened here.

My offhand private comment, which would have *stayed* private if I hadn't opened my big, damn mouth, was heard throughout the room and suddenly all eyes had shifted from Salk over to me. Every face was one big question.

"What did you mean by that?" Lawrence Singer said very slowly, very dangerously, lowering his glass without having taken a sip.

Now of course what I was referring to, in my oh-so-clever way, was myself. But I couldn't very well say that.

Mom immediately endeavored to jump in, saying dismissively, "Oh, that's just Vincent's sense of humor. Don't worry about it."

"I'm trusting your son with my daughter, Dina. I worry about everything. And, with all respect, I'd rather hear what he has to say rather than someone explaining on his behalf."

My mind raced. It seemed to me like I sat there, silent, for about half an hour, even though it was probably just a couple of seconds. Forcing a smile, trying to make light of it, I said, "All I meant was that, if we kill all the vampires, then there's nothing more for us to do. We're all out of work. And that would, y'know, really suck."

I hoped the joke would go over. It did: like a lead balloon.

"I do not understand," said Lawrence, "how you can possibly think that there being no call for our services would be some manner of tragedy. I think I speak for everyone here—except, apparently, for you—when I say that the day there would be no requirement for our services would be a glorious day indeed."

There were murmurs of agreement from all around the table. Basically the lot of them were taking the opportunity to just pile on.

Lawrence shifted his attention to my mother. "What kind of young man have you raised, Dina, that he would bemoan the loss of vampires in the world?"

"Now just hold on," said Mom, clearly starting to get worked up over the whole thing. "I raised one hell of a knight of our order, thank you very much. He was just making a joke."

"Our line of work cannot tolerate humor."

"No, *you* apparently can't tolerate humor," Mom fired back. "But just because you're a stiff doesn't mean my son has to be."

There was, of course, irony in that statement that Mom couldn't possibly know. Even so, as much as I hate to admit it, I was just a little bit proud of her, watching her tear into the guy.

"Dina, Lawrence—" Amanda began, apparently looking to be the peacemaker.

But Lawrence wasn't having any of it. All the glasses around the table had been set down, and Salk was looking incredibly uncomfortable. That was the only positive aspect of this fiasco. "I do not appreciate your tone, Mrs. Hammond."

Oh, now it was Mrs. Hammond. This was getting better and better.

"My tone wasn't for you to appreciate, it was for you to pay attention to."

"I am paying attention to everything, most particularly your son's behavior. And I have to say, thus far I have not been impressed by what I've seen. If he is going to be given the honor of marrying my daughter—"

At which point I couldn't take it anymore, and blurted out, "*Giving* me the honor? You're shoving it down my goddamn throat, and I can't say I appreciate it."

If I'd bared my fangs, I couldn't have gotten more of a collective gasp from the place.

Salk chose that moment to find his voice. "What are you saying, Vincent?"

"I'm just—" It was like the world was skidding out from under me. It was obvious that the Singers were a powerful and rich family, and if I just blew off their pride and joy, they might well crush not only me, but the entire garrison.

Once upon a time, garrisons occasionally got involved in full-blown feuds. It sounds idiotic; you'd think we'd all be on the same side. But that wasn't always the case, and I can only imagine the vampires sitting back on their collective asses and laughing while their would-be slayers tore into each other over some petty disagreement. It was one of the reasons that the Echelon had risen: to make sure that disagreements didn't wind up with a body count. We were, after all, hunters at heart, accustomed to settling problems through violence. It was natural that we would wind up turning on each other from time to time.

At this particular moment, though, I wasn't ruling out the possibility that there might well be a fatal blowback over this whole match falling apart, one that went beyond the sort of financial penalties that had been threatened. I suppose it depended just how old school the Singers and their garrison were. From the evidence I had at hand, I was starting to think that they were pretty damned old school.

I didn't exactly retreat, but I did everything I could to sound more frustrated than belligerent. "Look," I said, considering each word, feeling the weight of the world hanging on each one, "all I'm saying is that you guys have known about this for years. Me and my mom...we just had this dropped on us, out of the blue. And, no offense, but you guys are cutting us no slack in coming to terms with the whole thing. For whatever reason, my father didn't share any of this with us, and it's just..."

"It's a lot to take on," Amanda said helpfully.

"Yes. Exactly." I was starting to like her more and more, and couldn't help but wonder what in God's name she saw in a humorless killing machine like Lawrence Singer. I know love is blind, but at what point did it become deaf and dumb, too?

Or maybe there never had been any love involved. Amber had told me theirs was an arranged marriage as well. Maybe all she was doing was making the best of it, even after all these years.

That was when Amber, thank God, finally opened her mouth. "I totally get where he's coming from, Dad."

She does? I thought.

"You do?" said Lawrence.

"Dad..." She reached across the table and took his hand. "Our world isn't his. Our way of doing things isn't the same as his way. We just came rolling in here, assuming that they were like-minded, with no warning. I mean, come on. How much do *you* like it when somebody just drops something on you out of nowhere?"

He grunted. That was probably as close as he ever came to acknowledging that someone else had a point.

Backing up her daughter, Amanda said, "I think the ideal thing right now would be for the couple to just have some time to bond in actuality, rather than just in name. Have some time to get to know each other, see where things go."

"Maybe they could hunt together," Mom piped up.

"Yes, exactly! *Excellent* idea!" said Salk, as if Mom had just suggested for the first time in the history of mankind that maybe bread might be easier to eat if it was sliced first.

There were nods from around the table. Of course there were. This bunch was always up for even the suggestion of hunting. "Should we come with?" asked Kubrick.

Amber gave him a withering, pitying look. "We're grown Body Men, Kubrick. I think we can take care of ourselves. The whole point is that we need time to ourselves. Can't exactly do that if we have you looking over our shoulder."

Kubrick's response to this was to glare at me, as if I'd said it. Figures.

"Mr. Salk," Lawrence said, "are there any particular hotspots of vampire activity that my daughter and her Bond Mate could hunt?"

"Well, once upon a time, I would have said 42nd Street," said Salk. "But that got cleaned up when Disney rolled in."

"Central Park," I said quickly.

Salk looked at me in surprise. "Really? It used to be fairly bad there, but it's calmed down somewhat, I thought..."

"I've heard rumors," I lied. "The fact that it has been so quiet is exactly what's drawing vampires back there. They figure that we don't hunt there anymore which makes it perfect for them."

"That's exactly how the bastards think," Mom said.

"Okay, then," I said quickly, anxious to get the hell out of there. "It's settled, then." I got out of my chair and, ever the gentleman, helped Amber to slide hers out.

"Thank you, kind sir," she said with humor in her voice. "I'll run up to my room, grab some weapons, and meet you at the front."

"Sure, sounds great."

"Good hunting, you two!" called out Salk. "Come back madly in love with each other!"

This caused a ripple of laughter from everyone except Lawrence and Kubrick, both of whom continued to watch me as I headed out of the private room. I was beginning to get the feeling that if I didn't come back from the hunt, neither of them would be too broken up about it.

I was starting to think that I wouldn't be, either.

Eight
My Walk in the Park

It was a nice night and Central Park was only about eight blocks from the hotel, so Amber and I walked over. I was keeping a wary eye on the hour because I was going to have to get out to the brand spanking new location of Moveable Feast in Astoria by midnight if I was going to meet my contact there. But it was just pushing past eight o'clock, so I had plenty of time.

"Thanks for this," said Amber, looking rather fetching considering she had a bandolier of stakes tucked under her jacket and a silver knife slid into a sheath in her boot. She had been rather dressed up for the dinner, but now was dressed down into practical hunting clothes. Me, I was in jeans, turtleneck and black leather jacket, so I was good to go in any event. "This going out and hunting. It's just what I needed."

"Well, thank my mom. It was her idea."

"Believe me, I will." As we ambled down the sidewalk and drew nearer Central Park, she shook her head. "I know my father can get kind of intense sometimes."

"Really?" I said, acting in a very unconvincing manner as if I hadn't noticed.

She laughed lightly at that and then turned serious once more. "It's just, the things we do, all of us...they're matters of life and death. And there are times he acts as if...no, he's not acting. I think he truly believes that the responsibility for saving the world from vampires is entirely on his shoulders. He doesn't just go through police reports from our district. He spends entire mornings studying reports from all over the country. And I think that every vampire-related death, or even suspected death, that he stumbles over...it's like he takes it as some kind of personal failure, even though he was hundreds of miles away from it. He's just that dedicated."

"Sounds like a pretty intense way to grow up."

"It was."

We entered the park and were soon strolling along a random pathway. There weren't a ton of people around, but then I wasn't expecting there to be. One of those old-style horse drawn carriages that were so favored by romantic couples and tourists went clip-clopping by, with a couple snuggling in the back, a checked blanket pulled up over them. The air was crisp, but not wintery.

I saw that Amber was watching them roll past, and the edges of her mouth were turning up. "If you actually want to ride in one of those, we can get one over on 57th Street," I said.

She waved it off. "No, no. It's probably a big waste of money, and besides, I'm not really into that kind of stuff."

"You mean romantic?"

"Honest to God," she said wistfully, "I'm not even sure I know what romance is. I mean, I was already promised as Bond Mate to you, so it's not like I was going out on dates. And even if some guy was interested, well...Dad can be kind of intimidating. So romance wasn't really...I mean, I don't even know if I have the tools for it."

"Wait, wait." I slowed up walking, because something that should have been abundantly obvious was just dawning on me. "So you're saying you've never, yknow...dated..."

"Nope."

"Which means you..."

"Haven't ever anything, yeah," said Amber. "Probably one of the reasons Kubrick keeps looking at me like I'm some sort of hors d'oeuvres. Why?" She looked amused, but there was also a hint of concern in her voice. "Is that a problem for you? I mean, I'm assuming that you've, y'know..."

"Well, I'm not Casanova or anything, but yeah, I've been around." Which I had, but not all that much. There'd been the time with one girl in our garrison who was sick of her virginity and just wanted it over with, and I had the same status, so we fumbled through it and didn't do it particularly well, but at least it was done, although not well enough that either of us wanted a return engagement. She subsequently hooked up with another female Body Man and seemed much happier, which didn't exactly do wonders for my self-esteem.

And there was this one near victim of a vampire attack who didn't hesitate to show just how grateful she was. Several times. But since I'd been "recruited" to the other side, I'd been kind of avoiding any such get-togethers.

"Does..." I cleared my throat. "I mean...is that a problem for you? Because if it is, I'd totally understand if you were turned off or grossed out or..."

She laughed again, this time full throated. She had a really nice laugh. None of that snorting through her nose or stuff like that. "Look, Vince...I know I must seem incredibly naïve to you. Hopelessly behind the times, what with my being willing to sign on for the idea of marrying a guy that I haven't met before now."

"I wouldn't say 'hopelessly...'"

"Because you're being polite, which is sweet. I guess what it comes down to is trust. I trust my family to have my back. They do it when we're out on a hunt, and they do it when it comes to my living my life. I mean, if you can't trust family, who can you trust?"

The answer to that, of course, was nobody, which was pretty much where my head was at. I wasn't about to say that, though.

Fortunately, she wasn't waiting for me to reply. She was wearing her hair down rather than in the tight bun I'd seen earlier, and she brushed a few stray strands of it from her face. She really did have lovely hair. It had some sort of beautiful scent coming off it; strawberries, I thought. And she had the most sparkling eyes, when they weren't narrowed in contemplation of driving a stake into my chest. "Obviously I'd have no reason to expect that you'd be saving yourself for a girl you didn't even know existed. Hell, even if you *did* know I'd existed, I wouldn't be surprised if you were out, y'know, sowing your wild oats."

Which was, of course, part of the problem. My oats weren't going to be growing much grain anymore. I didn't say that either, although I was starting to think I could have had a very lengthy conversation composed entirely of the things that I couldn't say. Instead I went for, "I appreciate your being understanding."

"I *am* understanding," she said, and then to my surprise, she cupped my chin. "And I like Broadway musicals, hip-hop, and jazz. I love dirty jokes. I'm kind of obsessive with washing my hands and brushing my teeth, but I figure that's not so bad. I couldn't care less about football, but I'm a total baseball nut, probably because it involves long wooden sticks. I was totally bummed out for no good reason when they said that Pluto wasn't a planet anymore. I'm a sucker for cheesy medical programs with doctors who have hot bodies. I don't smoke. I like beer on tap, not bottled. And I think you're really cute and would like to get to know you."

She kissed me then, and the smell of strawberries almost overwhelmed me. Naïve she might have been, and inexperienced, but she kissed me with total confidence in her strength as a woman. Her lips were moist, but not too much so, and she wasn't wearing lipstick. Slowly her tongue started to slide into my mouth.

I felt my fangs starting to respond.

I avoided yanking my head back too quickly, because that might have either upset her or, worse, prompted her suspicions. But I did draw back, and she frowned when I did so. "Was I… doing it wrong…?" she said, fumbling for the words.

"No. God, no…"

"You're skeeved about my…lack of experience…"

I started to say "no" again but realized she'd handed me a gift. "Not…skeeved exactly," I said. "Just…I need to come to terms with it, y'know? I mean, when a girl's a virgin, that puts some pressure on the guy, which may sound a little weird…"

"A little," she said. "I mean, it's not like we're going to have sex right here in the park…" And then she cocked an eyebrow and, I swear, looked at me flirtatiously. "Are we?"

I felt my throat drying out. "What?"

"Just because I've been saving myself," and she ran a finger down my chest, "doesn't mean I haven't been wondering. And fantasizing. A lot. So you shouldn't assume that I'm…you know…not necessarily up for things. I mean, I'm a Body Man. So

I'm certainly as adventurous a girl as you're going to find."

She was coming on to me, right there in the middle of Central freaking Park. And she was totally serious. I could probably take her behind a bush right then and, well...take her behind the bush.

As much as I hate to admit it, part of me was interested. No, not *that* part. Well, okay, a *little* that part. The truth was that, were I human, Amber would have been great company. She was attractive, she was full of life, she was capable and self-confident. Sure, she was cool with the idea of her parents deciding who she was going to marry, but it was kind of sweet that she trusted them so implicitly. I hate to admit it, but I was a little jealous of that. Would I have gone so far as to marry her? Hell, I don't know. I'll tell you this, though: if I had, it wouldn't have been because of the money that would have been owed to her father if I didn't go through with it. It would have been because...

I'm not sure why because. I don't think I could have fallen in love with her that fast. Maybe in an arranged marriage, when you got past all the stuff about forming alliances and that bullshit, what it came down to wasn't the love that existed, but instead the potential for love. And I could see myself totally falling in love with her.

If I were human.

Which I wasn't.

Which, obviously, again I couldn't explain.

I laughed, trying to make light of the situation. "Well, I think your dad might kill me."

"Dad's not here."

"Are you serious? I mean, are you totally serious?"

She seemed to be considering it. "Kind of," she decided. "And kind of not. I guess I'm just trying to get you to understand that you shouldn't make assumptions about me."

"Well, you sure don't have to worry about that."

She reached up, pulled my head toward her and this time kissed me more sedately on the cheek. Then she pulled back and looked at me with slight concern. "Are you okay? You feel so cold."

"I'm like that all the time," I said lightly, trying to make sure there was no subtext along the lines of *because I'm kinda dead* that could possibly be discerned in the comment. "Poor circulation. Always having to shake my hands and feet like maracas in the morning just to get me jumpstarted. Consider yourself fortunate. At least I'm not one of those guys who sweats all the time."

"Lucky me," she said, but there was something in her voice that seemed laced with curiosity. That was, of course, exactly what I didn't want to have happen. Curiosity might be what kills the cat, but it wasn't going to be any less fatal for me.

Generally speaking, I'm not a big fan of those hansom cabs that trot around the park, but I'd never been happier to see one as I was at that moment, when it came rolling up drawn by a large black horse. I knew nothing about types of horses, but there was something that was definitely different about this one. The horses that pull the cabs always look downtrodden and bedraggled, like they have one hoof in the grave and three others on banana peels. This one, on the other hand, looked like it was brimming with power. I could see the play of its muscles beneath its horseflesh as it approached us, and I could have sworn that it was regarding me with a touch of disdain. It was ridiculous to impart that level of thinking to a horse, but still, there was just something about the animal that had me do a double take.

As opposed to most of the horse-drawn carriages around the park, this one was enclosed. It looked a bit more like a more stagecoach. The driver perched up and toward the front was heavily covered in a big, shapeless red coat with a hood pulled up against the rapidly chilling air, and he said, "Care for a romantic ride?"

The weird horse notwithstanding, I was grateful for the interruption. I wasn't especially inclined to take him up on it, but at least it would serve as a distraction. Once he went on his way, maybe I could then restart the conversation in a direction that would be potentially less lethal.

Amber waved it off. "No thanks. I'm not big on riding around. Rather stretch my legs."

"I know what's going on," said the coachman to me. "Your

boyfriend's too cheap to spring for the ride and you're just covering for him, right?"

"Yeah, right, that's it. You got me," I said.

'Tell you what. For the nice young couple: no charge." He waved toward the interior of the hansom cab. "Check it out. Nicest lined seats in the park."

Automatically, Amber moved toward it, apparently taken by the guy's hard sell. I, on the other hand, remained right where I was, because now I knew something was off. It was one thing that the horse seemed healthier and smarter than most such animals that hauled carriages around Central Park. But the idea of a New Yorker offering a free ride immediately rang false.

"Amber, wait," I said.

She stopped just at the cab and turned to look at me with curiosity. At that moment, the door to the cab banged open and a hand stabbed out, snake quick, and grabbed her by the arm.

"*What the hell*!" She twisted around and if she'd had even a second more to react, I have no doubt that she'd have been able to yank her arm clear. Her self-defense techniques were as good as anybody's and better than most.

But then the other hand of whoever was in the cab speared out and grabbed her by the throat, cutting off her air. At that exact same moment, the coachman snapped the reins and the horse launched forward, yanking Amber off her feet and depriving her of any kind of leverage. Taking advantage of her not having any grounding, whoever was in the cab hauled her in and the door slammed behind her.

The cab raced off, and I...

I didn't do a damned thing. I just stood there and all that went through my mind was, *Problem solved*.

It really would be just that easy. Whoever that was in the cab and whatever they had planned for her, when you come right down to it, it wasn't my business. There was no way that this was a simple mugging. Someone had targeted her. But they hadn't targeted me, because I'd been left behind, which meant that whatever the problem was, it wasn't one that involved me. Chances were that they were going to do something terrible to her. If it was vampire related—and since a Body Man was being snatched, the odds were spectacular that it was—they might hold her for ransom in order to strong-arm her garrison into something. Or maybe they were just going to kill her outright, either as a warning (which I doubted her father would take) or as revenge for a vampire that she or one of her people had staked.

If I had to guess, it was more likely that it was the latter. In which event, she was going to be dead. I would no longer have a fiancée, and certainly her father wouldn't punish my family financially just because his daughter had died through no fault of mine. It was a win/win for me, and sure, it sucked for Amber, but that's the way that went.

All of that went through my mind in maybe a second.

The next second, I was moving.

There was no doubt in my mind that, if the horse were unencumbered, I'd never have been able to catch up with him. My speed was supernatural, but I could never overtake a horse that powerful.

Fortunately enough he was hitched to a rig, and that gave me the opportunity I needed.

I ran after them, my arms pumping, never more glad that I didn't have to worry about being out of breath. I closed the gap quickly and then, with a burst of speed, the horse started to widen the distance as it sped along the road, which was closed off to cars or any other sort of traffic. Late-night joggers scrambled to get out of the way, yelling curses and shaking fists in anger. Someone saw I was in pursuit and shouted, *"Kick his ass!"* I appreciated the encouragement.

I chanced everything on a single leap. If I missed the carriage, I was going to wind up sprawled rather comically on my face.

Fortunately that didn't happen. Instead I managed to land on the back of it, my fingers just barely snagging the railing that ran around the top. For a few moments my legs dangled, my feet dragging on the speeding pavement, and then I firmed up my grip and yanked myself up and around, swinging myself to the side so that I was directly in front of the door that Amber had been yanked through.

I pulled on it hard. The door resisted, bolted from the inside. That didn't bother me none; I just pulled on it harder, ripping it right off its hinges and tossing it aside.

This was enough to get the attention of the driver, who turned and spotted me for the first time. "Hey! You dumb shit! You'll pay for that!"

I took the opportunity to flash my fangs at him and snarled back at him, "Bill me!" Then, retracting them, I twisted back around to look into the cab.

Amber was there, all right, unconscious. A vampire that I'd never seen before had his fangs sunk into her neck; it was probably the shock and blood loss that had knocked her out. There was blood spilling from her neck that the vampire was lapping up, and he looked up and glowered at me with furious red eyes, pulling his fangs clear of her. The wounds on her neck throbbed, blood continuing to seep out. He was dressed in a thick gray suit with, of all damned things, a black cape draped over his shoulders. His hair was tinted gray and in a widow's peak, and two other things stuck out for me. First, he had a V-shaped scar on the side of his face, and second, he was sporting a large skull ring on his right finger.

Everything about him screamed Old Country. But what the hell was an O.C. doing galloping around Central Park kidnapping a highly placed Body Man like Amber?

He hissed at me. Obviously he believed himself to be an alpha male type, and the hiss was a warning that I was to submit to his will.

I wasn't big on hissing. Instead I displayed my fangs again and told him precisely what I thought of his demands of submission by flipping him off. The hansom cab continued to rattle all around me as I held on with my other hand.

He was obviously less than thrilled by my manual response to his demand for my kowtowing to him. "Stay out of this," he said in a deep voice. "You have no idea who you're screwing with."

"If I did know, I wouldn't give a shit," I said, and thrust myself into the hansom cab.

I have to tell you: If you're ever in a battle to the death, doing it in a really enclosed place is about as crappy an idea as you could want.

V-face grabbed for me, doubtless wanting to put a quick end

to the whole confrontation by just ripping my head clear of my shoulders. I brought my arms up in a defensive block, knocking his hands away with my forearms, and punched him hard in the face. His head rocked back and he snarled in fury. He tried to strike back, but I brushed his fists away, preventing him from landing a clear shot. Amber's unconscious body was wedged between us and we couldn't really get at each other.

The speeding carriage suddenly hit something in the ground—a pothole, a fallen tree limb, somebody's dog, whatever—and it jolted me. It was just enough time for V-face's hands to thrust in through my guard and he clamped them around my throat. His mouth was twisted in a sick looking smile, like he knew he'd won and it was just a matter of seconds.

"I tried to warn you," he said.

But as he was busy reminding me of that, I was grabbing at the bandolier of stakes that Amber had strapped around her. My fingers wrapped around one of the stakes and I yanked it clear. The natural motion if you're going to try and stake someone is to bring the hand down and around in an arc, like you're throwing darts. There wasn't time or room for that, so I just slammed the stake upward as if I were throwing a softball underhand.

The stake drove up, under his ribs, and he let out a shriek like the damned, which is appropriate, I guess. I didn't get his heart because, well, he didn't die, so it was pretty obvious. But I might well have nicked it, because he was howling and thrashing about and obviously in a ton of pain.

"Take it outside," I said and, before he could do anything, including reach the stake to withdraw it, I grabbed him by the scruff of the neck and the back of his coat and flung him through the door. He sailed out headfirst. I had a brief glimpse of a downward slope that we were passing and then he landed on it and tumbled down it.

One down, one to go.

I hauled myself out of the cab and swung up onto the roof, keeping in a crouch since I had no desire to get knocked off by a low-hanging branch. The driver saw me coming, and suddenly he produced a gun from inside his coat pocket. He aimed and fired and I twisted around as the bullet tore across my upper arm. It hurt like a son of a bitch; it felt like someone had poured acid on my skin. *Silver. That bastard.* The fact that he was carrying silver bullets told me two things: He knew what he was dealing with, and he was human, because only a human could easily tolerate the presence of silver. I don't know what it is about the chemical composition of that particular metal that hurts my kind, any more than I truly understand why wooden stakes can end us, but it's just one of the inconveniences of being undead. Then again, regular people can be hurt by any kind of bullet, whereas most regular ones won't kill me, so I guess I have no cause for complaining.

On the other hand, a silver bullet in the brain would really suck. I had met a vampire who had taken a silver bullet smack in the gray matter thanks to a smackdown with a Body Man in Chicago. Before taking the hit, he'd been a brilliant essayist. Now he had to be fed blood through a straw because he'd literally forgotten how to use his fangs.

Tragically, I'd neglected to wear my bulletproof helmet when I'd decided to go for a stroll in Central Park.

I flung myself to the far side of the speeding wagon and off. This was one of those situations where I desperately wished that I could indeed change into a winged predator like Dracula or one of those guys. Instead the closest I could come was clinging like a bat to the side of the wagon. Through the cab's window, I saw Amber being jostled around. I thought that the blood flow was slowing down, but I had no idea whether that was because it was starting to clot or if her tank was just starting to run dry.

The driver didn't seem to know what to do first. He was looking down at me, trying to target me at what was now a lousy angle for him. At the same time he was trying to control a sprinting horse while holding onto the reins with one hand. That wasn't an easy job considering the way the animal was jerking the reins around.

I flattened myself against the hansom cab, making myself an even lousier target, counted to three, and then swung my body upward. I slammed my feet into the driver's chest just as he was trying to get a bead on me again. The impact sent him up and out of the seat. He flew through the air, his arms pinwheeling, and then he hit the pavement with what was, to me, a pretty satisfying crunch. He might well have been, indeed from all evidence was, a human, but he'd tried to kill me and I had no sympathy for him. Given the opportunity, I would happily have broken his neck. So I had no trouble with the idea of breaking his ass.

As I grabbed up the reins that had fallen from his hand, I couldn't resist shouting, *"You should've worn a seatbelt, asshole!"* When you're a vampire adding insult to injury just comes naturally.

My reflex was to slow the horse down but then I realized there was no point in doing so. Amber was suffering from shock and blood loss. I was going to have to get her to a hospital quickly, and that would hardly be served by slowing down the carriage.

Lenox Hill was the closet hospital. How did I know that? Because when you're a Body Man, you just make it a point to keep track of where all the hospitals are at any given moment.

The horse didn't seem to be aware that there had been a change in management. Maintaining a steady hand on the reins, I kept the carriage barreling down the road and looked for a crossover that would put me out onto Fifth Avenue. Within moments one presented itself, and the horse and carriage barreled out onto Fifth. But we were moving too quickly and the turn was too sharp. We sped into the middle of Fifth right into the oncoming traffic. Tires screeched and cars slewed to either side in order to get out of our way. *"Sorry!"* I shouted. *"Sorry!"* Drivers shouted back at me, and I can assure you that none of them was apologizing.

We had emerged on 73rd Street; the hospital was on 77th and Park. As cars scrambled to make room for us, I kept the carriage pounding down Fifth Avenue going against the traffic flow and then cut right on 77th. The carriage sped down the street and I guided it around cars that were slowing for such inconveniences as traffic lights. More cars slammed to a halt, more curses were hurled with that unique talent that only New Yorkers seemed to possess. I didn't care. Being undead tends to relieve you of worrying about things such as pissing people off.

The carriage rolled up to Lenox Hill's ER. I jumped off and moved quickly to the cab. Amber was looking deathly pale, but at least she was still breathing, so that was something.

And as I crouched over her, I noticed that I was bleeding from the place where the bullet had cut across my arm. It was at that moment I realized I could solve all my problems with a single stroke.

I could sponsor her. All I had to do was drip blood into her and that, combined with just how near death she was, would likely do the job. I couldn't be one hundred percent sure. It wasn't an exact science, and I'd never turned anyone before. But I was reasonably certain I could do it.

It was hard to believe it had taken me that long to realize it. I didn't need to bother with an emergency room. Nor did I have to worry about being a vampire engaged to—or, God help me, even married to—a human. All I had to do was make her like me and she would automatically be in the same fix I was. We would immediately be allies.

Or...

Maybe not.

For all I knew, Amber might be such a hard ass that she might decide that she would kill me if it was the last thing she ever did. She'd take me down and, once I was good and dead, she'd throw herself on her own stake just to avoid being like me. I sure wouldn't put it past her.

And besides, it wasn't like I was in love with my current status. Why should I want to inflict it on her? She wasn't a Wanna V, circling around the vampire lifestyle and hoping that it would embrace her. Just because I had decided to live with it—or whatever the hell it was I did with it—didn't mean that she was going to, or that she should have to.

The blood on her neck looked so inviting that I was tempted to drain her dry just because of what I was. But unlike the scorpion of the fable, I was able to fight my nature. Instead of sucking down her remains like a milkshake, I hauled her out of the cab and cradled her in my arms. "Sorry about this, kid. Would've been nice to be able to share the night with you." Then I hauled ass into the ER. I didn't bother to tie off the horse, not giving a damn if it decided to wander away on its own or, for that matter, if someone stole it. I had other problems to deal with.

A few of those problems showed up a few hours later while I was standing in Amber's room, waiting for her to come around.

Initially the hospital staff tried to keep me out, telling me that she needed to be kept in isolation and not even family members, to say nothing of fiancés, would be allowed in. Now we vampires, or at least this vampire, may not have the full-blown hypnotic powers that you see Dracula tossing around in movies. But there is a certain amount of charisma that we have going for us and if the target is pliable enough, we turn on the charm and get things done. It's probably a sort of survival mechanism that's developed over time since it can make intended victims more pliable. Nu Vs like myself usually have no need of it since the Wanna Vs come to us freely and of their own will, but you can bet the O.C.'s put it to use in order to exert enough influence over their intended victims that the poor saps don't fight back.

That's exactly what I did with the ER nurse, locking eyes with her and focusing all my will. I didn't hypnotize her exactly but instead charmed my way past her as she conspiratorially told me that if I went in without drawing attention to myself and kept it quiet, it wouldn't be any big deal.

Part of my desire to do so stemmed from genuine concern over her well-being. Amber was a nice enough kid, and even though the notion of our being married was a disaster in the making for reasons that she was clueless about, she still seemed capable and whip-smart and pleasant enough company. I didn't harbor any doubts that, if she knew what I really was, she'd stake me without a second thought. But for someone who would kill me and think nothing of it, she was a decent sort.

The entire business in the park, though, was preying on me. This was no random happenstance where a passing vampire had taken a shot at us because he was in the mood for an evening snack. She'd been targeted, and not by just some schmuck. The fact was that I'd gotten lucky taking the guy on. He reeked of power and old world style. I was reasonably sure that he wasn't just an OC. He was someone who was fairly high up in their pecking order. So why was a highly placed Old Country vampire gunning for Amber?

I had no answer, nor did I feel it was my job to provide one. As the typical target of Amber and her family, my emotional involvement in this whole business was pretty limited. What concerned me now, though, was just how far this unknown vampire was willing to go, and just how much they were out to get Amber. Had they followed us somehow to the hospital, or perhaps even had operatives on the inside? It sounds paranoid, I know, but obviously someone really had been out to get her, and I wasn't sure just how far they were going to take it. What that came down to was that Amber was completely vulnerable while just lying there unconscious.

And yes, granted, I could have just walked away and let someone dispose of her, thus solving my longer-term problem. But if I were okay with that, I would have just let him eat her in the first place and not worry about it.

I rang up my mother on her cell phone and gave her a quick rundown of what had happened. Naturally the first thing she asked was whether or not I was okay, which I obviously was able to tell her that I was. Then she expressed shock over what had happened in the park, but at the same time she didn't sound *too* shocked. The possibility of death stalked every single Body Man whenever we were out. We were, after all, essentially looking for trouble, and so it wasn't much of a surprise that on occasion trouble found us instead. She told me she'd take care of letting Amber's parents know, and then told me—not asked, mind you, but told me—to stay by Amber's bedside. "You never know with these creatures," she said with an edge of warning to her voice, apparently trying to make it clear that she was perfectly capable of taking care of business should it come to that. Frankly, I very much suspected that she'd be able to do exactly that, even if one of those creatures was her son.

I sat there for a time, watching Amber breathing, her eyelids fluttering every now and then. The machines connected to her beeped steadily, just like in the movies. At one point she moaned softly, her eyes dancing beneath the lids, and she thrust slightly with her hand in a stabbing motion I recognized all too readily. If she'd been a cat, I'd have said she was having a hunting dream. She was probably having it as a human as well.

And I was not human.

It was yet another reminder of the vast gulf that was between us, the hopelessness of my situation. Her head slumped to one side in her slumber, and I saw it there: her jugular, pulsing steadily in perfect time to the machine that was monitoring her vitals. Pure, perfect human blood moving through it, and if I drained it right here and now, there would be one less Body Man hunting my kind. I could come up with some sort of cover story easily. I was in the bathroom, I was out grabbing a late night snack, anything. And then some mysterious vampire, identity yet to be determined, must have snuck in and attacked the helpless vampire hunter in her slumber. How typical of that dastardly breed! Quickly, round up the troops and find her killer! The murdering bastard might still be around somewhere!

All my problems would be solved with one quick penetration of my fangs.

I don't remember walking over to her. One moment I was seated across the room, watching her, and the next I was standing over her and slowly running my finger along her throat, as if I were preparing to tenderize some meat. My fingertip rested on her jugular. The carotid, I was told, provided better eating because the blood was oxygenated, but the jugular would spurt less and the blood flow would be more controllable. I wouldn't have to worry about blood spurting onto my clothes.

So easy. So quick.

She moaned in her sleep and then, in her slumber, she brought her hand up and rested it atop mine. My instinct was to pull away immediately, but I left it there. Amber squeezed it then, ever so gently, not even conscious of it. She calmed immediately. Whatever was stalking her in her dreams, or vice versa, seemed to evaporate. Her moan slid into a soft sigh and her pulse rate, which had been creeping upward, slowed to a more normal rhythm.

A vampire hunter had taken comfort from the cold touch of a vampire upon her throat. It was so amazingly ironic that I wasn't sure whether to laugh or cry and settled for doing neither, but just remaining like that until she shifted in the bed and her hand slipped off mine.

I removed my hand from her throat and sniffed it briefly. It smelled like her. Not of perfume, but the pure human aroma that so many of them tried to hide with various scents and colognes, as if trying to deny their very humanity. Here's me, trying to hide my nature from others, and humans trying to hide their nature from each other. Send in the freaking clowns.

As I stood there, I heard quick footsteps, and some loud protests from nurses or whoever saying loudly that nametags or passes had to be gotten at the desk, and these people were going to have to turn right around and go through procedures immediately. No response was given them, which led me to believe that whoever it was was simply ignoring them, and the nurse's louder shout of "*Sirs!*" pretty much confirmed that.

The door had been hanging partly closed, but now it opened with a bang and there were Lawrence and Amanda Singer, with Kubrick bringing up the rear. They stood in the doorway, looking stunned for a moment, and then Kubrick pushed them aside. I doubt he would have been able to do that with Lawrence if Lawrence hadn't been so distracted. Kubrick came right at me, picking up speed with every step, and before I could move he grabbed me by the shirtfront and slammed me against the wall with enough force that it scrambled my brains for a moment.

"What the hell did you do to her!" he said with a snarl. His breath was thick with alcohol. He wasn't drunk, but he was sure uninhibited.

A great beast stirred within me, furious that this asshole thought he could shove me around like that. It pushed me to toss caution aside. I could feel my fangs trying to push through, and there was a tingling in my eyeballs that signaled the redness was about to surge forward. I could see myself picking up the startled Kubrick and throwing him with all my strength across the room, slamming into the Singers, knocking them all flat. Or maybe I would just snap his neck in one quick move. It would be so easy, so easy, because he'd left himself open for it and killing him would present no challenge at all.

I squeezed my eyes shut, took a deep breath that I didn't actually require in order to try and steady myself, shoving the murderous fury back down where it couldn't hurt anyone.

Instead I allowed just enough of it, the merest tip of the iceberg, to come into view.

Bringing my arms up from beneath him, I swept them side-to-side, breaking his grip effortlessly. He looked momentarily confused and, because we were so close to each other, I went for the simplest move: I head-butted him. My forehead slammed into his face and I heard a satisfying crack as his nose shattered from the impact. He cried out, clutching at it, letting himself react to the pain rather than the attacker, which is always a mistake. I started to jab toward his solar plexus with my hand like a spear. Had I completed the thrust, it would have driven right through his chest. I caught myself at the last moment, slowed my speed so that it wasn't an inhuman blur, and flattened my hand upward so that it was my palm that struck him. At full strength he would have flown out the door and not stopped until he struck the candy machine across the hall. As it was he simply stumbled backwards and struck Lawrence, who staggered from the impact.

"Stop it! Stop it!" Amanda was shouting, heading straight for her daughter. I sidestepped quickly and she fired me a confused look, as if she didn't know what to think of me. On the one hand I'd just smacked around one of her people in a hospital room where her vulnerable daughter was lying asleep. On the other hand, I was the one who'd been attacked, so how could she blame me for it?

Kubrick had his hand to his chest and was gasping for air a little. "Son of a bitch! I think he broke one of my ribs!"

"Good think you're in a hospital," I said sarcastically.

"This is no place for violence," said Lawrence, which was kind of belated as far as I was concerned. If you think someplace is no place for violence, why not try to prevent it rather than "tsk tsk" after people are getting smacked around.

A couple of burly guys in scrubs who I took to be orderlies were at the doorway, obviously out to keep things, well, orderly. "There a problem here?" one of them said, eyes shifting around as if he were sizing up individual targets. His eyes passed right over me. Not surprising; both Lawrence and Kubrick were big guys. I looked like a dwarf by comparison. He couldn't know that I was actually the biggest threat in the room.

"No," said Lawrence in that commanding voice of his. "No problem. That's my daughter in the bed. There was just some..." He glanced at Kubrick. "...raw feelings."

"Uh huh," said the orderly. "We need you people to get proper visitor IDs or we're going to call the cops. You can't just go walking past the nurses like you own the place. You understand that, buddy?"

"I'm not..." Lawrence cut himself off before finishing the sentence with the obvious *your buddy*. He paused and then said with forced civility, "Yes. I understand. If you wouldn't mind just giving us five minutes—?"

The orderly appeared to give this as much consideration as if the devil had just offered him a swap of his soul in exchange for a week-long orgy with the Laker Girls. "Okay," he said finally. "Five minutes. I'll be checking back." Then with one final, significant glower he gestured for his buddy to follow him and they walked out.

There was a moment of silence and then Kubrick, still rubbing his chest, said sullenly, "She was fine when she left us. Five minutes with you and she's in the goddamn hospital."

"Five minutes with you," I shot back, "and she would have been in the morgue. Because the guys who did this would have kicked your candy ass and sucked her dry. So how about showing a little gratitude, soldier boy, and save your attitude for somebody who's going to be impressed by it?"

"Gratitude?"

Kubrick looked like he was ready to throw down again, and Lawrence was about to rein him in, but Amanda short-circuited the whole thing by saying in a voice of iron, "So help me God, the next person who mouths off or starts something, I am personally going to kick the shit out of him. Understood?" When we didn't reply immediately, she repeated, *"Understood?"*

All of us muttered some variation on "Yes, ma'am."

She turned away from us then as if we were no longer worth her time, which as far as she was likely concerned, we weren't. Instead she took her daughter by the hand and stroked the top of it. Meanwhile Lawrence, apparently determined to seize control of the situation once more, said in his best *look at me and how commanding I am* voice, "Vincent…what the hell happened?"

I told him as quickly and concisely as I could. Obviously I held back some of the details of the battle, such as my displaying my fangs to the vampire I was fighting. But the gist of it was most definitely there. He listened, nodding, interrupting every now and then with a question. Kubrick, still rubbing his ribs where I'd clocked him, stood off in a corner and continued to make with the glowering.

When I finished, Lawrence stood there and processed it for a few moments more. Then, his voice tense, he asked the one question he'd obviously been putting off: "Did she drink?"

It looked like Amanda's spine stiffened slightly when he said that. It wasn't an unreasonable concern. If the vampire had, in addition to biting Amber, forced her to drink his own blood, then the Singer family was going to be due for a world of pain because they were going to have to deal with staking their little girl. Fortunately I was able to answer with authority.

"No," I said firmly.

"You're sure."

"Positive. I saw his attack on her; she was out of it. Also, I took a few moments to check her lips, teeth and tongue. Even if he'd somehow forced it down her in the scuffle, I would have seen blood stains."

"Okay," said Lawrence, and he let out a slow exhale of relief. Then he reached forward and clapped a hand on my shoulder. "Good job," he said.

Apparently this was more than Kubrick could take. He came forward, bristling with fury, and said, "Good job? Sir, with all respect, how can you say that? He let—"

"Shut the fuck up, Kubrick."

The voice that had spoken was tired and scratchy, but it was most definitely Amber's. Our heads snapped around and even Amanda looked startled because she'd shifted her gaze from her daughter to us and might have been, for all I knew, ready to tell us to shut up herself.

Amber gazed at us through half-lidded eyes. "Seriously, Kubrick. I mean it. Shut the fuck up."

"Language," Lawrence said more out of reflex than anything else. Then, apparently remembering that being a father meant more than attending to discipline, he said, "Are you all right, honey?"

"Well, my throat hurts like hell, but otherwise I'm fine. You," and she pointed at me, raising her hand ever so slightly, making it look like a huge effort. She waggled her finger. "C'mere."

I did as she asked. She took my hand and then, carefully so as not to dislodge the tubes that were sticking into her arm, lifted my knuckles to her lips and kissed them gently. When she spoke, she was looking at me but it was clear that she was addressing Kubrick. "He saved me, you big dumb ox," she said (which was how I, using my keen, analytical mind, knew she was talking to Kubrick). "I got sloppy. I let my guard down, and I almost lost my life over it. I was out for most of what happened, but I can tell you that if I'd been remembering a fraction of what Mom and Dad taught me, I wouldn't have gotten myself into that fix in the first place."

"You probably let down your guard because of him," said Kubrick, but he was sullen and unconvincing. Lawrence didn't even bother to look at him but instead simply rolled his eyes a little, a gesture that I have to admit I just loved.

I seized the moment of silence because I had to get out of there; I had an appointment waiting. "Look," I said, "I'm going to leave you guys here. You can keep an eye on her, and that vampire is still out there. I'm going to find him and kick his ass."

"I'll come with you," Lawrence said immediately, which I suppose I should have seen coming.

Before I could hit him with an excuse about what a lousy idea that was, Amanda saved me the trouble. "You're going nowhere, Lawrence," she said sharply. "Your daughter is here and she needs you. Let Kubrick go with him..."

"I don't think so," I said flatly, and no one challenged me on it.

As dramatic exits go, it wasn't up there with, "Frankly, my dear, I don't give a damn," but it was close enough.

Nine

My Two Visits, One of Which is Kind of a Dead End, But Not So Much

I felt relieved to be on my own again. It was good to be back on my cycle, clipping through the constantly stalled traffic of New York City and to be heading somewhere.

I rode past the place where I had left the horse and carriage and discovered that the horse was long gone. That, though, was quickly attended to: about ten blocks later, I found the horse. He was standing off to one side, comfortably eating the leaves off a Central Park tree that extended over the wall, while some bum lay unconscious on the ground. Police were in the process of gathering and summoning a van, or maybe a hearse. Made no never mind to me. I slowed down briefly and the horse caught sight of me. For the slightest of moments we exchanged looks, and I was reasonably sure he recognized me. Then I revved the engine and the horse went back to eating the leaves, and thus did we part company.

I cruised over the 59th Street Bridge, the same place where Simon and Garfunkel, sitting in unmoving traffic, had crafted a ditty about taking it easy and "Feeling Groovy." I'd never been much for writing songs. Or feeling groovy. Or anything, really. I wondered how it was that a couple of musicians could take something as routine as getting stuck in traffic and transform it into a catchy tune that hit number one.

I was able to dart through the traffic reasonably quickly, moving deftly from side to side past the crawling cars. I had never been that wild about Queens Boulevard on the other side, but at least it had opened up somewhat as I drove through it. I scuttled over onto the main section of the street and in a few minutes was cruising through Astoria. I didn't know the exact address, but I knew it was somewhere in the Astoria neighborhood and I was reasonably sure I could find it the way I always did.

Took me half an hour of endless patience before I finally turned it up: around a corner, down a half block, and there it was. It was an abandoned hotel that still had up signs about being for rent or sale. The signs were metal and bent, with rusted patches that were who-knew-how-old. I had every confidence in Duncan that he would wind up finding a way to cover all this. He might go for the simplest method and find the owner, make him over into "our own image," and deal with it that way. There was certainly no faster means of getting what he wanted than that. I'll grant you, it didn't do much insofar as my sense of feeling good about how the world around me went, but it had the merits of being efficient.

I moved around the building, looking for some manner of entrance, and eventually found a door on the far side. I knocked on it and, when no one came quickly, knocked again. This time there was some shuffling and when the door slid open, it was a brand new pair of eyes glaring at me from within. "Yeah?"

I didn't have time for the extended shit this time. "Name's Vince. Lemme in."

I expected that I was then going to have to go ten rounds of "Vince who?" Instead, to my surprise, the little window slammed home and moments later the door had opened right up. The door operator was shorter than the previous holder of the job had been. He also looked a damned sight jumpier. Couldn't blame him; there was little doubt that he'd heard how his predecessor had bought it when Lawrence and the hit squad had made their New York debut.

"C'mon in. He's expecting you," said the door operator. He glanced right and left past my shoulder to make sure there was no one behind me. Who that might have been, I couldn't even begin to guess. But if it made him happy then, y'know, what the hell.

The atmosphere was seriously restrained from the last

time. It wasn't all that surprising to me. People were still in the process of finding the place and acclimating to the new environment. Several floors above had already collapsed upon themselves, leaving plenty of room for the dance floor that now constituted most of the lower half. There were some Wanna V's around, and some vamps as well, but each side was more or less tending to itself and its own needs. The Wanna V's looked hopefully toward the vampires, but the vampires pointedly looked the other way. No one wanted to play with each other, and that was fine as far as I was concerned. I knew that, over time, the situation would change, but for now it meant that I had the Wanna V's mostly to myself, and that was always the simpler way to go about things.

I heard a soft footfall behind me and turned to see the guy I knew it was gonna be. Sure enough, Duncan the homeless vampire was standing directly behind me, studying me carefully. He was dressed much the same as he'd been last time; the only difference was the new shirt he was sporting to make up for the one that I'd previously stabbed. He looked me up and down and idly brushed some dirt off my shoulders. "Looking well, Vincent," he said in his standard, slightly indifferent tone.

"You too, Duncan, although," and I nodded toward the static group that was occupying the hallway. There was no DJ on tap yet, possibly because the previous one had been roasted alive. "The place isn't exactly popping yet."

He gestured lazily around the large area. "Of course not. These things are built over time, Vincent. After a sufficient period of adjustment, this area is going to be hopping. Trust me, you'll see."

"That's really great to hear, Duncan," I said, having none of the genuine enthusiasm that should normally have accompanied that kind of pronouncement. "Hey, you hear of any vamp with a v-shaped scratch on his face?"

"V-shaped?" When I nodded, he didn't answer immediately. Instead he was clearly thinking about it, revisiting the assortment of wounds that he knew vamps had sustained over the course of years. Finally, slowly, he shook his head. "Nothing's coming to mind. Which isn't to say something might not at some point in the future. But right now, nothing's ringing any bells. Why? Who is it?"

"Didn't say it was anyone."

He gave me only the slightest of amused looks. "It's obviously someone, Vincent. Whether you want to tell me or not is entirely your own lookout."

"That's true enough." I glanced at my wristwatch and saw that it was already 12:30. I'd been running late. Couldn't be helped, although now I was annoyed as hell.

"Looking for someone?"

"Yeah, but I'm not sure she's...hold on."

There she was, dressed exactly in the manner that she'd said she'd be in. Long red dress, black boa. She was obviously way too small for it; it sat upon her shoulders at least one if not two sizes too large. Must have been a borrow from her mother's closet. She was obviously used to wearing her darkened hair down, but this evening she had it done up in an elaborate wrap atop her head. My God, she was even smoking, although it was obviously something she was unaccustomed to since she would turn away and cough at least once a minute. She was standing off to one side, trying to keep a careful watch on the various denizens of the place. She was fortunate. I was reasonably sure that she wouldn't have to be concerned about her fun being destroyed by the hunters of the night

"That her?" said Duncan, watching where I was looking. "She's cute. Bit inexperienced, but cute. You thinking of—?"

"No," I said quickly. "She's a source, that's all, and maybe not even that."

"Yes, well..." He shrugged as if it made no difference to him at all, but we both knew that wasn't true.

I made my way down to where the Wanna V's were hanging. Vampires tended to move noiselessly as they walked. I could have done so as well. Instead I came down the stairs and entered the main floor with a steady *thump-thump* that practically screamed for attention.

The girls looked right toward me and then through me when they determined, with their endless powers of deduction, that I was merely another Wanna V like them. I paid no attention, instead focusing on the girl in the red dress. She, in turn, noticed me, and raised her eyebrows in a carefully dispassionate "is that you?" manner. I nodded ever so slightly and gestured for her to follow me. She did so, trying to walk with a slither but moving more with an odd kind of looping manner. I rolled my eyes. I didn't need this, but she was more or less the only source I had into this whole mess, and so I would have to just deal with it.

There was a small table for two off in the corner and I sat down, waiting. She joined me a few moments later. "The guy from on line?" she asked with no preamble.

No, just some weird guy who was hoping you would follow me so that I could—

Instantly I dropped the entire idle thoughts in my head. It wasn't going to help anyone. Instead I just nodded and extended a hand. "Vince," I said and she shook it limply. "And you are—?"

"Molly," she said. That was all. Just Molly. Fine, whatever.

"Okay, Molly. So how much time do you have for us to talk?"

"As much time as you want." She looked around once more and then, clearing her throat much more loudly than she needed to, she reached over and took my hand. "As much time as you need. I mean," and she suddenly seemed a bit uncertain, "you *are* a vampire, right?"

Oh, God. Not this again. But then I realized that all I had to do was be vague and I could get everything I wanted. I lowered my voice and, trying to sound casual, said, "You never know."

She gasped at that, seemingly coming to life for the first time. Her eyes widened and it was as if her entire body had just been jolted with electrodes. "You mean—?" She couldn't even fully frame the question. Dropping her voice to the barest of whispers, Molly managed to say, "You could...sponsor me?"

"You never know," I said again, and this practically sent her into spasms of joy that she very quickly managed to suppress by clapping her hands over her mouth. Before she could devolve into something that was going to be of no use to anyone, she settled for simply nodding.

"Tell me about when you first met Rodney," I began.

I was then going to ask if she actually *had* encountered Rodney before, but it wasn't necessary. "Ohhh, Rodney," she said, her voice wistful. "I'm not sure where to start. When I first met him, he was wearing a dark coat, black slacks and a black polo shirt. I guess he felt that black was really in this year. He looked right through me. Didn't have the slightest opportunity to talk to him about anything at all, really. The second time he had more or less the same outfit on, except it was a blue shirt. Again he looked right through me, but just toward the end, he smiled briefly before heading out. The third time—"

She fell silent when I put up a hand to stop her endless prattling. Having quieted her down, at least for a moment, I said, "Let's jump it forward slightly, if we could. Let's take it to a point where you and Rodney had actually, y'know, formed a *real* relationship. One that you could keep up to speed without having to worry about it."

"Oh." She seemed to understand. "You mean like to the point where he and Tracy were actually going together."

"That's correct."

She seemed a bit disappointed that the conversation was going off in a direction that she wasn't wild about. Obviously she preferred to dwell on her own obsession with Rodney than where his own interests took him. "After about six months or so, Tracy and Rodney had a real relationship going. Except it's hard to tell just how real it was, y'know?"

I started to shake my head but then I understood. "You're saying in terms of their relationship..."

"It wasn't going anywhere, yeah." She shrugged in a disconsolate manner. "What can you do, y'know? You hope that it's going to go somewhere..."

"Meaning that he would make her like him."

"Bingo." She touched her nose, just in case she thought I didn't get it.

I got it just fine.

"Annnnnyway," she went on when she saw I didn't respond, "she kept at it, but Rodney wouldn't do it. He'd feed on her pretty regularly, but always just enough to keep him going; never more than that. He was..." She paused and, in spite of herself, smiled. "He was kind of sweet, actually. Like, y'know, respectful."

"You're right, that is kind of sweet." Hated to admit it, but it was true. Either that or it wasn't true and Tracy was simply a typical brain case, the type of which was all too common in the venues where I happened to hang around.

"And Tracy, she didn't realize it, or at least didn't think about," said Molly. "Because this other guy came along…"

"Other guy." This caused me to sit up a bit more. "What other guy?"

"She met him on line at another chat site," she told me.

"And he was a vampire."

"Yeah."

This was beginning to get interesting. The impression I'd had was that Rodney had been a one-girl guy, at least to as much a degree as vampires usually allowed things to get. Yet now I was learning otherwise, and that was more than enough to pique my curiosity. "What's his name?"

"Dunno."

Dammit. "No idea?"

She shook her head. "Honest? I can't even say for sure that they met. They just had this thing going on line, and then…" Her voice trailed off. "And then it stopped. I mean, they stopped. I mean…she stopped. You know?"

"Sure I do."

Despite my best judgment, I reached over and rubbed the back of her hand. She let out a deep sigh and placed hers atop mine. After a few seconds of that I carefully extracted my hand from hers. "Okay, look," I said, "you don't know who she hooked up with. Right? Well," and I extracted a business card from my wallet, "here. My private number. If someone approaches you the same way that they came at Tracy, you'll let me know. Okay?"

"But what about Tracy?" She didn't seem to quite understand that the conversation was effectively over. Molly stared helplessly at the business card I'd given her. "I mean, this was a whole investigation into Tracy, wasn't it? She was my friend and—"

"She was a girl you knew. That's all she was. Isn't that right?"

It was more than a question. It was a strong suggestion that sank into her mind and seemed to clear away a good deal of the detritus that was rattling around in here. "Yeah, sure," Molly said tonelessly. "Sure, she was just some girl I knew."

"And now she's gone and you're not going to worry about her anymore." I kept my voice flat and even, devoid of any sense of urgency. Understand that I'm not much when it comes to the entire concept of hypnosis, but nevertheless I'm not exactly a slouch in such matters.

I got the exact response I wanted as Molly continued to nod, her eyes wide. "Not anymore. Not in the least."

"No, that's right. But if you do have some reason to call me, there's my card." I reached over and tapped it authoritatively.

"Yes, all right."

"Now smile."

She smiled obediently.

I patted her on the head. "Atta girl."

Then I got up and left her there. She continued gazing out on the people who were still checking each other out, scanning each other to see whether they were friend or foe, good or bad. I knew that it would wear off sooner or later, but I felt no need to hurry the process along.

I returned to Duncan and asked hurriedly as to Rodney's location. Duncan quickly produced the address, adding, "I have not heard from him since we relocated here. Understand that I try to allow for the uncertainties transpiring in people's lives, but he needs to return as soon as possible. Will you convey that, please?" I agreed to do so as soon as I found him.

It didn't take long, as it turned out. Rodney's place was over in Flushing, not all that far. It was nothing particularly fancy: the fourth floor of a five floor walk up, and there was a dust-covered sign indicating that the elevator was "temporarily" out of service. I suspected the "temporarily" part was going to last until such time as the tenants ceased paying rent in protest, at which point the landlord would simply sell the place off and walk away with a lined pocket.

At least that's what I suspected. On the other hand, maybe everything would be fine, and the repair guy was going to show up the next day. Anything was possible.

The moment that I entered the front hallways, however, I gagged. Fourth floor or not, the stench from Rodney's apartment building floated down to me with a determination that wouldn't be ignored. At first I couldn't understand how anyone else could possibly live with it, and then realized that my senses were far more attuned to it. Within a couple of days, the aroma would be so powerful that they'd be able to smell it halfway down the street. But right here, right now, it was impossible for me to miss.

There was a door that sealed the outside from the inside, and it took me only seconds to punch it open. The door flew wide and I was immediately into the main hallway and heading up the stairs. The smell grew more pronounced the further up the stairs I went, verifying for me that someone was definitely dead and the likely subject of the death was the late Rodney. An old man was coming down as I went up and he stopped and looked at me, confused. "Can I help you?" he asked.

"Not really, no," I said and kept going. Another few flights of stairs and then I was outside Rodney's apartment. One punch and the door flew open. I entered and, sure enough, there was the late Rodney, lying draped across his couch. He was wearing a pair of sweat pants and a blue t-shirt, and he'd been lying on the couch watching television. The TV was still on but softly; a repeat of *The Big Bang Theory* was on. Sheldon was at the moment losing control because Penny (what the hell *was* her last name, anyway?) had given him an autograph of Leonard Nimoy's. I loved that episode. Now I turned it off.

I went over to Rodney and studied him closely. His eyes were still open, as if in stage fright. I took the time to reach up and close his eyes for him. They didn't budge at first; it took me a couple of efforts to force them shut. I then glanced over his body and didn't see any sign of outside violence. I tilted back his teeth and spotted scrapes of blood still in it. He certainly had not died of hunger.

Quickly I looked around the rest of the place. There wasn't much of anything there. Some small bits of clothing, a few books, a single serving set of a knife and fork. Assuming that he hadn't been victimized or something, Rodney had been living a very empty life. So empty that it made you wonder who in hell would be remotely interested in ending it?

Then, in rummaging through the drawers, I discovered

the first thing that might actually represent something useful. Buried beneath an assortment of mostly threadbare clothing was a digital camera.

I turned it on and very quickly started flipping through it.

The images in the picture assortment were remarkably consistent. It was all some girl. Some of the photographs told me that they had been taken at the former Moveable Feast, and others were around the general area. Everything was at night.

All pictures of the same girl from different elevations. It became quickly evident that the photographer, whom we could safely assume was Rodney, had been obsessed with this one girl.

Tracy? Had to be. Okay, technically she didn't *have* to be, but still, I had a feeling. That was all; just a feeling. My feelings, though, had an annoying habit of turning out to be right.

What the hell were you up to, Rodney? What were you playing at?

Then I stopped cold.

The final pictures in the array of photographs were way more than familiar to me.

They had been taken from the same elevated angle as a number of the previous photographs. They were pictures of Tracy (or at least the girl I thought was Tracy) and she was leaning against the rails of some fence somewhere in the city. No, no just somewhere. It was, without question, around a lake in Central Park.

I believe the reason I recognized it so easily was because I knew the man that she was talking to.

It was the man whom I had been fighting, the one with the "V" wound on his face.

The girl whom I suspected was Tracy was chatting it up with the "V" wound guy whom I had managed to toss out of his carriage, and I had absolutely no idea why.

It was a lack of knowledge in my personal inventory of information that I very much intended to learn.

Ten

My Conversation with Amber Goes Nowhere

I lay in bed after returning home and tried to sleep, and succeeded exactly not at all.

I had dutifully called the cops right before I left so that Rodney would at least be attended to. Doubtless he'd be dumped in a pauper's grave and be forgotten about; many of us had long ago severed ties with our loving families and I had little doubt that Rodney had followed in that path. But at least his body would be disposed of, even if they had problems discovering exactly what it was that he had died of.

When I'd first arrived home, Mom had been up and waiting for me. She'd immediately started asking a barrage of questions, considering that she'd been informed of how badly Amber had been smacked around (that tidbit courtesy of Amber's father.) I'd made it abundantly clear at that point that I didn't have the slightest interest in bringing her up to speed; that I just wanted to go to sleep and be left alone. I had no clear idea who I'd been fighting and even less of a clear idea why they had launched an attack against my "fiancée."

This was information that my mother was perfectly happy to assimilate, or at least so she said. But the fact was that she wanted to know everything that had been going on, and I was hardly in any sort of position to tell her. All I wanted to do was get some sleep, and after making that abundantly clear to her, I went off to my bedroom to accomplish exactly that.

But once I stripped to my underwear, crawled under the blankets and tried to accomplish that very thing, it turned out to be the one thing I could not, in fact, do. My activities of the last twenty-four hours kept colliding with each other. Even though I managed to fall asleep for minutes, maybe even a whole hour at a time, my day turned out instead to be a mish-mash of events that refused to leave me alone.

There was Amber, charming and pleasant and, oh yeah, being dragged through the streets of Central Park by a vamp with a "Y" on his face who—when he wasn't busy assaulting my girlfriend/fiancée—spent his extra hours of the night chatting it up with Tracy-the-dead-girl.

Then there was Amber's dad, Lawrence, big and burly, a combination of Arnold Schwarzenegger and Denzel Washington, along with his crew of reprobates who were perfectly happy to go around and beat the crap out of my guys for no reason other than they saw them as mortal enemies which, by the way, they were.

I turned and slept and slept and turned and when it seemed as if I'd been doing that for an entire day's and night's worth of flipping around, I checked my watch and moaned to see that it was just past noon. Barely four hours had passed since I had gone to bed and now there I lay, peeking out at the sun behind the curtains and left wondering just how in hell this whole thing fit together.

I was no detective, that much was certain. This was way over my head, and I knew deep down—hell, I knew way up top—that I had none of the skills that were required to deal with all this.

There was a sharp knock at my door. I had no idea who it was; all I could think of was that it was my mother. "What is it, Ma?" I said, making no attempt to hide my impatience.

"Actually, Vincent, it's me. Do you have a moment?"

Immediately I sat up, keeping most of me hidden beneath the blanket. "Uh…sure, Mrs.—"

"Amanda, please." Sure enough, in strolled Amber's mother. She looked as self-conscious and uncomfortable as she had when we'd first met and she'd revealed to my mother that I was engaged to her daughter. My own mother was right behind her, standing a few feet back and letting this still-relative stranger take the lead. How much influence did the woman have over my mom, anyway? "I was hoping we could talk for a few minutes, if that's all right."

I toyed with the idea of pointing out that talking for a few minutes was something that never, ever went well. But I simply couldn't see the point in bringing that up. I rubbed my eyes slightly in order to put forward the notion that she'd awoken me. "Yeah, sure. Whatever. What's up?"

She came within a foot or so of the bed but then placed her hand upon the footrest. "I think it would be hard to express my concern over just how badly things went between us last night. The arguing, the testiness; Lawrence feels just terrible about it."

"Oh, does he. Well, I guess that makes it all okay, then."

"Vinnie," snapped my mother warningly at my sarcastic tone.

But Amanda put out a hand as she sadly shook her head. "No, he's right to sound irritated. We both know it. The little hunting job with Amber turned out to be great in theory and total disaster in real life. Absolutely nothing went as planned and now there's a great deal of frustration and finger pointing. It's just...it's not good, is what I'm saying."

"Well, you're right about that." I was trying to maintain my sarcasm, but it wasn't working particularly well. I kept feeling as if Amber was a decent sort who just found herself in the midst of dealing with a lot of crap, and having me along for the ride certainly wasn't helping. "So you're saying what? That you're here to apologize? Because if that's it, then hey, fine, I accept, we're done, we can move along."

Amanda took a breath and let it out slowly. "Your mother and I have been talking—"

Oh yeah, that *always ends well.*

"—and we were speculating that perhaps holding a public introduction for the happy couple might be the way to go."

"Oh God."

"Don't get huffy," huffed my mom. "It isn't out of nowhere. It is, in fact," she added with an edge to her voice, as if she'd been looking for a reason to blow her top and it was finally being presented her, "the common means of furthering the young couple's introduction both to each other and the world around them."

I wasn't listening (not that I'd been listening at any point up until when she'd actually spoken to me.) I knew perfectly well what a public introduction was. This big social event/convocation is held. The happy couple is brought forward, some more speeches are made (usually by the same people who made the speeches in the first place.) A lot of liquor is unleashed upon the population, and there is much singing and dancing and rejoicing. All of which is great if you're in the right mind to bear all of it. Me, I'd rather run screaming from the room, declaring that this entire idea more or less sucked rocks from beginning to end.

"A public introduction. Really." I wasn't doing much in terms of getting any sort of joy into my line reading. "You guys really think that's going to smooth things out."

"My husband certainly does," said Amanda.

"And if my husband were here," added Dina, "he would, too." Personally I thought it took a serious number of balls for her to say that, as if I was somehow responsible for the fact that he was not, in fact, there.

"Look—" I started to say.

The emphasis, of course, being on "started to say," because Mom was just getting warmed up. "Not only that, but Mr. Salk is saying so as well."

"He is?"

"He *is*?" Amanda had just echoed my own question. She was looking very strangely at my mother.

"Oh course. The moment you brought it up here, I immediately contacted Mr. Salk." My mother sounded surprised that Amanda was clearly startled by that. Without waiting for her to comment on it, Dina kept right on going. "He was all for it."

"Was he now," was all I could say.

"Of course. He pointed out that pissing off the Singers would be a terrible idea—"

"I wouldn't say we were pissed off." Amanda was looking more and more uneasy about the direction that the conversation was going.

Mom, of course, blithely continued. "And he also said, frankly, that you weren't doing much with your life and it would probably be a good thing for you to find something to, in fact, do. With your life."

"That was darn nice of him, to be so concerned about me."

Irony was not something that my mother truly appreciated. She smiled and said, "Wasn't it, though!"

"Look," Amanda said hurriedly, clearly wanting to find some way to assuage the feelings of anger that were clearly rolling out of me but were moving right past my mom. "Perhaps we can come back when things are a little more settled..."

"More settled?" Dina sounded astonished that there was anything about this charming deal that *wasn't* settled. "I don't understand how—"

"Let's let him get back to sleep."

"But he's already had four hours. How much more does a sturdy young fellow like him require—?"

"We're going." Amanda was nominally speaking to me but the force and thrust of the comment was actually aimed at my mom, plus whoever the hell else she might be thinking of bringing in there. "Right now."

"I'm not sure if that's—" began my mom.

Amanda shut it down immediately. "*I'm* sure." She forced a smile but it did nothing to touch her eyes, and I'm reasonably sure she was aware of that. "Come, Dina. Let's let the poor boy rest."

"I'm not certain if that's—"

"*I'm* sure," Amanda said firmly. She tossed an acknowledging nod my way and hastened both herself and my still chattering mother out of the room. The door closed solidly behind them, which I took to be Amanda's doing, and she kept the chattering going as she guided my mother in any direction that took her away from me.

"Jesus," I muttered as I flopped back onto the bed. This was hopelessly frustrating to me, especially when one considered that we still had no idea where, if anywhere, the bastards who had taken the money had gotten off to with it. For all I knew, Dad had it rotting away under a mattress somewhere, which was enough to remind me about searching for the money in the mattress.

Here was the worst aspect of the whole thing:

Amber was a really nice girl.

Smart, attractive, fun to be with. Yeah, sure, she had the blind spot for the whole undead thing, but really, who could blame her? It was what she had been raised to become more or less since she was a child. I couldn't expect her to throw away years of training just because she'd stumbled over me. Perhaps there was more to her than that, but perhaps there wasn't. And indeed if that left us with her being a hard-core vamp hater, who could really blame her? If I didn't know what she did for a living, I'd never know, if you get what I'm saying. So really, when you wound up giving it any thought, why would she not want to hook up with me?

Because she's a vampire killer, so where did I get off considering the possibility that she might find herself genuinely attracted to me?

Was that really all this was about? The notion that we had no business being together because her main social temptation if she was near me was to try and kill me?

Wasn't the real fact that she spent most of her time trying to be nice to me (not counting the earliest time when she mostly seemed determined to kill me) and all I was handing back to her was indifference? Hadn't I really been the one faltering on the job while actively ignoring all of her endeavors along this line?

She really was a perfectly decent girl. Shouldn't I be trying to accomplish some manner of our getting to know each other?

Of course not. Of course you shouldn't be doing any of that because we have no lives together. We never can. And until such time as you have the brains to admit that and get her to move on, then this is all just a waste of time.

That was really it. That was all that mattered, and everything else was nothing but a huge pipe dream.

With that entire speech in my head, I picked up the phone and dialed up the hospital. It wasn't any sort of real problem getting her on the line. I asked for her by name and they were immediately able to put me through. Her phone started ringing and when she didn't answer immediately, I thought, *Fantastic. She's not answering the phone and I can just leave the message on—*

"Hello?"

My teeth tightened. *Shit.* Even as that less-than-generous commentary came from my head, I was able to say aloud, "Hey. Just wondering how you're feeling."

"*Vinnie*!" Amber sounded so overjoyed that it made me just

want to blow my own brains out. *"How you doing, honey? They said they can let me out tomorrow."*

"That's, uh…that's just terrific. That they're letting you out, I mean."

There was a pause at the other end. *"What's wrong?"* she said finally. *"You don't have to be shy. There's no one around at the moment. It's just you and me."*

Well, that was the whole problem, wasn't it. The "just you and me" thing. When we were separate, everything was fine. She was a sporty vampire killer, and I was happily trying to avoid notice. It was only when we were "you and me" that everything seemed to turn to complete crap.

"Your mom was by," I said.

"Okay. And?"

"And she suggested we do this whole public introduction thing." Before Amber could begin to suggest anything to the contrary, I rushed on. "I just…I think it would be a mistake, don't you?"

"Why?"

"Why? Well, because…because I was with you for a little while and, boom, someone nearly took you out. What does that say to you?"

"All it says to me," said Amber, sounding confused, *"is that my wonderful boyfriend was able to make sure that I didn't wind up getting my dumb ass killed. Why, what does it say to you?"*

All things considered, you'd think that I would have had, at the very least, some sort of intelligent response to that. Instead I had nothing. I just kinda sat there and the most clever thing I was able to come up with was, "Well…I guess, yeah."

That wasn't even the beginnings of sufficient insofar as a response came. *"You guess yeah? How about you guess definitely? How about that the only reason I'm alive is because of you and everyone in my family knows it and believes it, and knows and believes in you while we're at it. How about that some of them, including some you haven't met yet, would love to have the opportunity to meet you? How about that, huh? I mean,"* and she paused as if only just now she was starting to understand, *"Don't get me wrong. If our getting married is anathema to you…if it's something that you want to avoid, then I totally understand—"*

"Avoid? No!" I said.

"Are you sure? Because you sound..."

"I sound excited," I assured her with as much fake muster as I could manage. "I *am* excited. I just didn't want to pressure you, y'know?"

"You're not pressuring me into anything. The only person who seems pressured in all this is you because of the idea of a public introduction..."

"No, hell no, nothing of the sort."

Long story short is that we went around about this for another fifteen minutes before we arrived at exactly where our two mothers wanted us to be in the first place: having this stupid public introduction so that everyone would get to know me and the young lady who had been dumb as a box of rocks enough to decide that we were going to get married. Another happy step on the road to inevitability, which would include wife and non-existent children and the eventual discovery that hubby was a blood-sucking monster who needed to be staked immediately.

I tried to imagine things transpiring damned near any other way. Perhaps I might become cured of the disease once more. Or maybe a man of the cloth would come along and—

Nah. I was screwed.

Life was good.

Eleven

My Secret Becomes Obvious to a Member of Amber's Family

The public introduction, or as it was more formerly known the Public Introduction Ceremony, was held in the large meeting hall that was the centerpiece of our Chevalier's community. It had been used for any number of purposes over the years. Having it as the centerpiece for the business that was about to transpire this evening simply seemed like yet another disgust for those who bore our names.

It had taken several days for the PIC "movement" to be pushed into production. It's not to say that people were unwilling to attend; they most certainly were.

There were plenty of thank yous and plenty of checks shoved into cards from Dunkin' Donuts. There were also assorted engagement presents from various members of our order, although some remained understandably suspicious. They'd known me more or less since forever, and the notion that I had acquired a girl of any sort—much less someone who was willing to put down actual full-time support to being my bride—seemed dubious at best.

"Where'd she come from?" "Who is she, man?" "She's adorable!" "She's exotic." "Sure she's not a vampire?" That last comment always got a chuckle, since it was generally assumed that naturally we'd be far too bright to be taken in by a vamp. I would dutifully smile and nod or shake my head; either way it seemed to come out the same.

We weren't much for catering, but there was certainly some

decent food to be had, not to mention wine to be drunk. That was Mr. Salk's particular state of mind, and he nursed it with great gusto and much detailed attention. He was the dutiful individual who was staying squarely atop the various drinking "needs" of the establishment.

He tended to start hanging around me way too much as members of the Garrison mingled with not only each other, but other Garrison members as well. This was, after all, an open party, and consequently any Body Men who happened to wander into New York City were certain to make it over to our Garrison's little soiree. It really didn't matter to them whether I wanted them there or not, or even if I'd heard of them. As far as they were concerned, if drinks were out, then so were they.

"Isn't this great?" Salk said to me, half in the bag, one arm draped around my shoulders. I would have been perfectly happy to break the little creep in half, but that wasn't really an option for me just then. "Isn't this absolutely fabulous?"

"Fabulous," I said, my voice little more than a faint echo. I desperately just wanted the whole thing to go away. I saw Amber across the room; she was speaking to several females and laughing merrily. She saw my gaze and waved to me. I managed a wave back, still trying desperately to figure out how I was going to get out of this. Parties, gatherings, all this stuff was just fine, but who knew how much longer it was all going to last? Sooner or later, we were going to start winding down to the specifics of the event, and that meant that the tough decisions were going to have to be made. The fact that Amber was clearly having such a good time—despite the presence of her still strained right arm, currently tied up in a bandage from the hospital—wasn't going to do a damned thing to deter the speed with which this was all happening.

"I have to admit, I really didn't see any of this coming. Between you and me," said Salk, his voice only a notch above a slur, "I didn't think you had it in you."

"Neither did I."

"You know I wish you the best of luck."

I managed a nod while imagining snapping his neck like a twig. I restrained from doing so, figuring that it might be taken amiss by some.

Then a deep voice sounded from near me and a firm arm draped around my shoulders. "Son," said Lawrence. He was holding a cocktail in one hand but it didn't seem to have diminished him in the slightest.

"Dad," I said readily, although it felt somewhat uncomfortable using the word.

Salk indicated in gestures that he was going to take his leave, and that did not bother Lawrence in the slightest. As Salk slid away into wherever he was going to plant his sagging form, Lawrence's arm tightened around me and I suddenly got the paranoid sense that the vampire killer had abruptly twigged to the true nature of his future son-in-law. Fortunately enough that did not seem to be the case as he said, "You don't have to call me 'Dad,' you know. 'Lawrence' will do."

"How about 'Larry?'"

"No."

"Okay, then."

Lawrence started to stroll through the room, slow and steady, keeping the arm tightly around me. I saw Kubrick and some of his people a few feet away, glowering at me. Thus far entertaining myself by watching them fume was the one bit of amusement I was getting out of this whole endeavor. I grinned and waved to them. They frowned even more.

"Vincent, I know that we've gotten off on the wrong foot."

"Wrong feet, actually."

"Fair enough," he said, permitting a very small smile. He didn't seem to want to acknowledge it, but I pretty much suspected he was under orders from on high: Specifically that Amanda had told him to make nice and this was about as good as he was going to get. "The point is, I think there's plenty of time to make things right between us."

"There is?" I wasn't thrilled with the way this was all shaping up.

He nodded. "I truly think you should give serious thought to coming back with us. Move to our side of the country. There's plenty of opportunities out there for you, not to mention that I can do a vast amount of positive things for you."

"That's really nice!" I was doing my best to keep my voice as up and positive as possible. "All in the vampire killing business, I assume?"

"Well, of course," he said as if anything else was too ludicrous to contemplate. Then he frowned. "Unless there are other things you'd be interested in looking into."

"I hadn't really given it any thought."

"Maybe you should start." There was no hint of irony in his voice. "It's a safe consideration, I suspect, that you're not exactly set up at the moment to support the both of you. Yes?"

"Pretty much." I was getting more uncomfortable by the moment. It wasn't as if I could just walk away from vampire hunting so that I could take up a life of waiting for the sun to set.

"Then I should put you together with my people. We have a variety of things that you could find to occupy yourself. Solid paying jobs with many entry points into other divisions."

"Working for you, you mean?"

He shrugged and gave that faintly distressing smile of his. "What can I say? I'm a big believer in nepotism. And if there's someone who feels that he's in dire need of my help, who am I to say no?"

"Well, that's...that's just great!" I said with absolutely no enthusiasm at all.

The lack of enthusiasm went right past him. Instead he squeezed me to him even tighter than before, so much so that I was worried he was going to break me in half. "That's terrific," he said, and I couldn't tell at that moment if he was being sarcastic or not.

At that moment I saw that Amber was waving toward me and gesturing for me to come over to her. The request could not have been better timed, because I was starting to feel as if, at any moment, my head was just going to freaking explode. Quickly I disengaged his arm from around my shoulders as I said hurriedly, "My, uh...your daughter is asking for a moment of my time."

"Of course," he said readily, although he didn't entirely seem to be done with me. "We can go over specifics later."

"Yes, we absolutely can," I said as my mind began to race. Just what specifics were we going to discuss? What edge of the Amanda/Lawrence financial kingdom was going to be shuffled over to me so that I could totally destroy it? Wow! What fun would that be!

Amber was still gesturing for me to come over. I certainly would have preferred heading in some other direction: one involving a path the hell out of town. Maybe I could haul myself back over to Duncan's latest Moveable Feast and just hide there for, I dunno, the rest of my life. It didn't seem the most practical tactic, but it sure as hell beat out the likelihood that I was going to avoid being detected indefinitely by a family of vampire hunters.

Quickly I crossed the floor, stopping only briefly to shake hands and pat the shoulders of those who stood between myself and my future wife/permanent girlfriend/total patsy. In the small crowd of females, including both Amber's mom and my other maternal organ, there were several other young women who were clearly close to Amber. Draping her arm through mine, she started introducing me to the ones I was unfamiliar with, rattling through their names as quickly as she could. I nodded and smiled and promptly forgot each name as quickly as it was provided me.

"And finally—best for last," said Amber, and she pointed me toward a woman whose back at that moment was to me. "My sister Hannah actually turned up. Hannah, this is Vincent. Vincent, Hannah."

Hannah turned to face me, a blood red drink in her hand. She smiled and stuck a hand out, and then both hand and expression on her face became frozen. It was no less so for me.

Because Hannah, my future sister-in-law, was the vampire who had transformed me in the first place.

Twelve

My Bizarre Evening Discussions

I knew I'd always remember the woman who had transformed me if for no other reason than that her hair was long and black and she had an exotic look about her.

This girl was nothing like that. She didn't seem exotic in the least, and her hair was cut short and now bright red. Other than that, though, it was her. I really don't know how else to say it: it's tough to forget the woman who killed you.

She had been shaking my hand, but her eyes had widened in pure astonishment when she realized who it was she was being all polite to. The astonishment had swiftly transformed into pure horror. It would take no more than the merest alarm for me to alert everyone that we had a classic, old-timed vampire squarely in the middle of our little gathering. And once I had done that, well...

Obviously Lawrence would demand to know just how in God's name I knew that his older daughter was one of the undead. To which, of course, I only had one reasonable answer, namely that I knew she was a vampire since *I* in fact *was* a vampire. Even if I came up with some bullshit excuse, if I revealed who and what she was, she would very quickly return the favor. So that would be a hell of a lot of screaming and shouting and swift murder in the heart of Garrison 13.

And that, in turn, would leave us what? Mom would be mortified beyond her ability to keep things under control. Meanwhile Amanda and Lawrence would be in the process of freaking out even as they readied a device to put Hannah out for her misery.

And Amber, oh my God, she'd be a mental case, losing fiancé and sister in one shot.

This entire situation was a complete disaster. In the long minutes that appeared to be counting down, I ran every way of getting myself out of this as possible and nothing was coming to mind save for the obvious. Which, as it turns out, is exactly what I went for.

"Hi," I said, still holding her hand in an affirmative and greeting grip.

Hannah managed a gulp of a response and said, "Hi," in response.

We continued to shake hands, neither of us aware that either of us had yet to release the grip on the other. The women were watching both of us and finally my own mother said, "You don't have to keep shaking hands, y'know."

Realizing that that was what we had been doing, we quickly released our grips on each other. I cleared my throat so loudly that it screamed to be followed by my saying pretty much anything. She cleared her throat and the same thing happened. Yet neither of us was speaking, and consequently we were garnering extremely strange and confused looks from the others, bordering on outright suspicion.

Hannah recovered before I did. "So, it's uh…it's a pleasure. Uhm…Vince?"

"Vince, right. Or Vinnie. Vin. Any of it's good."

"Well, that's good to know. Real good."

"Very good."

It should have been clear to anyone observing at that point that there was something completely wrong with the two of us. We were not behaving in a manner consistent with two total strangers meeting for the first time. And yet it appeared to go right past everyone. "So!" said Amanda, and the conversation continued from that point, more or less picking up on something else they'd been talking about. It distracted my attention for a few moments and then when I looked back, Hannah was gone.

In a low voice I muttered to Amber, "Where'd your sister take off to?"

"Oh, she's like that," said Amber, attributing it no consequence whatsoever. "She'll see something and it grabs her attention and poof, off she vanishes. I don't know how she does it."

I have a few ideas on the subject, I thought.

Begging off from further chit-chat, I started circling the room in a slow, steady manner, trying to spot her so I could confront her in a more direct manner. Even as I pursued her on foot, my mind raced as to exactly what I would say when I *did* confront her. What I'd always imagined doing was making an exception in her case and driving a stake right through her chest. I'd neither asked for, nor wanted, the life I was leading, and if I was being handed the opportunity to balance some scales, I was perfectly fine with that. But it wasn't happening. She'd vanished. Two complete circles of the room and then a third heading back in the direction I'd gone, and still I couldn't find her. In a matter of seconds, the bitch had completely disappeared.

Now what the hell was I going to do? Was she just going to allow Amber to get married to some random vampire? No, not random at all: the guy that she herself had transformed *into* a vampire. What kind of weird, twisted situation had I fallen into here?

I managed to stay another half hour or so and then begged off for the rest of the evening. Amber appeared somewhat upset to let me go, but she seemed to understand that even I had limits when it came to being out and about. She kissed me rather thoroughly and assured me that she would make up for my absence with the rest of the crowd. Honest to God, she could have banged them all at that point and it would have been fine with me. My thoughts and concerns were definitely elsewhere.

I headed back to my small apartment building. Reaching the front door, I stopped when my gentle push upon it caused it to swing wide open. The darkened front hallway seemed to call to me, saying, *Sure, come on in, Vince, what could possibly go wrong?*

I started to reach for the genuine stake that I kept secured just inside my jacket as I gazed into the darkness ahead; darkness which seemed like light to me. And then, just as I pulled it out, it was struck out of my hand. Hannah was right behind me. I spun to face her and she shoved as hard as she could, sending me off balance and tumbling to the floor of the entranceway.

She stomped in behind me and kicked the door shut, the sound of it reverberating through the small building. *"What the hell do you think you're doing?"* she demanded.

"Me?" I scrambled to my feet and faced her, my fists up, my legs in a crouch. "What do *I* think I'm doing?"

Hannah stood there with her arms crisscrossed across her breasts. "Does she know?"

"Know what? Your sister? About me being a vampire, you mean?"

"Yes, genius, that's right."

"*Hey*!" I dropped my defensive pose since she didn't appear inclined to start attacking. Instead, like a child, I pointed a finger at her. "You don't get to call me 'genius' or any other names."

"Some people would consider being called 'genius' a positive thing."

I paused, trying to come up with some kind of snappy comeback to that and realizing that I didn't really have any. So I went for a different angle. "I wouldn't be in this fix if it weren't for you!"

"What fix? Engaged to my sister?"

"Yes! Well, no," I realized I had to admit, "I'd still be in that fix. But the other one, about being a vampire. That I'd still be in. Because of *you*!"

She rolled her eyes and then rubbed the bridge of her nose, working to regain her composure. "Okay, look: I'm sorry, all right? If I'd had the faintest idea that you were going to wind up engaged to my kid sister, I'd never have sponsored you, okay?"

"I didn't need your help! I didn't ask to be sponsored!"

"No, you were asking to be dead," said Hannah in obvious annoyance. "You were going to go charging into Duncan's place like some sort of hero and you were going to get yourself well and truly corpsed. Is that what you wanted? To be corpsed?"

"I don't even think that's a word."

"*Whatever*!" she said, exasperated. "The fact of the matter is that I did you a favor."

"You turned me into a vampire! How is that a favor?"

"Because you're still alive, which is more than you would've been."

"How is that better?" I demanded to know. "If my mom finds out, she'll kill me!"

"Ohhhh, poor baby." She sagged against the door, looking tired. "You got anything in the fridge?"

"In the fridge? Like what? Blood?"

"Coke. Diet Coke. Beer. Anything. As long as it's fluid, I'm fine."

That took me off guard. "Really? I just throw up any normal food."

"Different strokes. What've you got?"

Moments later I was seated in the kitchen, watching the woman who'd transformed me into a vampire drinking a Schlitz. Of all the ways I'd imagined getting back together with her, this certainly wasn't one of them. Part of me still wanted to just kill her, but I was beginning to realize that, at least for now, that wasn't really an option.

"So what're you gonna do about this?" she finally asked me.

"About what?"

"About *what?"* She put the beer down and stared at me with clear amazement. "You're engaged to my sister! You have to get out of it!"

"Oh, do I?" It was my own frustration with her that prompted such a useless reply, but it was all I had.

Apparently she thought I was serious. "Of *course* you do! You're a vampire! She's a vampire hunter! There's not a whole lot involved in figuring out what the problem is going to be in the long term, because there isn't going to *be* a long term! Can you even get hard?"

"Wha—? *Yes*!" I felt a flush in my cheeks. "You mean sex? Yes, I can get hard! How can you even ask me that?"

"Because a lot of guys can't, that's why. Not in the normal, human sense, in any event. So that's why I was asking. If you know of a certainty that you can, then that's one thing off the table." She tilted her head at me slightly. "You sure?"

"Yes, I'm sure!"

"So how many women have you been with since you turned?"

"I wasn't turned! You turned me! And that's none of your damned business!"

Hannah rubbed her forehead as if she were stuck talking to the biggest idiot in the world. "Oh God. None."

"Shut up!" I said, which must have sounded wonderful. I mean, yeah, okay, the truthful answer really was "none." It simply hadn't come up before, and now certainly didn't seem to be the time.

"All right, fine," she said, obviously tired of discussing it. "You're a wild man in the sack. The point is, you've got to find a way to break this off! Amber's a sweet girl and she deserves more than being stuck with some guy that she doesn't realize can't ever provide her with a future!"

"And whose fault is that?"

"Mine, okay? I did a terrible and stupid-ass thing by allowing you to live instead of just offing you when I had the chance! Jesus!" She banged her hand flat on the table and nearly knocked over the salt and pepper shakers. "Happy? Does it simplify everything that we've got that straightened out?"

It kind of did, but I wasn't about to admit to it.

"So now that that's settled," continued Hannah, "it brings us back to what the hell you're going to do about this?"

"What would you have me do? Tell your parents that their prospective son in law is playing for the other team? How well do you think that's gonna go over?"

"Well, not that, obviously. But you'll have to tell them *something*. I mean, you can't seriously be considering—"

"I don't know what I'm considering. Amber is a great girl and if it weren't for the whole vampire thing—"

"Yeah, but there *is* a whole vampire thing, and you can't just ignore it! What are you going to do?"

"*I don't know*!" I was on my feet and waving my arms in frustration. If I swung them about anymore, I might well have gone into orbit. "I don't know, okay? I don't know what I'm going to do about the situation that *you* stuck me into. We clear on that?"

She stared at me for a long moment and then sank back into the chair. "God, you're an idiot," she whispered.

"Hey! It's not like I needed this, on any level. If you'd left me alone—"

"We've been over this. You'd be dead and I wouldn't be here wasting my time having this discussion."

"If it bothers you so much," I said challengingly, "why don't you just go tell her?"

"So she can ask how I know? Yeah, that's a great idea."

"Okay, then. So we understand each other." I sounded like I was boasting about it, but really I was covering up the sense of relief that I now felt inside. She had just made explicit the exact thing that I was worried about. Both of us had to keep our yaps shut for fear of exposing our own problems. That was something, at least. I wasn't sure exactly what, but something.

Feeling slightly buoyed, I chose that moment to rally a bit. "You should be thanking me," I said defiantly.

"Oh really?" She stared at me with the air of one who did not suffer fools gladly, but was making an exception in this case. "How do you figure that?"

"Apparently nobody told you, but your sister wouldn't be alive right now if it weren't for me."

"Yeah?" She cocked an eyebrow. Obviously she hadn't heard about it, but she was maintaining her reserve. "And how'd that happen?"

"We were taking a walk in Central Park, minding our own business..."

"Looking for vampires to stake."

"Well...yeah," I had to admit. From the face she made, the admission clearly didn't go over particularly well, but I pushed on. "But then some old-world vampire in a carriage grabbed her and tried to make off with her. And I came to her goddamn rescue. Got her away from some scar faced freak, I'll have you know—"

"Scar faced?" Now all of her interests were engaged. She sat fully upright and asked, "What kind of scar?"

"V-shaped. A wound on his face." The change in her attitude immediately engaged me. "Why?"

She didn't respond. For some reason I was now starting to feel seriously concerned. "Hannah...why do you ask?" There was no longer any sense of accusation in my voice. I was genuinely concerned.

As it turned out, I had every right to be. "Did he have grayish black hair? A widow's peak?"

"Yeeeeah." Now I was really worried. "You know him?"

"His name's Highgate," she said. "He's the right hand man to the Baron, the head of the Pride."

"The *Baron?"* It was all I could do not to laugh. "He's a myth!"

"You know how you used to watch old horror films, and they always bring up some guy and some other guy laughs and says he's a myth," said Hannah. "And then it turns out that, no, not so much with the whole 'myth' thing?" When I nodded she continued, "Okay, well...same deal here. Not a myth. Not any more than vampires are, if you want to look at it that way."

I had no immediate answer for that, what with actually being part of the mythic crew collectively known as vampires. Instead I said slowly, "And you're saying...what? That this Highgate guy has a scar?"

"Oh, definitely. I should know." She smiled ever so slightly at the recollection. "I gave it to him."

"You?"

"Yup." Hannah took a moment to appreciate the reminiscence. "He wanted me to join the Pride. Said I had too much going for me to be a member of the New V's. Actually, I think he just wanted to get into my pants."

"But..." I shook my head, not following. "But you're a lesbian."

She gave me such a pitying look that I was actually ashamed to have said anything. "No, I'm not," she informed me airily. "I simply said that to my parents in order to avoid having to deal with their match making."

"I wish I'd thought of that," I had to admit.

Her eyes were glistening with quiet fury. "So Highgate tried to eat my sister. It can't be coincidence. It just can't."

"Well, common sense would seem to indicate it wasn't."

"Which means we have to do something about it."

"We do?" I couldn't have been more surprised by the declaration. "Hey, I saved her. I've already done my part. Anything else you want done, shouldn't you have to do it on your own time?"

For a moment she looked surprised that I would say that. Then she recaptured any sense of confusion and tucked it away.

"I suppose I should," she said, her voice soft and even. "I suppose if I'm going to have anything to say to Highgate about it, that I should take care of it myself. Thank you for making that clear to me."

She emptied the rest of the mug and slammed it down on the table. "Nice talking with you, Vince. So look: whatever you decide to do, I'm sure it'll be fine. You'll work it out. You're a bright guy. And if you wouldn't mind telling my folks where I've gotten myself off to, I'd appreciate it a lot. There's a good lad." She patted me on the hand, one cold palm upon another. It held there for a moment and then she got up and started heading for the front door.

She almost made it there.

"Wait," I said, feeling a grim reluctance but also a sense of frustration.

Hannah stopped, turned.

"The Pride, huh?"

She nodded and waited, but this time there was just the hint of a smile on her face.

"There's one in Newark, New Jersey," I said. "Not that my Garrison knows, of course. There are certain things you just, y'know...don't do."

"Exactly. You really don't." She sauntered toward me and her smile widened. "Unless someone asks you very, very nicely."

I sighed. This evening was not turning out the way I'd wanted it to, at all.

Thirteen

My Trip to an O.C. Nest, Which is Freaky for an Unexpected Reason

It was just past the witching hour when Hannah and I hit the Jersey Turnpike, barreling down toward Newark astride my motorcycle. We both had helmets on in order to avoid any hassle with the police. Not that they presented a true threat to us, but the less aggravation we encountered along the way, the better.

Hannah kept her arms securely around me. In some ways, I was surprised. I'd have thought that she would insist on riding up front and that it would become an entire point of contention. Instead she seemed perfectly willing to sit securely on the back.

Once during the entirety of the trip, I tried to ask her about herself. Here was this woman who had had a massive impact on my life, and all I knew about her was that she'd bitten me and left me for...well, not for dead, but not for much of a life, either. But when I started asking how she herself had been turned, all she said was "Not now. Later. Maybe." And that was, for her, the extent of the conversation. Not being an idiot, I decided not to pursue. Maybe later. Maybe.

So half an hour or so passed with nary a word spoken between us. Every so often she would readjust her position on me, but that was about it.

Finally I said the only word that really meant anything:

"Here."

I guided the motorcycle off the Jersey Turnpike. I dropped money in the toll and kept going, down into the streets of Newark.

I had, in fact, been kind of full of crap when I'd talked about the Pride's nest in Newark. I knew of it, sure. Everyone on my side of the fence did. But I didn't know exactly where it might be. Theoretically I could use my vampiric senses to locate it, but that would take time.

Hannah, as it turned out, knew where it was. Over the next minutes, she guided me with a continued series of "Here's" that took me from one street to the next. It was difficult for me to tell exactly where we were as she navigated us further and further in. It began to dawn on me that I might be letting myself be led into some manner of trap. After all, I still didn't know for sure who Hannah was other than what she had chosen to share with me, and even that small degree might be total bullshit. She could bringing me directly into something and I'd have no idea of it until I was in over my head.

But I decided, y'know, what the hell. Life was too short.

"Here," she said abruptly, and it was a different "here" than I'd heard earlier. It was a definitive, pull your cycle over because we've arrived tone of voice. I nodded and did what she said, pulling over into a convenient parking space that was more like half a space, but plenty wide for my cycle. We slid off in two different directions and hung the helmets on the handlebars.

"Where?" I said.

She nodded toward a single building a short distance away.

It was a very select neighborhood, a series of townhouses running down the length of the street. Most of them were darkened since we were coming onto one in the evening, but there was one that remained brightly lit. There was the faint sound of music coming from it. I looked to Hannah questioningly and she simply nodded.

So that was it. That was where at least the east coast branch of the Pride liked to hang out. On some level, I supposed I shouldn't be surprised. If one is going to essentially have one's equivalent of hell on Earth, then it made sense that it shouldn't be trying to draw too much attention to itself.

We stood outside the building for a few moments, and then I muttered, "This way." I started off and then realized that Hannah wasn't following. Instead she was just standing there watching me, as if trying to determine whether I was worth coming after or not. "Will you—?" I started to say, stopping with impatience, and then she nodded and followed me.

Both of us were dressed in black, so we actually kind of went well together. I made my way around the back of the place, Hannah now right behind me. There was a door there, which I pulled gently on. It showed no indication of opening, so I yanked on it with greater force. This time it burst open, and I froze, waiting to see what would happen next.

Nothing did. Just because we were at vampire headquarters, that didn't necessarily mean that they had every inch of the place being watched. Why should they? Who in his right mind would attack them?

Hannah was right in behind me, peering over my shoulder. The hallway we were gazing into was nothing impressive; just a means of exit from the building. "Guess we're good to go," I said. "You in?"

She nodded. That was all the urging I needed, although I had to keep telling myself that she was genuinely "in" rather than simply steering me toward something catastrophic.

"Okay, then," I said and entered the building. She fell in behind me. I noticed, as if for the first time, that she was actually dressed quite nicely. Black blouse, black skirt and black boots. I could have done without the red hair, but other than that, it all came together very well.

I heard voices from up front and put up a hand, indicating that she should stop where she was. She had already done so, perfectly capable of hearing as well as I could. There was some discussion up at the end of the hallway and to the right, and slowly we made our way towards it.

It was at that point, faced with the prospect of coming face to face with one of the elders of vampirism, that it occurred to me I had no idea what the hell I was doing. I was going into this situation more or less blind.

Blind but determined to find out what the hell had gone on back in the cart in Central Park.

I realized that Hannah was standing just a smidge behind me, looking at me curiously. Nodding, I strode forward as if I had every right to be there and entered the far end of the hallway. I glanced left and right. Still not much of anything to the left. But there were still noises to the right, and that's where I indicated we should go with a brief nod of my head. Hannah followed. Perhaps she had a clearer idea of what we were going to encounter than I did. If that were the case, then it was a good thing that she was backing me up. Either that or she was walking me straight into disaster.

We kept walking to the right, then a left, and suddenly we were in a main hallway.

It was a wide enough area, lined with books on higher shelves. The bindings were pure and precious and obviously hadn't been cracked open in years, if ever. There were tables set up with small glasses of wine, and the various individuals there were moving from one table to the next, sipping carefully from each of the cups. Some of the members were carefully washing the liquids around in their mouths, keeping their eyes rolled skyward as they savored the various tastes.

A wine tasting. "We're in a wine tasting," I whispered to Hannah. She nodded in agreement, looking as puzzled as I was. If this was indeed some grand scheme intended to confuse me, it was doing a hell of a job.

I could tell they were definitely vampires because, well, I could. It was impossible for one vampire to throw a curve at another. We all knew each other for what we were.

One or two of them appeared to notice Hannah and myself, but simply nodded to us in acknowledgment. I, who had already picked up a glass of some sort of wine, responded with a slight nod in return. Then I quickly urged Hannah to do what I was doing, which she did. We stood there in the large room sipping the wine and making innocuous small talk with each other and some of the samplers. A few of them seemed to notice us, but weren't so much involved in what we were up to that they felt the need to bother us.

"This is impressive," said Hannah in a low voice as we worked our way across the room.

"Yeah, it is. I just wish I knew what it all represented. Any thoughts?"

"None that are coming readily to—"

Her voice trailed off. A number of cigarettes were being smoked in the relatively open air, making it a bit more difficult for me to see than others who were accustomed to such obstructions. But she had clearly spotted something and it took me a few moments to locate exactly what it was.

Standing at the far end of the room, drinking and chatting with the various guys who were higher up on the food chain than I was, was Jeremiah Salk.

Jeremiah Salk? WTF?

Hannah and I exchanged looks so startled that it told me beyond question that she'd had no idea what to expect, because neither of us had anticipated seeing the head of Garrison 13 drinking down with the heads of this place. Salk was eagerly talking about something with someone. He was gesturing widely and was obviously concerned about something. He was doing so at a door that was only slightly open, and on behalf of whoever else was on the other side of that same door. I couldn't hear him because he was on the far side of the room and the normal, peppy discussions that were transpiring throughout the rest of the room obscured my hearing.

Someone passed directly in my line of vision and a moment later Salk was gone. The door closed quietly; obviously he'd managed to talk himself in there with little to no effort.

"Salk," I said in a low voice to Hannah.

She nodded in response. "Yeah. I saw him."

"Shall we find out what he's discussing with his associates?"

"Absolutely." She was speaking in as low a voice as possible. "Question is: how do we do it so that they don't notice?"

"Not sure," I said. We were now standing just a couple feet from each other. The door was likewise right within our grasp. All we had to do was lean toward it and place our ears against it.

Suddenly something grabbed me by the shoulder and yanked my head away from the door. I was spun around to face several stern, very large, very angry faces. I could see that Hannah was hardly cooperative; a couple more of them were holding her by the back of the neck and her wrists.

"You," said the guy whose face was close to mine, "are not supposed to be here."

"You positive? Because I'm pretty sure that we are. But hey," I said with an indifferent shrug, "if you want me out of here, then I'll go. Oh, honey," and I called to Hannah, "I think it's time for us to get going."

"I agree," said the guy. And then his fist suddenly flew straight at me and before I could make the slightest move, blackness enveloped me.

Fourteen

My Visit to the Wine Cellar

The world slowly began to fill in around me and the first thing I heard was a sharp comment of, "Oh, good. You're awake. Nice of you to join us."

It was Hannah's voice. She didn't sound especially thrilled with me.

Slowly I opened my eyes and came to the realization that I was no longer in the hallway upstairs. Not a real surprise. I supposed I should have been happy that I was still in one piece. Unfortunately the one piece of me that was in existence was tied up. I actually looked up to see that my hands were tied over my head, suspending me from the ceiling. My toes were just barely touching the floor. I tried to pull back down on what was holding me upward and realized that it wasn't just rope, but some sort of heavy-duty nylon cable. I pulled on it a few times and saw that it wasn't intending to release me anytime soon. It was possible that further yanking on the cord might accomplish what I wanted, but I figured I had time, or at least a little bit.

It was darker in the room that I was now being held in, but my eyes were adjusting quickly. There were very few rooms that were too dark for me to perceive my surroundings, assuming I had a few minutes.

"Hey! Genius!" It was Hannah's irritated voice from nearby me and suddenly I felt a sharp pain in the area of my ankle. She'd just kicked me. Bitch. That wasn't what I needed just then.

Or maybe it was, because the abrupt pain caused my eyes to adjust more quickly in the dimness than they had before. I saw that she was hanging no more than a few feet away from me, likewise tied to the ceiling. "Nice of you to come back," she said and lashed out once more with a dangling foot. This time she didn't come into contact with me, the foot sliding past me.

"Stop it!" I hissed at her. "I don't need this shit right now! Where are we?"

"The wine cellar with the preserves."

"The what with the where?"

I started really looking around more closely at our surroundings, and suddenly my voice caught as I was truly able to discern for the first time just where we were.

It was a wine cellar, all right. I could see at the far end that there were stairs descending from above into the place. And there certainly seemed to be no stairs heading any further down, so I had to admit that there didn't seem to be much of anything around that qualified this as something other than a cellar.

Wine, though, I didn't quite manage to make out. What I did see was something far more horrific.

It was bodies. Human bodies. There were about a half dozen in all, at least from what I could make out.

Most of them were male, but there were some females mixed in. They had been stripped naked and were hanging upside down from the ceiling, their arms hanging to either side and attached to wooden supports that kept them immobilized. There were tubes feeding into certain parts of them. Something liquefied was being pumped directly into them. At the same time there were liquids being taken out of them, extracted into vials and collected into...well, into vials, I suppose. The drip was slow and steady, and it was painfully obvious why the liquids were being drawn off into the vials. They were being coagulated into individual samples to be kept for further taste testing. The human beings were a living, breathing means of collecting the blood that was pouring through their bodies. The drinks they'd been sampling upstairs weren't drinks at all; they were cups of blood that had been specially treated into making them something special. Off to the side, as if waiting for someone that it was going to contain, was a coffin. I knew it was empty at the moment because the top was open. Must have been there for storage.

"Holy shit," I muttered. "Do you know what this all is?"

Hannah sounded, at best, indifferent. "Yeah, obviously, they've got people in here tied up and turned into juice bars. So what? That's not my problem."

I had been turning slowly on the rope that was holding us, and now I managed to twist my body around so that I was facing her. "*That's* not your problem with it?" I found that extremely hard to believe. "How can that not be your problem with it?"

"Because they're vampires, dipshit, and oh, by the way, so are we." Hannah sounded impatient with the fact that she even had to point that out. "I don't give a rat's ass what they do in their free time. I just wanted to get my hands on Highgate, remember? He's in the middle of something and it caused him to try and take out my sister. I want a piece of whatever he's got his hands in and break it off and stab it into him. What, didn't I make myself clear on that?"

"Yes, you made yourself clear, and if you hadn't before, you certainly did now." I was definitely not in the mood for this. "So what do you suggest?"

"I suggest we get the hell out of here."

"Okay, fine, well..." I pulled on the cable once more and it seemed no more interested in parting now than it did the previous times I'd yanked on it.

"I tried that," said Hannah in irritation. "What, did you think I hadn't?"

"I really hadn't given it any thought at all." I turned my attention to the various "wine" samples. "Hey, you! Any of you! Think you can, y'know, come to and maybe give us a hand here?"

This supplication prompted no response at all.

"Any other ideas?" she said.

"No, none, sorry." I made no effort to keep my frustration out of the way. "I'd truly love to have some sort of convenient—"

"Hold it. Shut up."

I immediately silenced myself, because I heard the sound of a door opening at the top of the stairs. I honestly couldn't figure out why they'd secreted us away down there. They could easily have just shut us up permanently and been done with us. Instead they were dragging things out, keeping us alive while we waited to see what, if anything, they were going to do with us...

In fact, they *were* keeping us alive. I suddenly realized that I wasn't the least bit hungry. Apparently while we, or at least I, had been unconscious, they'd fed us some of their nicely and newly uncorked blood. How wonderfully sweet. It made me want to vomit. It also made me want more. A sample of the continued problems that were presented to vampires.

"Did they give you any blood just now? Or a little earlier?" I demanded of Hannah.

She looked puzzled for a moment and then licked her lips. Her eyes widened in surprise. "I'll be damned. They did. Bastards." Then she licked her lips again and tried not to smile. When she saw my annoyed look, she bristled and said defensively, "What?"

"Nothing. Never mind."

"You're going to be critical now, aren't you?"

"Will you shut up?"

"Fine." She did not in fact sound for one moment as if she was interested in shutting up, but she was willing to concede it since it was obvious we were about to have company.

Several of the vampires who brought us down here trotted down the stairs. They looked at us with a certain amount of disdain and then the foremost one simply snapped his fingers. At first I thought it would somehow magically cause the coils to separate all on their own. But no, vampires had to come up to us with long knives so that they could slice away at the ropes themselves. As they did, I briefly considered the option of launching an attack upon them, but I retained control of myself. Nothing was going to be gained by leaping into an attack against our "hosts."

I remained concerned about the people who were the substance of the wine cellar itself. "What about them?" I said, indicating the helpless victims whose bodily fluids were providing drinks all around.

"What *about* them?" was the only response.

"You can't just leave them here..."

"Vincent." It was Hannah, her voice sharp and warning. This was simply not the time to make a big deal about this. We need to be out, free, wandering around. Not making a pitch on behalf of the other prisoners in the wine cellar.

"Fine," I said with a deep growl. "Fine. Okay?"

"Okay," said one of the vampires. It seemed to make no never mind to him. He was perfectly content with the way things were. Whether the people were drained slowly in the wine cellar or else just brought upstairs and torn to pieces in one great orgy, either way was perfectly fine to him.

So with no further protest on our part, I allowed myself to be led up the stairs with Hannah on a short leash behind me. We kept the bonds on our wrists, which were now behind us. Whatever they knew or didn't know about us, the one thing we were definitely not going to be was allowed to have our hands free. I hate to say it, but I actually felt a little bit flattered that they seemed that concerned about us.

Either that or they didn't care all that much.

Up the stairs now and out into the main hallway, but brought in a different direction. I could still hear light laughter from the direction that we'd been in before, and I doubted very much that they were laughing about us. I didn't even know what time it was, which is always a dangerous thing for a vampire to lose track of. As I already mentioned, sunlight won't kill us, but it won't do us a hell of a lot of good, either.

We were led through the twists and turns of the hallway and then shoved through a fairly large open door. The moment we were through, it was slammed shut behind us.

The Baron was seated behind his desk. He'd been reading a novel—something about angels, I thought—and now he tossed it onto his desk and allowed us to take his full attention.

He was hugely tall, at least six and a half feet of him. I knew this because he rose from behind his desk, standing and looking down at us. He certainly had no scars on his face: if he'd acquired them at some point during his time, he had simply healed them or they'd gone away themselves, which gave me an idea of how deeply Hannah must have struck in order to permanently screw up Highgate's face.

The Baron was remarkably slender, with grey/black hair and a whitish Van Dyke beard that curved perfectly over the chin of his face. His forehead was very high and polished, and for a time he simply stood there, studying the both of us, but mostly me. Or at least that's how it seemed to me. This clothes were as black as Highgate's had been, and he looked as if he'd stepped out of the first act of an opera.

"So," he said, and when he spoke his voice was very low. "My understanding—and please feel free to correct me if I happen to be wrong about this—is that you are out to find Highgate. Is that correct?"

I looked in surprise at Hannah. She simply shrugged and said, "I told him before he locked us up. Problem?"

Fantastic.

Hannah then shifted her attention back to the Baron. "Do you know where he is?"

"At the moment? No. You see, Highgate endeavored a coup some months ago."

Coups were not as common in vampire ranks as any non-vampire might think they are. Yes, granted, there was a degree of testiness in the air between some of the factions of the Guardianships, but that's not why. It had entirely to do with the hostility between groups: New V's, Wanna V's, whatever other faction you might be currently abiding by. In this instance, though, it appeared that we might actually have some basis for discussion, especially if there appeared to be any hostilities between the Baron's group and those following Highgate.

It turned out there was more than plenty, and the Baron seemed happy to voice his frustration.

"A coup?" I said, as if I didn't know what the word meant. I suspected that we didn't need to worry about telling the Baron and company anything about us; I had a feeling that he was already up on us.

I was right, as it turned out, since he promptly addressed me by name "A coup, Mr. Hammond, that is correct. An endeavor to change leadership through physical means."

"So he attempted to conquer you through force of arms?" It was Hannah speaking, and she actually sounded more appalled than I did.

"He attempted." The Baron gave a small smile. "He did not succeed. It appears that our Lord Highgate had concepts for endeavors that were considered—oh, what was the word now—?"

"Unseemly?" suggested one of the vampires.

"Yes, exactly. Thank you, Tucker. He had various ideas for directions in which he wanted to take our organization. None of them," and the Baron smiled, albeit thinly, ""happened to be heading into that particular direction."

"So what happened then?"

"Nothing positive, I can assure you of that," said the Baron ruefully. "Let us just say that it came to a parting of the ways, as in Highgate was allowed to escape with his life."

"So that was that?" said Hannah.

He snorted disdainfully. "Hardly. That was simply the opening salvo. Although there is certainly not a good deal of love lost between the Pride and the Nu V's, Highgate wanted to convince others that I was being too 'reserved.' Yes, 'reserved' is how I believe he put it."

Something was beginning to fall together in my mind. "You're saying he wanted to get rid of the Nu V's?"

"More or less."

"How?"

"I don't know," said the Baron, and there was a look of frustration that he didn't really know how Highgate was going to go about his mission statement. "The scarred gentleman simply swore that he had 'huge plans.'" Before he spoke any further, he suddenly looked long and hard at Hannah. "You. You're the one who inflicted the wound on him, were you not?"

"I might have had something to do with it." Hannah shrugged her shoulders in order to convey just an additional bit of indifference.

"Well, that's interesting. Even entertaining. Yes, very entertaining." This time he actually allowed himself to smile broadly for a moment before reining himself in. "I'll tell you what, young lady. If you were interested in disposing of Highgate, then far from me to stand in your way." He snapped his fingers briskly once and just like that, our hands were being cut free from the binders behind us. We shook our hands out simultaneously, restoring a bit of the circulation to our hands.

"And do you have any intention of pointing us in the right direction? Toward Highgate, I mean," I said.

The Baron laughed lightly at that. "My dear fellow, other than the general confines of New York City, I couldn't begin to guess where Highgate is. Perhaps you haven't actually managed to determine how this works. I let you and your little killer girlfriend go, and in exchange, you do me the favor of disposing of this fellow that both of us would like to see go away. That's it. That is the entire deal, and it is one way straight out. If that is acceptable to you, then fine. If it is not, I can always have you tossed back down into the cellar where you can rot for the rest of your lives. It's entirely up to you."

Hannah didn't wait even a second. "We'll take you up on the whole 'getting out of here' card, if that's all right."

"It most certainly is."

"Wait," I said, and the Baron shifted his gaze back to me. It was obvious that he wasn't exactly wild about me, but at that moment I didn't care. I had other things I needed to know. "What about Salk? What's he doing here?"

The Baron's face, so serious a moment ago, now seemed nothing but amused. "Jeremiah Salk? May I ask what interest you have in him?"

I realized that the smartest thing I could do at that moment was play things cautious. "I know of him," I said curtly. "I know he's a Body Man and an enemy."

"Don't concern yourself about him," said the Baron, wiping it away dismissively as if cleaning a windshield. "I simply believe in keeping my friends close and my enemies closer. Do you believe in that credo?"

"More than you can believe," I told him, and I wasn't lying.

"Very well, then." He glanced off to the side of us and said calmly, "All right, it's late enough. You may depart."

"Depart? What do you mean?"

"Did you believe you were going to be staying here?" The Baron seemed amused by the notion.

"But...what time is it?" I said.

He slowly extracted a pocket watch. Apparently in the old days checking the time was kind of a big deal. He even clicked it open and nodded before declaring, "5:27 in the afternoon."

"In the afternoon? We've been here a whole day?"

"Half of a whole day. Would you like to stay later? We have some remarkable material on tap."

His off-hand comment, even borderline joke, about the people who were tethered downstairs, was enough to bring a chill to me. Unfortunately I didn't have the strength of will, nor the number of people on hand, that would be required to do something about it. This was reinforced for me as I glanced around and saw the warning stares from various vampires around me. There was a silent challenge there: the Baron is willing to let you go, but if you try something, we'll be more than ready for you.

Before I could say anything, though, it was Hannah who spoke up. "As much as that's appreciated," she said, "I think it'd be wiser if we were on our way."

"Yes, you're probably correct," said the Baron in a cavalier, do-as-you-will tone of voice. "Off with you, then."

"Off with us," said Hannah, and she pulled at my elbow. For a moment I didn't move. I couldn't move. I just stood there, staring at the Baron. His silent attitude of satisfaction was more than enough to prompt me to attack. But I was outgunned. We both knew it. So we were going to pretend that this was some sort of reasonable agreement between individuals who each had other things to worry about.

"Right. Off with us," I echoed, and allowed her to drag me out of there. The door to the Baron's office closed, seemingly by itself, but several of the Baron's men (and women) followed us along and out. The sun had just dipped below the horizon line, which made it low enough for our purposes.

My cycle and, miraculously, the helmets, were right where I'd left them. I swung my leg over it, strapping on the helmet. Hannah did the same. "They're not going to be thrilled with us."

"They?" I literally had no idea who she was talking about.

"They. Them. The ones who might have an opinion to voice about the intended husband of a girl..."

"Taking off with her sister for an entire night and day," I realized. Inwardly I moaned. Yeah, Hannah was right. Amber might indeed have something to say about that. They all might.

Fifteen

My Absence Doesn't Make Anyone's Heart Grow Fonder

The drive back to Manhattan wasn't much more verbal than the drive down to New Jersey was. We knew some stuff, but not much, and most of it seemed to have to do with internal politics of a group of vampires we tended to stay away from. So we knew that Highgate and the Baron's guys weren't exactly on a first name basis. I supposed that it gave me some useful bits of knowledge, especially when it came to knowing just who it was we were busy being at war with. Beyond that, though, there wasn't really all that much to go on.

Hannah, however, wasn't the least bit dispirited. In fact, she appeared rather chipper about it. "So Highgate managed to get himself cut off from the Baron." She was practically chuckling about it. "Figures."

"You really don't have any love for the guy, do you?"

"I told you. He came on to me and I scarred him. You really think that puts him in the top twenty guys I've ever met?"

Guess not, I thought, but it didn't seem like that was the thing to say aloud.

There was far more traffic involved in returning to the Garrison than there was leaving it the previous night. I dealt with it as best I could and continued to refrain from engaging Hannah in conversation. Somehow it didn't seem as if it was going to lead us anywhere good.

It was hard for me to get a read off her. She seemed friendly but distant. Obviously she didn't mind talking to me, but she certainly wasn't wild about it. And why should she be? She had transformed me into a vampire. How was one supposed to engage in chatty conversation after that. *So you were a vampire slayer! I was a vampire! Isn't that hilarious? So...you watching Dancing With the Stars this year?*

"Hannah," I said as I approached the tunnel, "we have to talk."

"No, we don't."

"Yeah, we do. There's things we need to discuss. About how you became a vampire, about why—"

"Again: no. We don't."

We glided into the tunnel, moving deftly down the middle line that served to divide the right and left sides. "Hannah—"

"No," she said more sharply. "Look, do you want me to get off here?"

"Obviously not." I wasn't thrilled by the dirty looks we were getting from drivers. I sure wasn't interested in seeing how they'd be reacting if one of us got off and started hoofing it. "I just want you to be honest with, y'know...everything."

"There's nothing to be honest about. I was a vampire; I made you a vampire because it seemed like a worthwhile idea, and because I knew you were going to get yourself killed otherwise. End of story. So if you have any brains, you'll stop making a thing about it like it's...I dunno...a thing."

I had no other response for that, and so let my lack of reply serve.

Amber, on the other hand, had plenty of response. So did Amber's parents and so did my mother.

"*What the hell were you thinking?*" demanded Amber.

We had returned to my house and, upon entering the living room, discovered an entire group of people waiting for us. Why they had decided to assemble in my damned living room was something I couldn't even begin to guess at. I had to chalk it up mainly to my remarkable luck.

Gathered in a group, sitting around and clearly in the middle of being worried about things that were none of their business, were my mother, my prospective in-laws, my prospective fiancée, and Jeremiah Salk. It was his presence in particular that I found especially annoying, but I didn't say anything about that because, really, what was I supposed to say?

Amber was on her feet first when she saw me enter and there was nothing but concern and compassion on her face. That lasted until she saw Hannah step into view behind me, and that was when the question about what the hell Hannah had been thinking emerged from her clearly angry mouth. She didn't give a damn about where my thoughts were, apparently. It was only Hannah's point of view that bothered her.

Naturally I found that to be kind of interesting, but I wasn't able to say anything about it because immediately my mother jumped in. All of her attention, of course, was squarely on me. "Where did you get off to? The both of you, overnight! It's...I don't understand—"

For some reason—probably because most of my thoughts were with Hannah and trying to get all that sorted out—I hadn't given any consideration to what I was going to say in regards to any of that. Realizing I had to cover it fast, I told the lot of them, "We were tracking down a lead on the vampire who attacked Amber."

"Were you?" Mom didn't sound especially impressed.

Lawrence, however, did. He took several steps forward and was standing practically in my face as he stared down at me. "And who might that have been?"

It was Hannah who responded. "Highgate. A vampire called Highgate." She stepped around us and subtly but firmly put herself between her dad and me. "I had a dust-up with him not that long ago. A year or so at most. Vincent and I here compared notes and when we realized we'd both run into the same individual, I thought maybe we could team up and get a few things done."

"Really."

"Yes, really," said Hannah. I noticed that she was exchanging quick glances with her sister, but Amber was now working on keeping her attention focused entirely on her father.

"And what did you find?"

At that point Hannah looked downward. "Nothing. Nothing worth discussing, in any event."

"What specifically?" Lawrence was clearly not about to let it go.

"*Nothing*, Dad," Hannah said with greater force, now looking back up and into his eyes in that defiant manner of hers. "We checked around; we went some places; we dusted some vamps. End of story. What we found didn't have a damned thing to do with Highgate's attack on Amber. I'm sorry about that, but that's the way that goes. And if you want to change that report into something else, you go right ahead, but it's still not going to be of any help to you. Okay?"

Lawrence seemed about to respond to her, but something—her energy, her aggressiveness, maybe just the fact that she was there—caused him to be taken aback. "Okay," he finally said.

"Wait..." Amber seemed appalled by her father's seeming understanding of her sister. "Okay? We're okay with that now?"

"Yes, we're okay with that," said Lawrence more firmly. "Do you have reason not to be okay, Amber?"

Apparently he was expecting her to fall back in her protests, but instead she bristled. "Yes, I have a reason! My sister vanished with my fiancé! So excuse the hell out of me if I wind up having kind of a problem with that!"

"Fair enough." It was Amanda who had spoken up. She seemed eager to try and reassemble her family into a single fighting unit. "She does deserve to know. Where did you two go?"

I noticed her use of "you two" in order to give me more of a reason for being part of the conversation. Before Hannah could say anything, I stepped in and said, "A nest, okay? We went to a nest. We asked questions. We kicked ass. We scorched a bunch of vampires and we found absolutely nothing that was of any use. Can we move on, please? *Please?*"

"*All right, fine*!" Amber fairly shouted, which was the most emotion that I had ever seen out of her. She regained control of herself and then dropped her voice down a notch. "Fine," she repeated, but then she could not help but add, "but you should have said something. You should have told us that was what you were going to do instead of just, y'know, disappearing."

"It was my idea," Hannah told her immediately. "And I thought it was too soon to drag you back into the field, Amber. Besides..." She turned to look at me. "If he's going to be my brother in law, then I wanted to have a chance to observe him up close."

"Really." It was Salk who had spoken up. Salk, who had to start yammering while not knowing that he was, of all the people there, the one who I'd most like to cave in his flapping mouth. "And what did you discern from your close range observation of one of my people?" *One of his people. God, I just wanted to punch him.*

Hannah looked me up and down as if she was visually dissecting a hot dog. "I'm…impressed," she said finally. "He has his act together. He's tough in a battle. If I had to go back out there with him, I'd do it in a heartbeat."

It was hard for me to determine whether she was full of crap or not. She certainly seemed sincere in her appraisal, but naturally she could also have just been saying what Salk needed to hear. Me, all I wanted to do was grab Salk and shake out of him the truth of his little visit with the vampires, but I didn't see how such an attempt would really go over too well.

There wasn't really all that much to say after that. Lawrence ushered his wife and daughters out of the room so that they could "reconvene" which, to me, meant that there was going to be quite a little discussion that was to be had between the lot of them. Salk, for his part, seemed inordinately pleased with the way things had worked out, or perhaps hadn't worked out was the better way to look at it. As for me, I was left with my loving mom, Dina. Yet rather than immediately start hitting me with a barrage of questions, all she did was offer to make me one of her burgers. Naturally I took her up on it, not because I was hungry, but because it was a step toward normality, which I could very much use at that moment.

Granted, I knew that normality would last only long enough for me to eventually reach a garbage can so I could upchuck the meat she was prepping me.

Still, it led me straight into a situation that I was not especially interested in discussing, none of which meant a damned thing to Mom who was prone to discuss anything and everything, no matter how ill-advised.

"So I thought the older sister wasn't interested in men," she said as she plopped the burger, dripping in juice, onto the roll in front of me.

"She's not," I said.

"Well, she's interested in you."

I had been about to dutifully bite into the burger, but that brought me up short. "No, she's not."

"Yes she is, Vince. I can see how she looks at you. She can't keep her eyes off you."

"Mom," I said with all the patience I could muster, "you know I love you. You know I care about what you say. But that's nuts. It just is. Hannah is not remotely interested in me in that way."

"Are you sure?" She seemed dubious over the proposition, as if the notion that anyone could *not* be nuts over me was completely preposterous.

"Yes, I'm quite sure."

"Well, then what about Amber?" She had taken the other burger for herself, but now she was leaning forward, staring at me with concern. "There are obviously some problems between her and her sister. So where does that stand with you? Is everything okay?"

I had no idea at all, and so of course said exactly what I always said when I was clueless:

"Everything's fine."

Why I kept saying that when it hardly ever was, I cannot even begin to guess.

Sixteen

My Next Few Days Go From Bad to Worse

Once having made their presence adequately known to the balance of Garrison 13, it seemed only sensible that Lawrence and Amanda's crew stay with us. Guest quarters were prepared for them, and the entirety of the Singer clan were set up. Amber herself was given a place to crash with her sister. From what I heard courtesy of people rooming near them, it was not exactly what one would call an especially fun time. Eavesdroppers recounted to me lengthy periods of silence interspersed with flurries of arguments and frustration. And unfortunately, most of the squabbles seemed to focus on the same thing: Me. How Hannah clearly had some sort of interest in me, except she didn't, except she did, and back and forth and on and on. Part of me was a bit flattered that my presence attracted that much attention, but most of me was just frustrated that the two sisters were arguing about me. I didn't need the grief.

When they weren't arguing with each other, the subject matter honestly wasn't all that much better. Most of the discussion amongst both them and the rest of the family seemed to focus on evening the scales insofar as the attack on Amber was concerned. In that case, there was absolutely no one in the group who was opposed to it. In fact, there weren't all that many people in my Garrison who were opposed to it, either.

"Something needs to be done!" Lawrence Singer was declaring the very next evening. The room in which he was ranting was the recreation room, filled with routine games, a wide-screen TV and such. Most of the time the members of Garrison 13 used it simply as a hang-out place where people would chat about whatever. Not that night, though. Singer was well and truly pissed about his daughter's condition. Amber, despite the fact that her arm was still a bit creaky, had decided to ditch the cast so that she could show no simple vampire attack was gonna keep her down, no sir. Salk was looking on as well, as were other assorted individuals in the Garrison. "And I'm telling you," Lawrence Singer continued, "it has to be done quickly! We have no reason to think that other vampires are not, even now, crawling all over Central Park, looking for people who are hardly in shape to fight back against their evil intent!"

Now I have to tell you, in case I haven't made it clear up until now: Lawrence was a hell of a speaker. He could thunder out pronouncements like nobody's business, and when he stood there and bellowed about how someone should be doing something about a situation, damned if you didn't just want to go out there and *do it*. It's not as if Garrison 13 was lazy. We definitely were not. So when he was standing there and declaring that we should get our collective acts together, get off our asses and leap into battle against the unknown vampires of Central Park, why then by God there were going to be a ton of people who had a whole, "Let's go do it!" attitude.

Even me. I hate to say it, but even I was standing there believing fervently—with every ounce of my fervence, whatever that was—that we should head out *en masse* to Central Park and start kicking vampire ass. Not that I was about to say it, because naturally there was the whole business with me figuring that the last thing I needed was to find myself pulled into a hunter/vampire bash off. If I wound up battling the wrong vampire, there was very chance I'd wind up exposed for what I was, and that was certainly not something I needed.

But Jeremiah Salk, on the other hand, was among those who seemed rather taken by the idea. "I think you're making valid points, Lawrence," he said to the angry family head. "If we know of a certainty that there are vampires in Central Park, then perhaps we should be out this evening in the midst of a good old, solid dust-up. Let me speak to the others on the ruling council about it right now and we'll see what we can work up!" He sounded so jazzed about the idea that it seemed more or less to be a done deal. Lawrence looked proudly to his family and they beamed at him in admiration. Why not? Dad was getting it done.

Except he didn't.

Because when Salk reappeared from the emergency sessions meeting that he had organized, the conversation did not go as he, Salk, had clearly planned.

"Can we speak privately?" he said to Lawrence Singer when he emerged from the council session.

Perhaps sensing that things had not gone as planned, Lawrence decided that rushing into hiding was not, in fact, the best way to go. Instead he said, brusquely and gruffly, "Anything you have to say to me, you can say in front of my family and friends. Are we launching a raid into Central Park this evening?" I noticed that the normal follow-up of "or not" had not been added to the question.

"Not at this point," said Salk.

"May I ask why?" It was a far more even-handed question than I would have expected Lawrence to pose.

"Lawrence, I'd far prefer if we could find a private place to—"

"May I ask why." There was no longer a question mark to the question.

Salk let out an irritated breath. He was fully aware that everyone in the rec center had stopped whatever they happened to be in the middle of and were now listening to every word he was saying. He glance heavenward in a "why me?" manner and then said gamely, "There are five people on the ruling council. Only myself and one other decided in favor. The rest felt that a single assault on one person did not constitute—"

"That single assault was on my daughter," said Lawrence, his voice rumbling. "And I very much suspect that if it were on a daughter of this Garrison, the vote would have gone quite differently."

"I don't disagree, and if you would be willing to take the time and explain—"

I have to give full kudos to Lawrence Singer, I'll say that much. I very much suspected that in his native Garrison, what he said went. Here he was on new ground where he was clearly but cautiously welcome, and just because he wanted something didn't make it so. With all of that, it was impressive that he kept his shit together as long as he did. "Take the *time!?*" he practically bellowed across the room. Anyone remaining who wasn't paying attention to him by that point certainly was by then. "What do you mean, take the time? I don't have to take the time! I'm Lawrence Singer, and what I say goes! We do not need the full cooperation of Garrison 13 in order to launch whatever type of maneuver we care to undertake!"

Salk actually balked at that declaration. "Excuse me, Lawrence, but you actually do! This is our Garrison—"

"And this was my daughter! And she was assaulted by a vampire in your backyard! And if you're not going to do anything about it..."

"I never said we weren't going to do anything about it!"

"Excuse me, but you most certainly did!"

Well, that was it. We were off and running. Lawrence and Salk started going at it, back and forth about who said what, and who was responsible for what, and where was the rest of the council, and how dare they, and where do you get off saying how dare anyone says anything. And then someone else started shouting, telling Lawrence to back the hell off, and immediately Kubrick was in the middle of things, and on and on. I mean, I could go on for a couple of pages about how what should have been a simple discussion blossomed into a full blown mass argument that would have had vampires laughing their asses off. It would be very entertaining and not really move the story along one iota, but it sure as hell would be a lot of fun nevertheless.

The problem for me was that I noticed immediately what no one else seemed to be tumbling to: Amber had walked out. This was all on her behalf, after all, and seeing her gone somehow seemed to undercut what the whole thing was supposed to be about.

Quickly I went to Hannah, who was standing over to the side and watching the dust-up with what could only be termed mild amusement. I asked her where her sister had disappeared to and Hannah just shrugged. "Does it make any difference to you?" she asked with indifference. If I'd been paying the slightest bit of attention, I'd have noticed that the indifference seemed to carry with it some genuine interest in what I was thinking regarding Amber. But I was not, in fact, paying that slightest bit of attention, and so I simply walked out and left the rec room to its concentrated shouting match.

I went down the main hallway, found nothing, and emerged into the street. There I spotted Amber across the way, walking briskly with her hands curled into fists. I shouted her name and she didn't slow down in the least.

Left with no alternative, I sped up. She blinked in surprise as I seemed to appear out of nowhere next to her. I started talking quickly in order to distract her from that minor miracle. "Where do you think you're going?"

"I'm going out."

"Where?"

"Why do you care?"

"Because I do," I told her in frustration.

"I'm going to the Park, okay?"

"No, not okay."

I grabbed at her wrist, but she shook off my attempt to stop her. Nevertheless it worked because she spun to face me. "I'm the one who was attacked! I should have the right to go back and see if they're still waiting for me out there!"

"If they are, then you can make them wait a little longer."

"Why do you even care?"

"I do! I do care!" I said in frustration. "I really like you!"

"But not love?"

Well, that was the question, wasn't it. The million freaking dollar question to which I had no answer.

I mean, what if I was? Let's go for the whole enchilada and say that yes, I was slowly but inevitably falling completely head over heels with her. Where was I supposed to go with that? What was I supposed to do? Marry her? It'd be like making her a widow on her wedding day. Share my secret with her? Yeah, that was going to end well.

"What?" she prompted me when I didn't respond immediately. "You don't think I deserve the truth?"

I didn't know what the truth was. How the hell were we

supposed to be together? How was I supposed to love her?

I told her the only thing I could: "I honest to God don't know what the truth is. All I know for sure is this, and that's that you should stay the hell out of Central Park right now."

Amber stared at me for a long moment, and then simply said, "Thanks. Thanks a lot."

With that pronouncement, she turned and stalked away from me. I saw, however, that she wasn't heading out of the area. Instead she was stomping towards the apartment building that her parents and she had been set up in. Reflexively I wanted to start after her, but then I decided that nothing good was going to come from that. She was still pissed off with me, and there was nothing for me to say that was going to change the level of upset that was currently fueling her. Running after her wasn't a choice, nor did just standing where I was and watching her leave seem like a useful option.

I turned to discover a dark shadow was leaning over me

I let out a startled, bird-like yelp.

Lawrence was standing not six feet away from me. Any closer and I would have sworn that he could pull the thoughts right out of my head. He was leaning against the nearest building, studying me thoughtfully with a laconic air. "My daughter going somewhere?' I sure didn't like the way he'd said that.

"Heading back to your quarters, Mr. Singer." Somehow it suddenly didn't seem like the time to be addressing him with the happy pleasantries of first name basis.

Unfortunately he was smart enough to notice it, and cool enough to comment on it. "Mr. Singer, now. Not doing 'Lawrence' anymore?"

"I would love to call you that. I would love to—"

"Shut up."

"Okay," I said immediately. I realized I didn't have to say anything else; he clearly had it all planned out. All I had to do was listen.

He strolled toward me slowly, hands draped behind his back. "I heard your little chat just now," he said. His voice was calm. I wasn't sure whether or not to be relieved about that. "Would it be safe to say that there is no romance being shared between the two of you? My daughter and you?"

"I wouldn't say that," I lied quickly. "There's certainly lots of—"

Now he brought a hand around and raised it, a single finger pointing into the air as if he were indicating something floating in front of us. "I'm not a fool, Vincent. Do you think I'm a fool?"

"No, sir, I do not."

"Then kindly do not do me the disservice of treating me as if I were one." He was keeping himself well reined in, but I was certain he wanted to start tearing into me. And why not? I had made his little girl miserable. "The fact of the matter is, as of this point in time, it is becoming extremely obvious to me that you do not reciprocate my daughter's feelings. And I am certainly not going to force her into a loveless marriage."

I wasn't sure how to react to that. For all I knew, he was trying to draw me somewhere. So I settled for a fairly non-demonstrative, "That's good to hear."

He continued to speak, as if that entire exchange settled, for all time, exactly how she felt about me and me about her. "Once we've done the work that your bickering Garrison is unwilling to do, we will be on our way."

"Well, that's a shame," I began to say, and I had an entire series of back-ups about how much we were going to miss them and how maybe they were running out too quickly.

"You, of course, will be required to repay me the $100,000 I gave your father, and our deal is over. I won't even charge you interest."

I gulped deeply. "Well, that's, uh...that's damned great of you and everything," I managed to say. "About not charging interest and everything. Real nice. The problem is that I don't have it. And wherever my father stashed it, and whatever he did with it, he sure didn't tell us. He might have it in a bank; he might have lost it years ago. We—and by 'we' I mean me and my mother—we really don't have anything that we can tell you right now." I gulped a second time. "That's all we can tell you at the moment. Which isn't to say that we don't have every intention of looking everywhere..."

"That's very kind of you," said Lawrence coolly, which made

me feel better right up until he said, "But I don't have any intention of waiting around while you scramble to repay me. I will simply look to your Garrison to recoup me the funds."

"But that's no better!"

Lawrence clearly didn't see how it wasn't, in fact, better. "If it serves as a problem for your Garrison, then I'll appeal to the Echelon if I have to. They'll back me up on it."

"I've no doubt they will!" I said, unable to keep the escalating alarm out of my voice. "That's not the problem, though. You're gonna wind up breaking our Garrison!"

"That," said Lawrence calmly, "is your problem, not mine."

And for just a split second, I leaped at him. I covered the distance between the two of us, jammed my fangs into his throat, and down we went. I drained him even as we fell so that when we hit the street, I was already alone. Lawrence Singer lay there with eyes wide and a dead, empty mouth hanging open. I scrambled to my feet and started considering rapidly everything I was going to do, and all the options that were in front of me at that moment. I had killed him, but hey, he'd had it coming; he'd been a dick. Instead everything was now going to depend upon how quickly I could pull everything together and hammer this entire thing into a how-do-we-cover-this scenario. Several ways presented themselves and every one of them was better than having this loud-mouthed jerk demolish our Garrison just because my father had taken him for a shitful of money.

But then just as quickly it all fell away. Lawrence Singer was still standing there, alive and hearty, and aside from the fact that I was wavering slightly, I had made no approach upon him. Instead I was simply standing there, trying to cope with what he'd just told me, as Lawrence Singer turned away from me and headed off to be with his family.

Kill him, that's all, just go for him, my inner voice commanded me. *His back is to you and he has no idea what you are. Just go for him, assault him, take him down, suck him dry. None of them would admit it, but any move that takes him down would be roundly appreciated by everyone in your Garrison. Just take him for your evening feast, just—*

This was getting me nowhere. Instead I headed for the one

person who, as much as I hated to say it, might be the only person who could be of any use to me at that moment.

Jeremiah Salk was still standing in the main rec room when I got there. Nothing much had changed. He was still animatedly arguing with some of the Singer clan: Kubrick, as I might have guessed, and one or two others of Lawrence's front men. When Salk saw me coming, he turned to me as if he was intending to haul me into the midst of the discussion. Instead I grabbed him by the wrist before he could get so much as a word out. "Come with me," was all I said as I hauled our standard bearer with me and out of the hall.

As soon as we were alone, I turned the surprised Salk toward me and brought him up to speed with our little financial disarray. As he listened his eyes widened, and when I paused for breath, he immediately leaped right in. "Where are you going to come up with that money?"

"I don't have anywhere to come up with it!" I told him in exasperation. "That's kind of the point! Do we have it?"

"You and me?"

No, not you and me, you idiot! "'We' meaning the Garrison, Salk," I said, greatly forcing patience onto the situation.

"What? No! I mean, we have some money in our emergency funding, yes. Twenty, thirty thousand or so. But not the $100 grand that you'd be looking for, and certainly not what Lawrence would want."

"Then what's the worst that happens? Bottom line it for me."

"Bottom line?" He thought about it. "Well, if the Singers appeal to the Echelon, and the Echelon backs the Singers—which they likely will," he added, just in case I thought something that suited us would happen. "Then there's a decent chance that Garrison 13 could be cut off from the Chevaliers entirely. That would mean that we wouldn't be able to use the Echelon as a resource."

"Do we use them as a resource now?"

"Yes! Very much so. For additional help, for training. For all sorts of things. We would be completely on our own. Whatever spare monies we have left to ourselves, we would likely burn through very quickly, and then…well, I don't know what, then.

Vincent," he said with a growing sense of urgency, "I don't ask a lot of you, but I'm asking you now: fix this. Find a way to repair this situation immediately! Because we don't have the wherewithal to withstand being shunted off on our own! Do you understand what I'm saying?"

Of course I did. He wanted me to fix matters with the Singers so that I was madly in love with Amber. That way she and I could be married and live happily ever after. That was the ideal plan. Failing that, then I should come up with some manner of situation so that we wound up together nevertheless. Come up with something, anything, that made sure we stayed together. It wasn't really much more complicated than that.

In the meantime, Salk was hanging around in a vampire lair in New Jersey doing who-knew-what-all down there. But I was the one who was under pressure to solve this problem that was entirely of my late father's making.

"Thanks, Salk," I said to him grimly. "I'll get right on that."

Seventeen

My First Break in Ages, Except Not So Much

With everything that was going on, the last thing that I expected was to discover the phone ringing when I walked into my home. But I did. And since it wasn't as if we received a ton of phone calls, it felt as if the phone were braying at me.

I grabbed up the phone and heard on the other end, *"Hello? Hello? Is this Vincent?"*

"Yeah, this is Vincent. Who's—?" Then I recognized the voice. "Molly?"

Molly. The vampire girl, or more correctly the Wanna V girl, who'd spoken to me a day or so ago. It had been a longshot that she would ever get back to me, much less that she would contact me so quickly.

"Yeah, this is Molly," she confirmed. *"Look, I needed to tell you—"*

"Calm down," I said. I pulled a chair over and sat down in it. "Just grab a chill pill and then tell me what's going on."

I heard her take a deep breath over the phone and then let it out slowly. *"He contacted me,"* she said.

"He? He who?"

"I've no way of knowing for sure," she said, *"but I think it's the same vampire who wound up getting in touch with Tracy."*

Immediately I was sitting up straight, all thoughts of relaxing forgotten. "Are you sure?"

"No, I'm not sure. That's why I said, 'I think.'" She sounded vaguely impatient, as if she couldn't believe I was being that stupid.

Still, I didn't want to go running headlong into something just because it seemed to fit into some manner of wish fulfillment. "Okay, okay. What makes you think that?"

"Well, because he's saying some of the exact same things that he said to Tracy."

"What things?" I couldn't recall her getting especially specific. That didn't necessarily mean anything, but still, it was of concern to me.

"About all the great things about being a vampire. About how it's something she should really consider, and that if it was really something she'd care to pursue, then he'd be happy to help her."

"He said all that? Because you didn't tell me that."

"I figured, you know, that you'd know all that already. You didn't?"

"No, I didn't." Now I wasn't sure what to think at all. It certainly *sounded* reasonable, but nevertheless, I felt like there was something in all of that that I couldn't quite put my finger on. Still, it wasn't so completely off base that I could simply toss it aside. "You've been talking on line?"

"With the guy you mean? Yes, absolutely. Like, practically right after I got done talking to you the other night. Do you think it's coincidence?" she said breathlessly.

Might be. Might not be. Either way it was something that had to be addressed. "Okay, look. I want you to arrange a meeting with him for tonight."

"Tonight? I'll do my best. I mean, he did say he was interested in getting together."

"Good. How about—?" My mind raced. "Chinatown. Do you know Chinatown?"

"Know it? I've spent half my life in it."

"Okay. Do you know the corner of Centre and Canal Street?"

"Absolutely."

"Fine. That's where you meet. Tonight at..." I glanced at my watch. It was barely past seven PM. "Eleven o'clock. Does that work for you?"

"It works fine! Oh, Vincent," and she sounded so excited. *"You really think this is the guy who was responsible for what happened to Tracy?"*

The truth was that I had no idea at all. It might well be someone who wasn't the slightest bit involved in any of it. It could be some random guy who happened to sound to her just like the guy who had taken out Tracy. But there was no way to be sure.

"I'm hoping so," I told her. "I'm sure as hell hoping so."

After I got off the phone with her, I considered assembling a squad of men to come with me. Even more to the point, I thought about bringing Amber or even Hannah. Either of them would be extremely valid individuals to have backing me up. Backing up? Hell, they'd take the lead in a heartbeat. Amber was dying to have a whack at the guy who had nearly capped her, and Hannah seemed to consider it her personal endeavor to take out Highgate, assuming it was indeed him involved in this entire mess. Both of those, however, were reasons that ultimately I decided to go out myself. I had no need of other hunters who were massaging their personal frustrations and vendettas when it came to pursuing their own endeavors. I was in a far better position to remain neutral in the midst of this whole thing, and that's what the situation needed: Neutrality. Yes, I wanted to put paid to Highgate, but I wanted it done on my terms.

I set out early for Chinatown and made it to the intersection in plenty of time. I didn't bring my motorcycle this time, but instead simply went by subway; there was a station stop right at the corner of Centre and Canal Streets. By 10:30 PM, I had chosen a place on a rooftop nearby and was spying down with a pair of binoculars. I had a genuine stake on me since I wasn't envisioning having to fake stab anyone. If Highgate did indeed show up, I had no reason not to try and spear his ass, although I was initially hoping that he'd have something to say in the conversation that would inevitably ensue.

I stayed crouched on the flat roof. There was some laundry nearby that was fluttering in the night breeze. I figured that whoever's it was, wasn't about to do anything save for leave it there overnight. I kept the binoculars securely against my face, watching carefully. There was Molly, sure enough, walking back and forth in a little circular pattern by 10:45. I wondered what was going through her mind. Was she excited? Did she have the slightest idea that she was working with a vampire? I'd been coy enough about it when we met at the Moveable Feast, but she certainly seemed to have figured it out. She hadn't bothered to wonder why in the world one member of the vampire society was trying to track down another, but that was probably because she didn't give much of a damn. She just wanted to become one of us, and it didn't matter to her all that much which of us was willing to accomplish the deed for her.

You'd think I'd have realized at that moment, but no. I was too freaking stupid to worry about it. If I'd given it any thought of all, I could have avoided a hell of a lot of hassle. Instead I just went with it, giving it no real consideration so that I could wind up totally regretting it later.

Molly continued to walk back and forth and then she stopped dead. It was as if something had spoken to her softly. She turned to face a man who was standing a short distance away. He simply seemed to have appeared there out of nowhere; one moment he wasn't there, the next he was. I adjusted the binoculars for a closer look and if my heart had been beating regularly, it would sure have skipped.

It was Highgate. No doubt about it. He was tall, with the same coat and beard and I was pretty sure that, even from where I was upon the rooftop, I could make out the scar on his cheek. It was definitely him.

I wished at that point that I'd had the brains to put some sort of speaker device upon Molly, but I hadn't planned to meet up with her before hand. So instead I was confined to remaining upon the rooftop and looking down upon the two of them as he slowly approached her. His bearing was pleasant enough, and she moved toward him, chatting off-handedly in a manner that suggested she was warm but guarded. Good girl. Smart girl. She was handling it perfectly.

I was confident that there was no way he was just going to take her on the street. He was going to go somewhere private with her. Somewhere they could chat, somewhere they could interact. Somewhere that he could start devouring her throat and then drip his own blood down her mouth. Or perhaps—and who really knew—somewhere that he could just drain her whole and leave her there to rot. It was impossible to tell from where I was exactly what he had planned for her.

Quickly I got to my feet and started to head across the roof in pursuit.

That was when the fist hit me squarely in the face.

I fell backwards, having been caught completely flatfooted. My feet went out from under me and I hit the floor. Desperately I tried to shake it off, tried to see who and what I was dealing with.

There had to be a half dozen vampires descending upon me. While I'd been busy spying on Molly and Highgate, they had found me, moved into position, and were now completely ready to commence tap dancing on my face.

Set up! You were set up, you moron! Even as the realization went through my head, I rolled to one side and started to scramble to my feet. Perhaps I could manage to throw myself over the roof. It would cause me to land hard on the ground several stories below, but at least it would give me distance.

No chance. One of them pounced upon me even as I began to get to my feet and shoved me back down again. A second yanked a burlap bag upon my head. I didn't need to breathe, but I did need to see. I struggled furiously and that was when the fusillade began: a series of kicks and poundings to the upper part of my body that were clearly designed to hammer me into unconsciousness.

At first I managed to resist. I twisted and turned and at one point nearly managed to yank the burlap bag from me. But all six of them—at least by my hurried count—were operating in tandem with each other. As much as I struggled, I was being hammered into unconsciousness. The only thing I had going for me was that I wasn't out cold yet, and so ultimately I did the only thing I could: I lapsed into a state of fake unconsciousness and played dead. Honestly, there really wasn't all that much playing involved. I was barely keeping myself together as it was. Pretending to be out cold was maybe a degree or so up from the truth of the matter.

"We got 'im," growled one of the vampires, and another said, "Let's go." I did not for a moment think that the "let's go" meant that they were just going to head out and leave me there on the roof, and it turned out I was absolutely correct. They hauled me off the roof and down the stairs, then through a back alley and into another building. Even though the bag covered me, I could tell that I was being hauled into a store that hadn't been active for a while. It had been burned out. Whatever it formerly had been, it was now simply a symbol of its former self.

My hands and arms were tied even tighter than they had been before, and then the mask was yanked off my face. I was indeed surrounded by a store that had once been something else: maybe a deli, maybe a tailor, it was impossible to tell. Molly was there and she was speaking eagerly to Highgate, who was looking down at her with the sort of upper vampire superiority that so many of his kind enjoyed displaying.

"See? I got him here!" Molly told him with great enthusiasm. It wasn't as if he truly needed her to remind him of her involvement in getting me there. It was just the kind of thing little bints like her enjoyed saying. "I got him here, just like I promised. So what now? Do you finally make me over into a vampire?"

Jesus Christ. All this insanity and all she wanted to think about was getting transformed into a vampire. I knew the Wanna V's were consistent in their desires, but sometimes they were down-right obsessive. She had no idea that she was truly in any sort of danger. It was entire possible that Highgate would drain her of every drop in her body, just to be rid of her. If I were him, that's what I'd certainly do.

Instead, to my utter astonishment, Highgate said to her, "Absolutely. We will definitely make you one of us." He ran a finger along her jaw and smiled down at her. It made me want to hurl as I stared at her through narrowly slitted lids. Upon hearing this declaration, Molly audibly swooned. I was amazed that she didn't just pass out right there and then.

"However, " Highgate continued, "before that happens, I have one last assignment for you."

"You do?" said Molly. She seemed a bit disappointed. Wanna V's were all about being transformed, and hearing anything along the lines of, "But wait, before that happens" tended to be something of a downer for them.

"Yes, but it won't be too much of a hardship," he assured her.

He took her chin in one hand and smiled down upon her, which immediately relaxed her. "I want you to go to the Moveable Feast."

"The one in Astoria, you mean?" She seemed a little puzzled, which made sense considering we were nowhere the hell near Queens.

"That is correct," Highgate assured her gamely. "It's going to be your last night as a mortal, after all. I want you to spend your time supplying as many vampires as possible."

"Supplying?" Clearly she wasn't following.

To Highgate, however, it was all remarkably simple. "Yes, that's right," he said. "The thing is, there are quite a few vampires out there—including many of the ones who inhabit the Moveable Feast—who would want to have nothing to do with me or any of my kind."

"Really?" She couldn't believe it. Me, I thought it was kind of honest of him. He was right; there *were* a lot of vamps out there who wouldn't have wanted to have a damned thing to do with him.

"Really," he confirmed. "There are plenty out there who just want to live their unnatural little lives, keep below the radar, and not cause any problems. These are the kinds of vampires that I'd like you to supply to me."

She still wasn't getting it. "Supply in what way?"

"Get me their names, their addresses. Contact information. Just provide me with means by which I could get in touch with them. Just so I could present my concerns to them myself. And as an additional incentive, make certain that as many of them as possible sample you."

"Sample me?"

"Of course," he said as if it were the most natural thing in the world. "You can do that, can't you?"

"I suppose. Sure. If you think it will help."

"Of course it will." He kissed her forehead and she sighed.

"Yes, absolutely, Highgate. And after that—?"

"After that," he assured her with such sincerity that it would have been touching if it hadn't been pure bullshit, "you will definitely walk as one of us."

“Thank you!” She threw her arms around him and squeezed him as tightly as she could. Then she took the time to glance toward me, with my arms and legs bound. “You understand, don’t you, Vincent?”

Pretending that I was unclear on any of this, I managed simply to say, “Eh?”

“Your promises were nice, but his were better. It was just a case of helping myself. You get that, right?”

“Yeah. Right. Sure,” I managed to get out. What I really wanted to say was, *You raving lunatic. You are risking throwing away your life and you don’t even understand why.* But I didn’t say that because I didn’t want to give away just how conscious I was. Not to mention that even if I said it, she very likely wouldn’t understand it.

“Don’t expect him to comprehend, my dear. He cannot.” Highgate at that point took her hand and squeezed it fervently. “All he cares about is his own interests. You have to attend to what’s important to you.”

“Ow!” she abruptly yelped.

Immediately Highgate released his grip upon her. “I am so sorry,” he said with great apology in his voice “Did I squeeze you too hard?”

“A little,” she said, shaking out her hand.

“My greatest apologies.” He rubbed the hand gently and even kissed it on the knuckles, immediately prompting her to smile once more and practically melt into him. “I have a car just outside that will take you to the Moveable Feast. Do all that you can and then return here, and all will be well.”

“Yes, Highgate,” she said with a tone of wonder and adoration. She looked at me once more with supreme regret and then headed out.

And just before she departed, I noticed a small spot of blood on her hand. The hand that Highgate had just squeezed so fervently.

It told me everything I needed to know.

Eighteen
My Neck is on the Line

Highgate stood in the doorway, waving cheerily to young Molly as the car, a nice Lincoln Towncar, pulled away from them. Then he closed the door, still smiling until the moment that it shut. Then the smile faded completely away. Instead he stared straight at me with no sense of generosity or any gentler emotion other than clear impatience and even puzzlement.

"So what is your story, eh?" he asked.

"I have no idea what you're talking about," I said. "I was just hanging around, minding my own business, and the next thing I know, your guys are attacking me."

Highgate raised a hand as if to wipe my comments off a board that only he could see. "Please. Save it. First of all, do you seriously believe that I don't recall your attacking me in my own conveyance?"

"What conveyance is that?"

Once again he waved it off as if my words meant nothing to him, which obviously they did not. "I had assumed," he continued as if I hadn't spoken, "when you initially assaulted me that you were a Body Man. Were that the case, naturally I would have simply killed you out of hand."

"Really." From his attitude, it was clear to me that being cute wasn't going to get me anywhere. I shoved it aside and sat up a bit straighter, straining gently but firmly against the ropes that were holding me down. "Didn't seem to me like you were having any luck the first time you tried to kill me."

The response that I got as a result of my snippy reply was a firm shot against the side of the head from one of the vampires. None of them seemed especially pleased that I had the temerity to speak in such a way to their beloved Highgate.

Highgate, for his part, didn't seem bothered one way or the other. In fact, he smiled slightly. "There is something to be said for that," he admitted. "In any event, naturally I figured out quite quickly that you were one of us. That alone spared your life."

"That and the fact that I kicked you out of your carriage."

"Yes." He paused a moment, his mouth closed tightly, as if trying to determine what the next best thing he could say would be. "So tell me: Were you put in place by the Baron?"

"Excuse me?" Of all the questions he could have asked me, that one caught me by surprise. "The Baron?"

"Don't lie to me. You know who he is."

"Yes," I said cautiously. The moment seemed to require caution. "Yes, of course I do. But there's no reason to assume that he brought me in."

"And why not?" Highgate seemed surprised that I might even put forward such a notion. "This is the second time that you have crossed my radar. The first time was in the park and it thwarted my ability to destroy young Miss Singer."

"So it did," was all I said.

"And now you show up a second time."

"A time that you arranged."

"Yes." Highgate saw no reason to deny it.

"How did you know to contact Molly over me?"

"I didn't." Highgate smiled slightly at that. "She contacted me."

"She knew who you were?"

"She knew enough."

I'll be damned. Clever girl. I'd underestimated her.

"So I ask again, now that we're being all candid with each other," Highgate continued, "if you were put in place by the Baron: Were you considered to be a monitor, perhaps, to make certain that all procedures are being followed? Perhaps you've been put in to keep an eye on Jeremiah Salk and make sure he's following orders?"

I had no idea what he was talking about. I considered the notion of trying to play like he was putting forward valid notions and that I was playing him along, but I couldn't bring myself to do it. "Highgate," I said slowly, "I have no clue what the hell you're talking about."

"Vincent—" he began.

I didn't provide him the chance to continue. "I don't know the Baron beyond having run into him once. *Once.* And even then he just seemed interested in you. He wouldn't install me as a monitor. I'm not sure what I would supposedly be monitoring. And if I had something to do with Salk, the ideal thing would be that I had a means of telling him to keep his nose out of my business. Last time I saw him," I added as something of a lie, "he was trying to make nice to the Baron, and he was clearly following some kind of orders. What those orders might be, I haven't a clue. Beyond that," and I shrugged as best I could considering I was tied up, "I got nothin' for ya."

Highgate had lit a cigarette and was calmly sucking on it. He studied me for a long time and at one point he even extended the cigarette to me as an offering. I shook my head. He nodded and went back to drawing on the cigarette for another minute.

"You don't know," he finally said. "You honestly don't know. Well, far be it from me to illuminate matters for you. Better for you to die in ignorance, along with those pathetic excuses for vampires at the Moveable Feast."

The moment he said that, that was when it suddenly became clear to me. "You poisoned her," I said with what amounted to a low, revering whisper. "The girl. Molly."

"You saw me do it."

I had. I had seen her react as if she were in pain the moment he withdrew his hand from hers. I'd been sure that I'd just seen something, although I was not one hundred percent what. "Yeah. I saw you do it."

"Digitalis." He saw no reason to screw around. "I poisoned her with a specialty version of digitalis, carefully treated to be lethal to vampires as well. She will die, just as her little friend did. But before she does, she'll take plenty of the pathetic Nu V's along with her."

"But I don't understand why?" I was desperately trying to wrap my head around it.

"Because she and her friend, Tracy, were part of my pilot program," he said. "And once I've refined the poison for maximum potency, I'll target the entire Nu V food supply. And we'll be rid of those pathetic excuses for vampires once and for all. Do we understand each other, my dear fellow?"

Slowly I nodded. "I think we do. The only thing I don't understand is why you've told me all this."

"Well, I'd think it should be obvious," said Highgate. "I want to kill you. And I'm going to kill you. Right now. Gentlemen," and he nodded to the vampires.

They came at me from both sides. One of them was wielding a large, bladed weapon. The other five were preparing to hold me immobilized so that my head would be kept stationery.

That was the point where I realized that I had completely miscalculated. Highgate wasn't kidding. They were going to snuff me, right then, right there. And there wasn't a damned thing I could do about it.

I tried to pull away, to exert a last minute burst of strength, but it did me no good at all. My head was being kept immobilized and the largest of the vampires was coming right at me with the blade. I had maybe a couple of seconds left, and there was absolutely nothing I could think of to say or do that was going to stop him.

And that was when a flashbang grenade crashed in through the window.

I was the only one looking directly at the scuffed up, steamed over window when the grenade came bouncing in, and thus the only one who knew to close his eyes. The others stopped just long enough to see what the origin was of the crashing sound, and that was when the flashbang detonated. The sound was as deafening as any of the flashbangs ever were, but at least I could still see and that was what gave me the advantage, no matter how momentary it was.

I opened my eyes, saw that everyone was temporarily blinded, and I threw everything into what I had at the moment. I'd been pulling at the bonds, but now I tossed all that I had into it in one great shot, and the bonds tore loose. I pulled my hands in either direction and just like that, I was free.

At that moment the front door burst open and my jaw dropped as I saw Hannah Singer charge in. She had a blade in one hand and she swung it at the very first person she saw: Highgate.

But Highgate had been fast enough to shield his eyes, apparently, because he caught the blade and brushed it aside. He strode forward and slammed his elbow up and in, striking Hannah squarely in the chest and knocking her off her feet. She went down heavily and for a moment he was right over her.

The moment, however, was all he had. I had managed to push aside his men and snatched the blade from the nearest one of them. With a quick whirl, I whipped the blade around and sent the head flying from the man who had, only moments before, been about to behead me.

Without slowing or foolishly waiting for their eyes to clear, I lunged forward and took off the head of a second before the first had finished falling. A fast turn, a dodge, and I whacked the right leg off a third one. He screamed, going down, and I brought the blade up and around quickly and knocked the third one's head off, quickly and neatly.

Highgate saw what was going on and that was more than enough. He didn't have a blade handy to combat me with, and I suspect that even if he'd been holding a sword in either hand, he would still have been reluctant to take me on one-to-one.

He gave no thought to the rest of his men at all. Instead he was out the door in half a second, banging through it and sending the various pieces of it flying in all directions.

I immediately forgot entirely about his accomplices; I only wanted Highgate. I charged through the door, looked right and left.

Gone. The bastard was gone.

I looked straight up just in time to see him scaling the front of the building. *Oh no you don't,* crashed through my mind. Immediately I started up the building after him, snarling deep in my throat, determined I was going to take the bastard down. I thought that right up until I saw a statue coming straight toward me.

Son of a bitch. That was all I had time to think before I threw myself to the side. There was nothing for me to grab onto and I fell. The building whizzed past me and then I hit the ground, having only time to leap to the right before the statue—a twisted and deformed gargoyle—struck the ground, shattering into at least a dozen large pieces. The statue already forgotten, I looked up again.

No sign of Highgate. He was gone. There was always the chance that I could go in pursuit of him, try to chase him down, try to find him, stop him. But I knew already that one of two things was going to happen. The more likely was that I would not find him at all. The less likely, but equally less appealing, was that he would find me by leaping out of some hiding place along the way and taking me out. Neither option seemed especially appealing.

So instead I retreated to the place where he and his crew had been about to annihilate me.

There I found several more dusty corpses and a winded but determined Hannah, glancing around while holding the sharpened blade. There was no blood on it. That didn't surprise me terribly; there was no reason for there *to* be any blood on it.

"Sorry," she said when she saw me. No longer interested in it, she tossed the blade to the far side of the room, ignoring it as it clanked to the ground and then lay there silently. "Didn't mean to keep playing with it."

"You're certainly entitled to," I said.

"Highgate got away?"

"Yeah. Sorry about that. Although you could have gone after him."

"Could have. Didn't. Maybe next time."

"Next time. How the hell did you know about *this* time?"

"I heard you," she said matter-of-factly. "On the phone. Talking to the little ditz who went off to try and serve as a stake to any vampires stupid enough to take her on."

"You were there in my house?"

"Yes. I was waiting there to talk with you. Except you were too busy talking to other people. And when you spelled out where you were going and then decided to take public transportation for no reason I can think of, I decided to take your bike, which is what *you* should have done."

I was going to argue her on the point, but was having a hard time doing so, mostly because she'd turned out to be so damned right. "Yeah, well, okay, I'll give you that one."

"Damned decent of you," she said. Then she shrugged. "What can I say? I was worried that you were getting into something that was gonna be over your head."

"You were worried about me?" I wasn't sure what I was having more trouble with: that she'd been worried about me, or that she was admitting to it. Either one seemed kind of out of character for her. Then again, what did I really know about her character, when you got down to it.

"Yeah," she said, "I was worried about you, okay? I made you, so that sort of makes you my responsibility." As she was speaking, she was actually adjusting my collar so that everything fit smoothly. Then she patted it down and added, "So now what?"

"Now what? You mean, now do we go after Molly and prevent her from doing something stupid out in Astoria?"

"More or less, yeah. Me, I don't really give a damn, but if it means something to you..."

"Yes, it means something to me. And I'm getting the feeling it means something to you as well."

"Don't get smug," she said firmly. "There's no reason whatsoever for you to assume anything when it comes to me. We understand each other?"

"Perfectly. Now where the hell is my cycle?"

Minutes later we were aboard my motorcycle and barreling toward Queens. We tore through the streets of Manhattan as quickly as we could and then up onto the bridge that would take us up onto the BQE, the Brooklyn-Queens Expressway so that we could make it back to Astoria as quickly as possible.

The entire time Hannah kept her arms wrapped around my midsection. She said nothing; she simply chose to maintain her firm grip on me and even, for a brief time, rested her head against my back. Neither of us was wearing helmets this time. Whenever we passed a police car we just lowered our heads and barreled forward at top speed. Nobody stopped us. I guess they felt that if we wound up smearing and shattering our heads, we would have no one to blame but ourselves.

I couldn't entirely say they were wrong.

Nineteen
My Worlds Collide

The only thing that saved me when I arrived at the Moveable Feast was the fact that Hannah was holding onto the back of my cycle. I'm telling you, that *had* to be the only thing.

Because when we pulled up to the Moveable Feast, the armed forces of Lawrence Singer and company were already there.

I couldn't believe it. I simply could not believe it. The neighborhood was as run down and indecent as ever, and yet the presence of the vampire hunters was practically a blinking red light. As we pulled up, I sensed them immediately, and Hannah's stiffening behind me underscored the fact that she sensed it as well.

"My God," she murmured as we pulled up. "They're everywhere."

Not everywhere, really. Not technically. But they were in enough places to make it seem that way. There had to be at least half a dozen of them in the vicinity and more at the outer edges. Behind garbage dumps, behind cars, leaning against traffic lights and trying to look nonchalant. I'll tell you right now, there are fewer things more obvious in this world than a vampire hunter endeavoring to look nonchalant.

Sure enough, there was Lawrence, with Amber, Kubrick and several others by his side. They saw us come rolling in and immediately they gestured for us to join them. We rolled over on the cycle and Lawrence was all over us. "What are you doing here?" he demanded as we took positions behind some conveniently set up cardboard boxes.

I hadn't really come up with a good answer. Nor was I

doing any better thanks to Amber's just staring at us, clearly astounded, from a corner of the alley. "I'm doing the same thing I'm always doing," I told them out of reflex, since I really didn't have anything better. "Chasing down vampire places. Which this happens to be, after you forced them to relocate. The better question is, what are *you* doing here?"

"The same thing as you." It was Kubrick who was now speaking, and his attitude and tone of voice didn't sound any better than the last time I'd heard it. "It seemed to have more potential than Central Park. You two were planning to go in all by yourselves?"

"I was checking it out," I said icily, and then added as sort of a last minute thing, "And Hannah was helping."

"Yeah. I was," she said. "Anyone have a problem with that?"

Amber very much looked as if she had a huge problem with it, but she chose not to say or do anything about it. Nor did she even glower. Instead she simply kept her face unreadable, and that was—I have to tell you—more disconcerting than anything else that she could possibly have done.

We had both disembarked from the cycle and now the curve of Hanna's mouth brushed my ear ever so slightly. "Stall them," she whispered. Naturally I got it immediately. I was to keep the vampire hunters here while she went in and made sure that any vampires within got themselves the hell out.

Stall them. Perfect. And how the hell am I going to do that?

Lawrence seemed ready to just accept my presence there as something that happened. "All right, then," he said matter-of-factly. "So you're here. Fine. The both of you can take the western entrance..."

"Whoa, whoa. Hold on there," I said. I was speaking way faster than I was actually capable of putting thoughts together, which is always a very dangerous approach to take. But it was the only approach available to me since I certainly didn't have anything more sensible to have happen. "Where the hell do you think you're going?"

Lawrence's dark eyes blinked at me in confusion. "We think," he said slowly, "that we are going in. Why? Where do *you* think we are going?"

"I think you're going to stay right here until we get this all sorted out," I said. I hated the way I was sounding. I was coming across like some sort of two-bit organizer of vampire-hunting activities. What the hell was up with that? Since when did I wind up sounding like a watered down version of Jeremiah Salk? It was almost embarrassing to have to listen to. Nevertheless, I had to keep going in order to provide Hannah as much time as she required. "You can't just go running into—"

"We most certainly can, Vincent," Lawrence cut me off. He was clearly not thrilled about the direction that this conversation was taking. "The fact of the matter—if you must know—is that we received the specifics about this place from the same arena of our movements as we did the previous one."

I wasn't entirely sure I was following. "Are you telling me that the Echelon—?"

"Yes, the Echelon told us about this place, just as they informed us about the one in New York City, if you must know." Lawrence was clearly not happy to be providing this information, but he didn't see any other way of accomplishing what he needed, or at least what he felt he needed, to do.

"But this is the property of Garrison 13. I don't understand how you guys suddenly managed to get the final say on what goes on around here."

Kubrick rumbled, "Trust, obviously. They trust us to get things done. They don't trust you. Simple as that."

"No, *not* as simple as that! Whatever else may be going on, New York still remains the bailiwick of Garrison 13. I don't care what you think; you just can't go wandering into our neck of the woods."

"Yes, we really can," said Lawrence. His voice was stone-cold level. He was clearly not happy to be stuck in this position, much less having to argue over it with one of the young Body Men... not to mention that the Body Man was at least still nominally considering still becoming Lawrence's son in law. That, however, didn't seem to carry much impact at that particular moment.

"If this wasn't cleared by Salk, then—"

"Then here are all of we, not caring." This was obviously Lawrence's last comment on the subject. As if I were no longer there, he started calling for his people to get into position. He did not, at the moment, notice that Hannah was nowhere to be found. Amber was glancing around, though, and it was clear that within a second, maybe two, she was going to zero in on the fact that her sister had suddenly disappeared.

I did the only thing I could think of.

I shoved Lawrence Singer. Hard. Hard as I could, or at least as hard as I could and not tip off just how much harder a shove I could have made it.

Lawrence staggered under the impact and would have fallen, had Kubrick not caught him. He stared at me, eyes gaping, as Kubrick helped him back to his feet. "Are you out of your mind?" he demanded.

"You're not going in there," I said, pointing toward the building that housed the Moveable Feast. "Not until everything gets cleared through Salk."

"I already told you: we have this cleared through the Echelon. And you will not get in my way again. Do we understand each other?"

Okay. Shoving him clearly had not gotten the message across. Time to kick it up a notch.

I hit him.

Understand, I could have belted him hard enough to send him into the middle of next week. Hell, I could literally have knocked his head off. One solid punch from me and he'd have been a dead man.

As it was, I simply settled for getting his attention. The punch was a solid right cross and it knocked him off his feet and onto his ass.

That was all that Kubrick needed to launch an attack. This assault was what I had been waiting for. He came at me quick, but I sidestepped him and drove two quick jabs into his upper chest. He staggered, arms out to either side, and I slammed both hands together and into his face. Down Kubrick went, and a quick strike from my right foot kept him there.

But Lawrence was now back up and he was absolutely livid. This, of course, presented me with a serious problem. I could easily pound the living crap out of him, yet how would that be of any benefit? All I'd show is that I was far more capable than my simple build might indicate. And that, in turn, could add to more of the kinds of questions to which I had no ready answers.

So when Lawrence drove his fist forward, even though to me he was moving in slow motion, all I did was move my arms to block his thrusts. His arms slammed into mine and I deflected them. He came at me, quickly, angrily, steadily, and all I did as I backed up was continue to knock aside any and all of his attempts to hit me. The blows came so fast and furious that it was far more about the shots he was taking than it was about the blows I was deflecting.

I counted off maybe thirty seconds of his assaults and then carefully planted my feet. On the very next swipe he took at me, I went down even though he hadn't in fact connected with me. I lay on the ground, huffing and puffing even though I didn't really need to. I maintained the determined expression on my face, though, to convey to Lawrence that—down I might be—but out I most definitely was not.

Lawrence stood over me, hands curled into fists, breath coming raggedly from his chest. Kubrick was near him, urging him to continue the attack, but Amber had now forced her way between her father and me. "Get back, Dad," she said with furious urgency. "I said *get back!*"

At that moment Lawrence wanted to snarl at her. It was incredibly obvious to me. He wanted to snarl, to shout, to tell her to get the hell out of his way because she had no business interfering in the first place.

But he did none of that. He hesitated, presumably because—faced with his protesting daughter—he had no idea how exactly he should be behaving. This provided her the opportunity she required, and she placed herself between us firmly as she said, "Get away from him, Dad. Now. *Now!*"

Briefly he rallied. "You do not tell me what to do, little girl."

"Yes, I do. About this, I do." For a moment she seemed just the slightest bit intimidated by his anger, but then she rallied. "This is his town, and his area, and his state, and his...his everything. And if he says that you have to get Salk to sign off, then you have to get Salk to sign off. It's that simple. And if it's *not* that simple, then it should be."

There seemed to be so much that Lawrence wanted to say to her. Say what you will about him—and God knows I could say plenty—he managed to keep himself pretty well under wraps when it came to responding to his youngest daughter. His teeth gritted, he managed to get out one word. Fortunately it was the one word that was needed for the situation:

"Fine."

That was it. A simple "fine."

"Thank you, Dad," she said, but he was already not listening to her. Instead he was busily barking orders to the rest of his crew, telling them to stay put until they had a sign off from Jeremiah Salk, and by the way, did anyone have a number for him?

I remained securely on the street, looking up, as Amber knelt down next to me. She looked me over briskly as Lawrence continued to minister to her desires, although he kept glancing at me every so often. It seemed to me that he was practically begging me to offer some manner of serious obstruction. Knowing the uselessness of such a plan, I stayed right where I was, maintaing my gaze upon him while simultaneously keeping as much to myself as I could. Amber went over my face, touching dampened cloth to it in order to keep control of any swelling that might result from getting whacked around by her dad. There wasn't any, of course. I'd been too smart and defensive for that. I had to hope that witnessing the absence of marks on my face wouldn't provide too much of a tip for her. At one point she frowned slightly, but otherwise she didn't appear to be making any note of it. Leastways that's what I hoped.

"Can you get Salk on the phone?" she said in a low voice.

That wasn't actually what I wanted to accomplish. I was waiting for Lawrence to do the actual contacting. But Lawrence was still busy speaking with his people, and frankly, I didn't expect that Salk would necessarily be especially supportive. *Let him through! We have enough problems!* That's what Salk's contribution to the evening's proceedings would be.

But Amber was asking in such a straightforward manner, and I didn't really have any basis upon which to refuse her. So I pulled out my cell phone and started doing what I could. I hesitated then, because off the top of my head I couldn't remember his direct number. Why would I? How many opportunities did I have to call him up?

And then, even as I sat there and tried to remember what Salk's phone number was, there was suddenly a massive shout and rush. Before I could do anything short of shout in protest, Lawrence and his crew were charging en masse toward the building housing the Moveable Feast.

"*Sonofabitch,*" I snarled, all in one word, as I scrambled to my feet, shoving Amber unceremoniously aside. She called out a frustrated objection as she fell back, but I had no patience or thought for whatever it was that she had to deal with. I was instead charging in after Lawrence's people, fighting to keep up.

They weren't even bothering with flashbangs. Instead they were charging with crosses and crucifixes held up in front of them. Those, of course, would do them no good if they encountered vampires who were interested in fighting back. The vamps would smack aside any such religious emblems and instead proceed to devour anyone who was waving a religious icon in his or her face while expecting some protection.

The scenario that such an attack could create was absolutely terrifying to me. It wasn't as if I was especially concerned; I already knew it was simply a matter of fate because they hadn't been willing to believe that humans were not, in fact, dumb as a bag of rocks. No, what terrified me was Amber and her family winding up as a bunch of blood-drained corpses. I didn't want any of that to happen.

"*Hold it!*" I shouted, but it was too late. They were battering down the doors and windows of Moveable Feast, kicking their way in while wielding their utterly useless religious icons. I stopped thinking about Amber, who was behind me. Instead I plugged everything I had into getting into the building as quickly as I could. I moved so quickly that I left Amber far behind, charging in through the nearest open door and waving my arms wildly, shouting, "Hold it! Wait!"

Then a hand suddenly clamped onto my shoulder and pulled me back before I could draw any attention to myself. I didn't even have to look to see that it was Hannah. *"Shhhh!"* she practically spat in my face.

I looked around and immediately saw what she was trying to draw my attention to.

There were no vampires. Not anywhere.

Lawrence and his guys were going over the people that they'd found in the place, flashing them with special lights, making sure that they were what they said they were: perfectly human people who were just having a good time.

That was when I understood. "Got all the vamps out?" I said so softly that only Hannah could possibly have heard me.

She nodded.

"And then got back outside?"

"Barely." She was speaking just above a whisper. "Of course, having you get into a boxing match with my father certainly helped."

Then I realized that I needed to focus on matters of greater importance. "Molly. If the vampires fled, chances are she's still here. We need to find her."

"Why?"

"Because she's dying."

"Let her," said Hannah. Clearly not the most generous of individuals.

I decided that continuing the back and forth with Hannah was going to go nowhere fast. From behind me I heard Amber shouting my name, but there was no time to chat with her. Instead I quickly made my way through the dancers and kids who were "having a good time and had no clue at all what any of these guys were talking about." That was their trope and they were sticking closely to it. Lawrence's angry theatrics weren't cutting any ice with this crowd the way they had the first time.

Obviously there had been secret means of escaping the place built in, and the vampires had availed themselves of it. Whether or not the hunters would return at some point in the future would be something left for another day.

I moved quickly through the fans who were still doing everything they could to look up with blank, confused eyes at Lawrence and company and ask what the problem was.

Everywhere I looked, though, I didn't see Molly.

And then I did.

She was at the far end of the room, pushing her way toward an exit, and there was nothing but fear on her face. Lawrence hadn't spotted her yet because, if he had, he would have gone right toward her. Fortunately I managed to impose myself between his clear sightline of her and I started right toward her.

So did Kubrick.

Son of a bitch. He certainly had a knack for being where I didn't need him to be. This time, though, I didn't have the time to deal with him.

Molly saw Kubrick coming about the same time that I did, and I had no time to do anything else than what I did: leap. Kubrick never saw me coming. I landed on back of him so quickly that he was knocked to the floor and I just barely had time to strike him from behind. He tried to get to his feet, but the world was clearly spinning around him and he collapsed forward, his eyes fluttering closed.

I vaulted off his back and Molly backed up, her eyes wide. She'd seen everything, which was more than the others had. "You *are* a vampire. I knew it!" she said in a strangled whisper.

There was no time to screw around. I shoved her hard and fast, pushing her back to the furthest point in the room.

She gasped as I practically slammed her up against the far wall. "I'm sorry, I'm so sorry," she managed to say. "I was just—"

"Shut up," I told her. I had no time for screwing around. "Listen to me very carefully: Highgate's poisoned you. Any vampire who drank of you is going to be dead in a very short time. Do you understand what I'm saying to you?"

She stared at me. "What?"

"I said Highgate's poisoned you. Any vampire wh—"

"Drank of me?" It was starting to filter through. "Poisoned... are...are you saying—?"

"Yes, exactly." It was a relief that she seemed capable of jumping to the end of the thought rather than dwelling endlessly on the first part. "And we need to get you out of here. Right now."

"And take me where?"

"To a hospital!" My frustration was starting to boil over. "We need to get you to a hospital! Do you understand that?"

Slowly she managed to nod, and then did so even more vigorously. "Yeah. Yeah, okay."

Quickly skirting the perimeter of the place, I guided her toward an exit. And unfortunately, naturally, I heard the sharp retort of, "*Hammond*!" from behind me. It was Lawrence and he was heading very quickly my way.

"Not now," was all I could say.

"Yes, now." His face was a mask but the fury within him was palpable. "Who is this? Where are you going—?"

"I'm taking her to a hospital." The truth was the only thing I could think of to fall back on.

Lawrence looked her up and down. "She looks fine to me. Hasn't been injured. Have you been injured, Miss?" She didn't reply and he didn't wait for her to do so. "See? She's just fine."

"Lawrence—"

He took a step closer, so close that I could shove my hand into his chest and extract his heart before he could make the slightest move to stop me. I could show it to it, wave it at him, and use it for a hat while he keeled over. Then, with any luck, while everyone else was standing there looking horrified, I could haul Molly and myself out of there.

Or I could get cut down before I could take another few steps. Yes, Lawrence would still be dead, but that would serve as cold comfort at best.

"I'm pregnant."

Both of us turned away from each other and stared at Molly. Her face was impassive, but there was a very authentic hint of urgency in her voice. "I'm pregnant," she said again, "and I need to get to a hospital because...because I think I may be having a miscarriage."

Lawrence was clearly incredulous. "You were pregnant and decided that the best thing you could do during that time was to try to convince someone to turn you into a vampire?"

"I have no idea what you're talking about." It sounded like her entire throat was starting to cramp up. "I just want to get out of here and take care of my baby."

"Who's the father?"

"That's enough," I said, mustering as much frustration as I could. I had her firmly by either arm and said, "I'm getting her out of here and if you want to stop me...."

Lawrence was ready to give me more problems about it, and then he noticed Kubrick lying off to the side. He frowned. "What the hell happened to him?"

"No clue," I said immediately. "Found him like that. You really need to keep a closer eye on your people."

I glanced around and saw that Hannah was no longer anywhere nearby. Fine. Let her go do what she felt comfortable with doing. Before Lawrence could say anything further, I pushed past quickly with Molly. "Nice meeting you," she managed to mutter to Lawrence before he was behind us, still looking down at the unconscious Kubrick.

Seconds later I had pushed Molly through the open door and out into the crispness of the street. I started looking around desperately for a cab and didn't see any, and I wasn't thrilled about the prospect of riding along with her clinging onto the back of my cycle. Unfortunately I wasn't beginning to see a lot of alternative.

Especially when she passed out.

"Poisoned?" she suddenly said as if she were still processing that piece of information. When I tried to verify that, yes, Highgate had indeed poisoned her and the best thing she could do about it right now was allow me to haul her ass to a hospital, that was when it turned out to be too much for her. Her legs appeared to go numb, her eyes rolled up into the top of her head, and a second later she slipped into unconsciousness.

Oh, fantastic, was all I could think. I swept her up into my arms and looked around desperately. I knew where the local hospital was; I *always* knew that. But getting there was going to be a bit of a problem. I shouted toward a passing cab, but the "Off Duty" sign snapped on and it kept on going. *"Aw, come on!"* I bellowed, which didn't deter the cab in the slightest.

I was going to have to run. That was all there was to it.

I turned around and just as I did, another occupied cab came rolling right up behind me. I stepped out of the way and then, to my astonishment, the vehicle screeched to a stop. The back door flew open and out stepped, of all people, Amber Singer.

Her face was impassive. She took in the now unconscious form of Molly in one glance and then said briskly, "Get her in."

This certainly was not the time for hows and wherefores. Without hesitation I shoved her insensate body into the cab as fast as I could. "In the back with her," Amber ordered and I did as I was instructed. Amber then clambered into the front seat, getting a startled reaction from the driver, a rotund black-haired guy. "Where to?" she said.

I told her the address of the nearest hospital. The car immediately took off, and as it did so, Amber turned in the front seat and said briskly, "Okay. We're heading to the hospital. This is my cab, and *you* can just say nothing." That secondary part of the sentence was directed not to me, but to the cabbie. He responded with a shrug and a miming of zipping his mouth closed. The cab pulled away and Amber turned her attention back to me. "As for you, you are going to tell me what the hell is going on. Do we understand each other?"

"Yes, ma'am," I said, and I did.

Twenty

My Interview with a Vampire

Naturally I didn't tell her *every*thing. Starting off with, "Well, your sister turned me into a vampire and it's been downhill from there" didn't seem to be the best way to kick things off.

So I told her as much as I thought was reasonable considering the circumstances, and did it with enough sincerity that it sounded right. Actually, it was remarkably easier than I would have thought. All I did was start my narrative pretty much from the time that I had initially met her, when I was supposedly first entering the previous incarnation of the Moveable Feast. I told her how my subsequent investigation of the attack in Central Park had resulted in my winding up at the same location she and her family had. I expressed my frustration over how the place had obviously cleaned out of whatever vampires had been there, leaving us with only the obvious Wanna V's.

As I told her all of this stuff—some of which she already knew—I noticed that the cabbie kept glancing back at me with widening eyes. This was obviously stuff that was not remotely within his range of experience. I think he was trying to figure out whether we were just teaming up to yank his chain.

The entire time I kept wishing that Hannah was along for the ride. For some reason I felt as if having her voice added to the mix would have brought Amber down from the ceiling.

Amber listened carefully, interjecting questions here and there. The cabbie kept trying to appear as if he wasn't paying attention and repeatedly failing spectacularly. At one point he couldn't stand it anymore and asked, "Are you people serious about this vampire stuff, or are you just screwing with me?"

"Kind of both," I told him. He didn't seem especially thrilled by that answer, but it was the best one I had for him.

As Molly slumped against me, my fingers darted through her clothing. In her small jacket, I found her ID and flipped it open. Her name was Molly, all right. Molly McGuire. Jesus Christ, she was only seventeen; she wasn't turning eighteen for another two months. She lived in Flushing, and it left me wondering how in the world she had managed to get herself over to the original Moveable Feast, which was in Manhattan. Subway, probably.

Minutes later the cab roared up to the E.R. entrance of Mount Sinai. The moment we pulled up, I leaped out of the car and hauled the unconscious Molly through. Her breathing was already starting to sound shallow to me. If Highgate had been planning for Molly McGuire to be well enough to last until morning, he had sadly mistaken her staying power.

I ran into the hospital, Amber following in after me once she'd taken care of paying off the cab. I realized belatedly that I should have offered to help pay for it, but my mind was too much with Molly.

I'll tell you this: if you want to get attention in an E.R. then the best way to do so is by running in with an unconscious body. That immediately gets people coming over to you, demanding to know what's going on. They didn't seem especially worried about helping me; they just wanted to know what the hell I was doing there.

"We were at a party," I said and then nodded toward Amber. "The three of us." Amber looked momentarily surprised but then nodded. I pushed forward: "And then I saw that this girl taking what looked to be digitalis into the bathroom. I waited a few minutes and when she didn't come out quickly, I banged on the door and burst in. She was unconscious. Right, Amber?"

"Completely out," said Amber. She escalated her voice and made herself sound even more concerned. "She was just, y'know…out."

"I don't know what's wrong. I don't know—"

"We need a gurney!" shouted the E.R. nurse who had obviously heard enough. Moments later a gurney had been rolled out and I eased Molly onto it. As I did so, I slipped Molly's identification to Amber and said in a low voice, "Call her parents. Right now."

"And if they don't want to come?"

I hadn't even entertained that notion, although it was certainly a possibility. Who knew what their relationship was like? But that wasn't important to me; all I cared about was getting them out of Molly's house, because there were things there that I wanted to take a look at. "Make them," was all I said.

She nodded and stepped off to the side, taking Molly's contact info with her.

Meanwhile Molly was being wheeled into the back of the hospital and a nurse was coming up to me with a clipboard and a determined look on her face. She shoved it into my hands and said, "Fill this out, please. Both sides."

"Both sides." It asked for plenty of information and I didn't have much of any to provide other than the obvious stuff. Nevertheless I sat down and started whittling away at it as best I could. Periodically the nurse from the front desk would glance over toward me as if to make sure that I was doing what I was supposed to do. I would nod at her and keep writing, even though I didn't have the slightest clue whether I was providing accurate info or not. I figured that, worst came to worst, her parents would fix everything once they got there.

Amber came up to me as I reached halfway through. She dropped next to me and said in a low voice, "They're on their way."

"Both of them? Mother and father?"

"Yes. They were kind of freaking out. They knew their little girl was involved with some 'weird stuff,'" and she took the time to put quotation marks around the select words. "But they had no idea just how weird it was. They should be over here in about..." She glanced up at a clock on the wall. "...fifteen minutes. Twenty at the outside."

I hesitated before I asked, "And Molly? What's the story with her?"

"She..." Amber licked her lips and pushed forward. "She's slipped into a coma. But they have her connected to maybe a hundred tubes. If she had any more stuffed into her she'd look like a Christmas tree."

"Okay." My mind was racing. "Okay, here's what you do. Finish filling this out," and I shoved the clipboard at her.

Amber seemed more suspicious than cooperative. She didn't immediately take the clipboard for herself. "And while I'm doing that?"

I considered not telling her anything in particular. *Better to keep matters as vague as possible.* I quickly realized, however, that might not be the best way to approach matters. We needed to be on each other's side, no matter how many suspicions were floating around at the moment. So I decided yet again to go for reality. "While you're doing that, and while you're bringing Molly's parents up to speed, I'm going to head over to the house they just left empty."

"Why are you assuming it's empty? What if they have other kids?"

Shit. "Then I hope you're wrong and they don't. Because otherwise this thing is going to get a bit tricky. Make that a lot tricky." Even as I said that, I was firing off a fast message to someone who could help me out. Less than thirty seconds later, I got a response: *On the case.*

"Vince," she said firmly and I turned to her with a certain degree of exasperation. "You simply cannot expect things to go back to the way they were."

"I don't know where anyone or anything is at the moment, Amber," I said honestly. "I mean, what are you saying? The way we were? The way that Molly was? I dunno what's what or where or with who and oh, by the way, I don't think you know either. So we can just wait things out, or we can try to get ahead of the curve. Me, I'm for the latter."

"And what's getting ahead, uh…get us?"

"With any luck" (which I was perfectly willing to admit we hadn't really had) "it gets us the guy who attacked you in the Park. I thought that's what we all wanted. Is it what you want?"

"Yes." Her lips twitched in clear annoyance. "But you know what, Vince? We're not done here."

"I didn't think we were."

With the understanding that she would remain and try to smooth things over with Molly's parents, I immediately headed out. I had Molly's home address tucked in my pocket and it took me only a minute to flag down a cab and get a ride over there.

I watched the area change around me as I went. Busy streets with businesses, most of them closed at this point in the evening, evolved (or devolved, depending on your point of view) into small apartment buildings and eventually small, shoulder-to-shoulder homes. Nothing particularly fancy, which was good as far as I was concerned. The less festive the home, the less likely it would be that I'd have to contend with house alarms. It simply wasn't aggravation I needed.

The cab dropped me off. I sent him on his way. Didn't figure there was any reason to have a witness watching my every move. The house was a single family dwelling, quite small, and all the lights were off. I didn't see any sign of a car in the driveway. So far everything was running strictly according to schedule. Unless, of course, someone was asleep inside, in which case I was quite likely screwed.

Five minutes passed. It was easily the longest five minutes I'd ever experienced in my life. I imagined Amber waiting back at the hospital, very likely trying to figure out exactly what she was going to say—if anything—to Molly's parents. I had hardly left her with the easiest endeavor in the world. But I had every confidence that she'd be able to handle it.

Then, as we rolled into minute number six, a small car pulled up. Moments later the inimitable Tyler, the Garrison's resident computer expert, extracted himself from the car and bounded to his feet, shaking them out in order to get rid of whatever cramps he might have picked up. He shook out his long hair rather briskly and said cheerfully, "So okay. What've you got?"

"Computer belonging to a teenage girl. She's been emailing a vampire named Highgate, and I'd be astounded if she simply deleted them after reading."

"Oooo." Tyler didn't exactly sound like a bunch of raw nerves. "Teenage girl's computer. Sounds pretty rough...oh. Wait. No, it doesn't." He had a bag slung over his shoulder and he was already marching toward the front door of the house. "C'mon.

Let's go before somebody spots us." It didn't seem terribly likely that someone would, considering the darkness around us, but it made sense that we should watch out for anyone who might be trying to stop us.

We strode up to the front door, big as brass, and it took Tyler only a few seconds to jimmy the lock on the front door. We took a few steps in and paused, waiting to see if an alarm would go off. Nothing happened. The house remained quiet.

"Where's the computer?" whispered Tyler.

I looked at him with not a little surprise. "How the hell would I know?"

"You don't know her?"

"No!"

"Okay, well..." He glanced around and then up. "Probably up in her bedroom."

We headed briskly up the stairs and, after a few moments, zeroed in on the room in question. It could not have been more different from a standard vampire-worshipping girl than one could have imagined. There were standard R&B posters, books about history...nothing, in short, that tagged her as a vampire wanna-be. I suppose in retrospect that makes a certain degree of sense. She wanted to keep her hidden world, well, hidden. No point in having it otherwise, or at least so I supposed.

Booting up her computer wasn't all that much of a trick: It was password protected, but a little experimentation brought us the password of "TEAM EDWARD," which should have been predictable. Seconds later I was sifting through Molly's hard drive.

"Stand back," said Tyler and I proceeded to do as he said. Skidding out of the way, I allowed him full reach so that he could manipulate it as he saw fit. His fingers seemed to fly over the keyboard, brushing aside a lot of useless crap like fan fiction about various novel vampires. What in God's name did this girl think our lives were like, anyway? I found myself hoping that, in the event she managed to survive what had happened to her, she'd decide to be quit of the entire world and do something more appropriate for her age. Like...I dunno...Dora the Explorer or whatever.

Her emails were flashing across the screen and suddenly they stopped. Tyler zoomed in on one subset and nodded. "Got it. This is from Highgate. There's a couple." He skimmed the content and shook his head. "Jeez, what a douche. He's talking about getting together."

"Already happened."

"The result?"

"Nothing good." I leaned in toward the screen. "Can you tell where he's sending them from? I figure it's a longshot but it's a place to start..."

"Not a longshot at all," said Tyler. "The public library. New York Public Library. The one with the lions on the front."

"I know which one it is. I saw *Ghostbusters*. Are you sure?"

"Positive. It's where the IP addresses are coming from."

"Could he be faking it?"

"Sure." Tyler shrugged. "But why would he? Does he have a reason to hide from her?"

"No. He poisoned her. He has no reason to think she'd be coming after him. So . . . okay, then," I said, determination growing within me. "Then I think it's time that somebody did."

There was no way he was going to be at the computers this very evening. Nevertheless, it was all I had to do for the rest of the night and so I figured I might as well do it.

I returned to the Moveable Feast, keeping easily to the shadows and out of the view of some of Lawrence's men that I saw still lurking about. I spotted Hannah briefly, but she didn't appear to be paying me the slightest bit of attention. She was just standing there, arms folded, watching the proceedings. Apparently they'd decided to hang around for a while to see if any vampires happened to show up. I doubted that was going to happen: Duncan would have already circulated word that, at least for the time being, the current location of the Feast was off the chart. Whether he had someplace new lined up so quickly, I couldn't even begin to guess. Fortunately it wasn't anything I needed to worry about particularly long.

My cycle was parked off to the side and I managed to retrieve it, gun it, and get it the hell out of there. I thought for a moment that maybe someone was watching me—Hannah, probably—but there was nothing in my way and so, minutes later, Astoria was in my rear view. Good riddance.

I rode through Queens, across the 59th Street bridge, and toward the library. It was after hours, so naturally there wasn't going to be an easy way in.

That didn't present much of a problem for me, though. Least, I hoped it wouldn't.

For some reason, the place looked quietly menacing in the darkness. I had no idea why that would be. It was just a big place filled with books. Nevertheless, there seemed to be an innate threat that I was reasonably sure wasn't simply left over from old movies. I put it aside as briskly as I could. I was a vampire. I was the individual that others were afraid of in the night. It wouldn't hurt if I could remember that.

I made my way around the building several times and finally spotted a window on the second story that was partly open. For all I knew, someone left it that way deliberately. I took a few steps back, then charged straight at the building. I leaped through the air and landed perfectly right at the window sill. I hung there for a moment, congratulating myself on the jump, and then I hauled myself up and through the window, sliding my way into the New York Public Library.

It was incredibly dark, but that was of no relevance to my eyes. To me it might as well have been midday. That didn't mean I wasn't going to be careful. It was incredibly likely that there were guards around in the darkness. It wouldn't be hard to avoid them; they'd be walking around with flashlights and such. Me, all I had to do was stick to the shadows and I should be fairly okay.

I went quickly from floor to floor, room to room. The problem was that there were computers everywhere. He could have availed himself of any of the stations and it wouldn't have presented an issue. It left me with only one option: go from place to place and, once I was done, start over again. Even that plan was a guarantee of absolutely nothing. There was no reason to assume that Highgate was going to show up here this evening or, for that matter, any evening.

But it was all I had. And if I had to keep doing this every evening, then that's the way that went.

At one point I actually ran into a guard. He was strolling around, waving about his flashlight, looking to see if anything was amiss. There was nothing handy for me to hide myself behind, so I simply stopped moving and blended in with a darkened corner. The guard walked right past me.

Then he stopped.

I froze, prepared to leap at him, take him down. He waved the flashlight around, trying to determine the source of whatever it was that had caught his attention. My fingers itched. After everything that had gone on, part of me was eager for the opportunity to just tear into something, and this guy would do as well as anyone else.

But then he shrugged and kept moving. I didn't know whether to be happy or depressed and decide to go for the former.

The moment he was sufficiently gone, I went back to moving. I glanced at my watch; it was going on two in the morning. I wasn't accomplishing a damned thing, but I really didn't see much else that I could do.

Three o'clock in the morning came and went, and I was sure that I was wasting my time. I figured that by the time 5 A.M. rolled around, I'd have to pack up and head out.

As it happened, it didn't require waiting quite that long.

It was steaming toward four o'clock in the morning, and that was when I heard something clicking steadily. It was several rooms away, and anyone with normal hearing wouldn't have been able to pick it up.

But I did. I sure as hell did.

It was probably some secretary. Or a kid. Or a guard.

Or Highgate.

I made my way quickly down the hallway, passing several large rooms that presented no interest to me at all. Just ahead of me was some sort of special file room. Probably one of those places that was dedicated to devoting tons of studying to shelves filled with some small and precise aspect of research that a dozen or so people in the city cared about.

I stuck my head around the corner and looked in.

Highgate was seated at a computer. He was typing away remarkably quickly, and his mouth was edged into a narrow smile. The scar on his face seemed almost as if it was burning in the dimness of the room. His heavy coat was draped over a nearby chair, along with a hat. He still had the sophistication of when I'd encountered him the other night, but his mind was clearly on other things.

I knew exactly how this was going to play out. I was going to creep forward. Even as I did that, I slowly extracted my knife from my sleeve. I would come up behind him, get the drop on him, put the knife to his throat, and he would tell me everything I needed to know. Then I would kill him.

Simple.

I began my approach. Simple, quiet steps. I swear, anyone could have been standing in front of me and they'd have had no clue as to whether I was there.

His back remained to me. Each stealthy step drew me closer and closer to my target.

Ten feet away from Highgate, my cell phone went off.

I muttered a silent curse and automatically grabbed it out of my pocket, but it was too late. Highgate was on his feet, staring at me, looking puzzled at first before the surprise settled into recognition. And recognition promptly segued into grim determination.

I took barely enough time to glance at my cell and see that it was Amber calling. Then I shoved it back into my pocket and turned to face Highgate.

He wasn't there.

"Son of a—!" was all I was able to get out before he attacked me from behind. I slammed forward, banging into the computer table. The computer was knocked clear off the table and crashed to the floor.

I spun to face him and he was leaning over me, grinning with determination. He cocked his right fist and slammed it down. I barely got out of the way and then his right leg lashed out. It caught me midsection, knocking me flat onto my back.

"Idiot!" he said, barely above a whisper. He came in fast and attempted to stomp his foot into my face. I practically threw

myself to one side. His foot came down, and then down again and again as he chased me through the small, enclosed area.

I managed to get just far enough ahead of him that I could scramble to my feet. He backed off and we circled each other, fingers twitching. For long moments we just watched each other, moving forward, back, trying to find an opening.

Suddenly there was a long, elegant knife in his hand. The blade edge gleamed wildly in the low light. He flipped it back and forth, one hand to the other, like some sort of bizarre ballet.

"That's pretty nasty," I said, my gaze following him steadily.

"It's going to be more than nasty," he whispered. "I'm going to carve you up slowly, Vincent. I'm going to start with your fingers. Just your fingers. Then work my way up the arms, first the left and then the right."

I let him go for a little while. He made it all the way to my hips before I got bored and shot him.

The move was so quick he never even saw it coming. One moment my hands were empty and the next thing he knew I had a .45 in my right hand. I fired off a quick blast and it took him in the shoulder. Highgate let out a pained scream and stumbled backwards, keeping himself upright. He tried to bring the knife around and I simply shot him again. Nothing in the face and nothing near the heart. Nothing that could possibly have lethal consequences. But it sure as hell hurt as it slammed into his other shoulder. Highgate cried out once more and this time dropped the knife as he stumbled backwards. I kicked the knife away and advanced.

Even now I can't believe how quick he was. He came at me so fast that even though he was suddenly closer, my next shot went over his head. Highgate came at me fast and low and he slammed into me, lifting me off my feet. We kept going and crashed into a shelf. Books thudded off the shelving all around me. Highgate shoved against me, his face right in mine, snarling furiously, all resemblance to his more polished self gone. I tried to aim my gun at him but he pounded me repeatedly in the chest. I felt something crack beneath one of the blows; something in my ribcage.

I fired the gun again but my aim was off despite the proximity.

The blast went just past his head and he slapped a hand around. It knocked the gun from my hand, sending it flying across the room and skittering along the floor.

I head butted him. My skull crashed into his nose and he let out a startled gasp. I struck him a second time and then a third and he staggered from the repeated impact. It was enough to disorient him and I shoved him away from me.

"Freeze!"

I whirled. It was the guard, or one of the guards; I'd never gotten a good look at him. He had a gun in one hand and a walkie-talkie in the other. "Neither of you move!" he shouted and then he started to provide his location over the walkie-talkie to whomever was listening on the other end.

I did the only thing I could think of: I grabbed the nearest book and threw it at the guard with as much velocity as my vampiric strength would lend me. It flew straight and ricocheted off the guard's forehead. For a moment I almost felt badly; the man had to be in his late 60s, maybe early 70s. This was way beyond anything that he was expecting on an average night. As the book bounded away the guard went down and he lost his hold on his gun.

It hit the floor and skidded straight into Highgate's grasp. He picked it up and didn't hesitate to start firing at me.

I wasted no time scolding the annoying fates that had dropped the weapon into Highgate's hands. Instead I took the only available course of action: I charged him, worrying about nothing except getting my hands on him.

Highgate backed up and continued to fire. Guns were clearly not his thing. Most of his shots missed. A couple struck home. One hit me in the thigh, another in the upper chest. I staggered from both impacts but kept going. The closer I got, the less accurate his shooting became, and then I plowed into him. He grunted as we went down, crashing to the floor, and then we were struggling. No art, no artistry. Just balls-to-the-wall wrestling for position. He snarled, he thrust, he clawed at me.

And finally, finally, I got the upper hand on him. My legs had encircled his; my arms had gotten down and under his and then up and over, and moments later I had a full nelson clamped on him. Highgate struggled furiously to pull free but I had him too solidly. He wasn't going anywhere.

"Tell me what's going on," I said, my voice barely above a hiss. "Tell me what's happening and I'll let you go."

He didn't seem to notice that I had said anything. He was still struggling, still trying to pull away from me. He was incredibly strong, but fortunately enough—at least in the position that we were in at that moment—I was stronger. The longer I held him in that manner, the easier it became for me. *"Tell me what's happening,"* I said again. "I know you were tossed out of your little club. The Baron told me to keep an eye out for you. Tell me what's going on. *Now*!"

"You idiot!" Highgate snarled at me. "You think you know anything? About anything? You know nothing! I've looked you up, Vince Hammond. I know who you are. I know what you're a part of. You and your supposed Echelon, running the Chevaliers for generations..."

"I know all about myself. What I don't know is—"

"You know nothing." He seemed to delight in that pronouncement. He grinned widely, the extensions of his fangs visible beneath his lips. *"The Echelon is run by vampires*!"

It was all I could do not to lose my grip on him at that moment. Indeed, he sensed a lapse and tried to pull away, but I yanked him back into my grasp at the last possible instant. "You're lying," I said with both intensity and uncertainty. It made no sense, what he was saying. The Echelon was the top ruling council in the entire anti-vampire hierarchy. For him to claim that vampires were actually running it...it was like saying that Nazis had been secretly running the Allied Forces in World War II. That Hitler had been Churchill's boss...

"Generations," he repeated. "Old World vampires, to be precise. Do you want to keep trying to strangle me or—?"

I let him go. I suppose partly it was because I was hoping that he would continue fighting and that, in doing so, I would then be able to come right at him and kill him before he could say anything else.

But he didn't attack me. Instead he lay on the floor, rubbing his throat, making no further effort to come after me. He must have sensed that he had managed to engage my interest, even though the things he was saying were utterly appalling.

We both lay on the floor for a moment, Highgate rubbing his throat. Then, slowly, he managed to sit up.

"You're lying," I said again, but here he was, sitting up, and I wasn't attacking him. So it was pretty damned obvious that I was willing to listen to what he had to say.

He took a deep breath, let it out. "Shortly after the French Revolution, they insinuated themselves into the Chevaliers. Over time, they created the concept of the Echelon—the highest ranking members of the group—so they could ride herd on the ranks of vampire hunters and make sure that they would never be able to wield their power again in a manner similar to the Revolution."

"You mean just running rampant? Killing entire families?"

He managed a nod. "The Echelon managed to keep their friends close, and their enemies closer."

Well, that I actually had no trouble believing. I had been doing more or less the same thing ever since I had been transformed into a vampire in the first place. "Plus," I said slowly, "that way they could monitor the activities of the Chevaliers and keep them away from O.C. interests."

Highgate actually had the nerve to smile at that. "So you understand, do you, Hammond? I admit, you're somewhat smarter than I originally gave you credit for."

"Thanks. Means a lot coming from you. But…but if they were part of the Old Country vamps, and so are you…"

"Why the separation now?" He shook his head in what was clearly disgust. "Because I felt they could be of more use nowadays than they currently are. They are interested mostly in maintaining the status quo. But me: I wanted to use them as a means of 'thinning the herd.' Weeding out unworthy vampires in both the Nu V and the O.C. ranks. The Baron," and he distended "Baron" into five syllables instead of the normal two, "disliked the notion. He had a lack of vision. We parted ways under somewhat…violent circumstances."

"Meaning he tried to kill you."

"He did," said Highgate.

"Just as you killed the other vampires who were part of Moveable Feast."

"They were fools. Amateurs," said Highgate in disgust. "They had no business existing as one of us."

As much as I hated to say it, I tended to agree with him. The dead vampires from Duncan's herd really were kind of idiots. Well…maybe not total idiots. "One of them followed you, taking pictures while you hooked up with Nu V's and used them for your own purposes."

He shrugged. "Why should that be of any consequence to me? Let him take pictures. He can take all the pictures in the world. He'll still be just as dead." He tilted his head and studied me, as if seeing me for the first time. "And he is dead already, is he not? He is, isn't he?" When I couldn't bring myself to answer, he actually laughed in my face. "How charming. How utterly predictable. Drank of one of the girls I poisoned. Idiot."

We were both on our feet now, but he was making no effort to attack. He glanced once toward the unconscious guard and then seemed to forget about him. Instead all of Highgate's attention was upon me. "Why are we fighting, Hammond? Seriously? We are so much more alike than you could possibly wish to admit."

"We," I said firmly, "are nothing alike."

"Oh, please. You were in the wine cellar, were you not?"

"How the hell did you know that?"

"Because," he said, as if discussing something of utter indifference, "I have people watching the establishment of my former associates. They saw you brought in. You did not emerge until well into the next day. My assumption is that you were caught and imprisoned, and the wine cellar would be where they would do the imprisoning. Feel free to correct me if I am wrong."

"Okay, yeah, fine," I said with obvious irritation. "They stuck—me…" I saw no reason to drag Hannah into all this. "…into their wine cellar. So what?"

"You saw what they had there. The people being kept prisoner there. And what was your reaction, eh?"

"I thought it was terrible."

"No, you did not," said Highgate. "You may have thought you

were appalled by it, but you were not. Not really. You, who are so quick to look at vampires such as me and deem us enemies, but really, you had no real depth of reaction. Don't you see? You have no soul anymore."

"I have plenty of soul, Highgate."

"No," and his voice actually seemed to drop in sympathy. "No, you do not. You may think you do, but you don't. Depending upon your specific religious beliefs, that is a sad thing or a convenient thing. I leave that for you to judge. But it is something nevertheless, and it is what curses you and curses me and the rest of us. You were in the wine cellar, and you saw those people trapped down there, helpless, hopeless. And the fact is that you did not give them the slightest thought. Instead you're just seeing humans for what they are: sources of nourishment. You are every bit the monster that every other vampire walking around is. You're just too arrogant to admit it."

We stood there, facing each other for a moment in long silence.

Then he turned away from me to leave.

I picked up the fallen gun and, in one smooth motion, shot him in the head.

Highgate went down without a noise. The fact that there was no noise wasn't all that surprising considering the entire front of his face had been blown away. The most easily recognized mark on his face, the "V" sign that Hannah had inflicted upon him, was nowhere to be seen.

As he flopped about on the floor like a beached salmon, I pulled out a lengthy knife from my boot. Then I dropped down behind him, shoving my knee squarely into the top of his spine. Much to my surprise, he actually managed to get out a few words.

"Said...you'd let...me go." Actually, the words were more slurred. It came out more like, "Sedjulemmegooo," but I was able to make out the gist of what he was saying.

"I will," I told him flatly. "I'm letting you go straight to hell."

I brought the blade down upon his throat. I'd love to tell you that I knocked his head from his body in one easy shot, but that was hardly the case. His neck was made out of old combat boots and initially resisted my endeavors to part it from his body. The next thirty or so seconds were filled with grunting and gargling and, in the end, a high-pitched screech. The entire time he was trying to throw me off his back and having no luck at it whatsoever. Finally I managed to shove the knife all the way down and the curved blade clanked against the floor. Highgate's body straightened out rigid, the fingers opening and closing spasmodically. Then it seemed to sag directly into the floor somehow, and moments later the entire body fell in upon itself. I got to my feet and managed to step out of the range of his corpse. The body began to vibrate, spasming all its own, and that was all the time required for a body to return to its natural state.

I paused only briefly as I headed out, making sure to pick up those items—aside from photos—that would surely be part of any manner of editorial material. Once I was satisfied, I checked the guard over once more. He seemed fairly unconscious and I was inclined to make sure he remained that way.

Moments later I was outside the library. By the time any other guards in the place discovered the display I'd left, I was already on my cycle gliding away from the impossible-to-distinguish mass of mess on the library floor.

Twenty-one

My Decision Not to Give a Crap Anymore

And that was it. It was over.

Considering everything that had been in front of me, it really hadn't been that difficult.

As soon as I was en route, I flipped back the phone in order to discover why it had been Amber phoning me. She was calling to tell me, after all this time, that Molly was stable. Near as I could determine from the message she'd left me, the hospital had indeed managed to determine the nature of the poison that had been pumped into her, and had immediately swung into action to counter it. I didn't know if they'd pumped new blood into her or tried to extract what was there or perhaps some bizarre combination of the two. All I knew was that, although Molly was still not in the greatest condition, she wasn't deteriorating. So that was something at least.

I made it back to my house without further problems. The sun was going to be coming up within an hour or so. It wasn't the closest I'd ever cut it, but it certainly wasn't the worst.

I staggered up the stairs, shedding jacket and then clothing as I approached my bed. My room was its customary darkened condition and, stripped to my underwear, I tumbled face forward into bed and immediately fell asleep.

And in my sleep, I dreamt.

Highgate was gone. The guy who had assaulted Amber was dead. I knew this because I'd killed him myself, and it wasn't as if there was a duplicate one of him hanging around. I had forgotten to ask him why, exactly, he'd targeted Amber, but it wasn't too difficult to figure out. It was one of two reasons. Either he'd been planning to secretly turn her so that she'd be playing for his team (and something told me he'd been underestimating exactly how that was going to wind up. I could easily see a transformed Amber making the death of her sponsor the very first thing on her to-do list.) Or he had simply decided that he was going to off her because she was in town and she was hunting vampires. Simple as that. And when the rest of the family had gone hunting in response, he would have had his own people out there ready to take them down.

It wouldn't have been all that difficult, really. I hope no one out there thinks that vampires are *really* daunted by the prospect of hunters. There are simply too many things they think they know about us that really aren't true and will just wind up getting the hunters killed.

In any event, my dreams should have been clear. With Highgate gone and Amber safe, I should only have needed to worry about the vampires themselves and, specifically about keeping them safe from hunters. Moreover, there were the things that Highgate had said about the Echelon and the notion that the highest aspects of my vampiric world were, in fact, vampiric. Was it really true? Were the highest ranks of the Garrison, or more specifically the organization to which the Garrison responded, actually in the throes of vampires? It was incredibly difficult to believe. And yet maybe it wasn't. It *did* make a certain degree of twisted sense. For decades now, stretching well back into the 19th century, the Echelon had risen as a power group within our ranks who had managed to take control and oversee every aspect of vampiric life. They were in charge of overseeing training, they were in charge of...hell, everything. Didn't it make a horrific amount of sense that the individuals who were in charge of how we lived our lives were, in fact, on the other side? They could easily manage to control us, keep us in check. *The enemy of your enemy.* Something like that.

And then there was the matter of the people in the wine cellar. As appalled as I was to admit it, there was something to be said for what Highgate had pointed out. I tried going back into my head from that night. I knew that I had been appalled when I saw them strung up against the ceiling like a gathering of Christmas turkeys. But once the surprise had worn off, had I actually had any compulsion to try and free them? Or had I simply accepted it? Down in New Jersey there was a vampire nest where captives were held so that the club members would always have something they could drink from. How sad that was. Oh well. On to the next thing.

It shouldn't have been that way.

Should it have?

Should I have been concerned about the

(food)

people? The people who were just hanging there

(helpless)

to be consumed by the…by the…

(monsters, ghouls, demons)

people who resided in the

(den, nest, evil hideout)

club?

I kept waking up, falling back to sleep, over and over, unable to get things settled in my mind. I was finding it difficult to remember how I would have felt, how I should have felt, before I became…what I was.

And in one of the many times that I awakened, I came to the realization that I had not once, not *once,* thought about doing something to help the people who were the main course in the wine cellar. Why was that? What was wrong with me? Was I turning into something that I should not, under any circumstance, have been?

At one point when I woke up, I discovered that I was thick with sweat. Yes, I'd been sleeping, but in many respects I hadn't been. I got up, pulled a towel out of the bathroom and scrubbed myself down. I went back to sleep, and yet as I did so, the dreams were continuing to lash out at me. *Do something. You have to do something. Except…no you don't. Or do you?*

Hannah. Help me.

The name, the sentiment itself, leaped out at me as if jamming claws into the base of my throat. I awoke, crying out Hannah's name, a move that alone might have gotten me severely questioned.

Hannah. She was the one to talk to. She was the one whose guidance I needed because she had turned me into what I was.

Easy to say. Harder to do. Since matters had deteriorated between the Singers and myself, they had relocated back to the Plaza 25, the hotel that her family owned. Which meant that the only means I would have of talking to her would require that I talk to the rest of her family as well.

Great. This evening is just getting better and better, and it hasn't even started yet.

My phone took that moment to start ringing. I glanced at the ID and saw that it was Amber again. At least I wasn't fighting a vampire at the moment. I snapped the phone open and answered it.

"Thank God. Where are you?" she asked immediately.

"At home. I was..." I mentally fumbled a moment and just went for the obvious. "I was about to come over there."

"Really." She sounded dubious. Who could blame her? Ever since she'd set foot in town, I'd done nothing but yank her around, and not for one minute did she deserve any of it. I still hadn't given her any sort of guarantee that I wanted to marry her. Plus, for all I knew, by this point she wanted nothing to do with me.

"Yeah, really," I said after a moment. "I think we need to talk."

"So do I."

"But first, we have some people we need to save."

That caught her flatfooted. *"What people? Who needs saving?"*

"I'll tell you when I get there. That work for you?"

"Okay. Okay, sure."

I knew I shouldn't ask...every fiber of my being warned me off...but I asked anyway. "Is Hannah there with you?"

Immediately I could feel the temperature drop by at least twenty degrees over the phone. *"Yeah, she's here. Why?"*

I was hardly in a position to achieve total honesty. "Just trying to count up how many people we have in a potential raiding party. I'm on my way over; be there in a few minutes."

I quickly hung up before she could say anything else.

Minutes later I was rolling across New York, having narrowly missed having to go five rounds with my mom; she'd had the perfect timing of being in the bathroom when I headed through the living room. The last thing I heard was her shouting after me, "Wait! Wait! We need to talk!"

The more I thought about the people hung up in the basement of the vampires, the worse it became to me. I couldn't tear my mind away from it, no matter how much I wanted to. It was as if I'd had to be reminded of how I should think about these things.

So before I left, I stocked up. I went to my workshop and acquired the weapons that I was going to require in order to take on the vampires. It was an unusual situation for me. Typically when I prep for a hunting endeavor, I take weapons that aren't going to do any real harm. After all, I'm not *really* out to kill vampires. They are one half of my true family. This time, however, I had to get ready for fighting the real thing. That meant genuine stakes, genuine cutting implements, genuine everything. By the time my mother had gone upstairs to check on me and see if I was ready to face the day, I was on my motorcycle and speeding through Midtown toward my destination.

Minutes later, I rolled up to Plaza 25. I entered and quickly got directions to Lawrence's room. No great feat of investigative legerdemain involved: I asked at the front desk, they called up to the room and received permission from the guy there to let me come on up.

I knocked firmly on the door. Amanda opened it. She would have been surprised, of course, if I had not called up from the front desk. As it was, she was expecting me. I entered and whistled softly at the room. *Very* impressive. Some kind of fancy suite, the type you usually hear about only when it's being destroyed by some drunken rock star. This one was clearly between thrashings, and it was really nice. Soft white carpets that stretched everywhere. Full kitchen, and a piano in the living room because that's what you always have in your living room.

Lawrence was standing a few feet away, looking at me stiffly. His eyes were narrow, his jaw tight. Everything about him screamed tension. "So it's you," he said, not even bothering to make any polite chit chat. That was fine. I wasn't at my chattiest.

"Yeah, it's me," I agreed. "Listen—"

"I have had enough of listening to you."

"Lawrence!" Amanda was clearly annoyed with her husband's tense reply to me. I had to give her credit for an endless amount of determination. Just because her husband was in a mood didn't mean she had to be, or that at least she had to give into it. "Come on. He's here to..." She paused and then looked back at me with a glimmer of uncertainty. "Why *are* you here?"

"It doesn't matter why he's here," said Lawrence Singer. "As far as I'm concerned, even if Amber begged to marry him, and even if he wanted her, why should we bring him on?"

Despite the fact that I kind of agreed with him, his off-hand dismissal bothered the hell out of me.

But he kept on talking, removing the opportunity for me to say anything that would have likely been pretty stupid anyway. "He has no real interest in assaulting vampires. He doesn't know how to work as a team. He fights us as if we're the enemy. Frankly, I don't care what he has to offer anymore. All I want is the money that I paid in for the dowry and we can all go about our business."

That, of course brought us back to a hundred grand, which I was hardly in a position to provide. But I knew I could provide the next best thing: vampires to destroy. I knew that I could just go through my own Garrison, but that didn't seem the best option right then. I wasn't sure who to trust and who to go to, especially considering that everything wound up going through Salk. He was the last person whom I wanted as a part of this. If I was going to pull off this little raid of mine, it would have to be with people outside of my usual Garrison. At that particular point in time, the only people who filled that qualification were the members of Singer's crew. So it was going to be Lawrence Singer or no one at all.

"Believe it or not, Lawrence, that's not why I came," I said. "I stumbled upon a nest the other night and I want to mount an offensive against it."

"Use your own people," Singer said automatically.

"I don't trust my own people."

"Well, that's your problem, isn't it." But Lawrence had spoken too quickly, and he knew it the moment he said it. Endeavoring to compensate for his hasty dismissal, he cleared his throat and then, trying to sound as off-hand about it as possible, said casually, "Why don't you trust your own people?"

There was no way around it. "Because Jeremiah Salk was there."

"There where? Wait...*there*?" He exchanged startled looks with his wife. She shrugged helplessly; clearly she had no idea what I was talking about. No reason she should. "Salk was at the vampire hideout?"

"Yes. Having nice conversations with the guys who were running it. Salk isn't a vampire; I swear to it." It was easy for me to do. I could tell vampire from human, and Salk was certainly no vampire.

"You've *been* there?" Now he was beginning to sound dubious. I suppose on some level I couldn't blame him. I was dumping a lot of info on him.

"On a stalking tour, yes." I paused and then added the one bit of information that could kick matters over the top...or sink them completely. "Hannah was with me."

"Hannah!?" Lawrence was stunned. He looked ready to have his head explode.

Amanda immediately called her older daughter's name. A few moments later, Hannah emerged from a room at the far end of the luxurious suite. She looked at them questioningly and then her eyes stopped upon me. They widened slightly in obvious surprise but then she immediately reined it in. "Hey," was all she said.

"Hannah," said her father gravely. He had not moved from where he was standing, next to me. "Did you and Vincent here go to a vampire hangout somewhere in New Jersey where Jeremiah Salk could be found hobnobbing with the beings that ran it?"

If she'd been asked the question earlier, with no preamble, she might well have lost her ability to respond with something other than shock. As it was, though, she managed to keep her face impassive, although I could tell it was taking a good deal of effort for her to accomplish it. "I...seem to recall something like that happening."

"You ran around to a vampire outpost with Vincent here," Lawrence said slowly, as if trying to parse out the entire endeavor, "and didn't bother to tell me?"

"No, Dad, I didn't tell you." She folded her arms across her bosom and struck a defiant pose. "And if you have a problem with that, then it's your problem, not mine. I go where I wish, with whom I wish."

Hannah was damned lucky her father was not, in fact, a vampire, because he looked ready to leap upon her and rip out her throat. "Where do you get off—?" he began.

I physically placed myself between them. "Excuse me, but I have no interest in standing here and listening to this. I'm sure it'll be incredibly fascinating for everyone in this room except me, but tragically for the rest of you, I really only give a damn about me. Hannah and I saw a number of people piled up in the basement there, being used as ongoing sources for harvesting, and I think it's time we did something about it."

"'Ongoing sources of—' You mean they're eating people in there? Slowly?"

"Very," I said. "And I wanted to do something about it, and I thought you might want to help. If I'm wrong, then I'll just let myself out and—"

Now Amanda stepped in, firm and decisive. "Of course we want to help. If people are in trouble, those are the exact people we should be helping. Isn't that correct, Lawrence?"

"Yes. Yes, of course," Lawrence said quickly. It was difficult to tell whether he wanted to maintain his status with his wife or if he truly believed it. Whatever the reason, he was now committed to it. Apparently forgetting that he wasn't wearing a jacket, he smoothed out his crisp white shirt and then immediately took command. "Vincent, where is this place, anyway?"

"Newark," I said briskly. "I can lead you there."

"I'll get my people together. We'll meet in the downstairs lobby in ten minutes."

"Okay, then."

"Vinnie." It was Hannah's voice, sweet as pie. "If we could talk for a minute…?"

Yeah, I wasn't looking forward to this.

We walked quickly into her room and just before the door closed I caught a glimpse of Amber. She had emerged from her own room on the other side of the suite, and when she saw me with her sister, her face got the oddest look on it. A look of pure anger and fury, but contained, as if she'd had a lot of practice doing so. Then the door to Hannah's room swung closed, blocking her from my sight.

I turned around just in time for Hannah to slug me.

I went down, collapsing to the ground. It was only a glancing blow; it left no mark. But it hurt like hell.

"*You idiot*!" she whispered. "Are you *out* of your *mind*?"

"Listen..."

"No! I don't listen! I don't have to listen! Not to you! Not to anyone!" She started to pace, ruffling her hands through her hair. "I cannot *believe* this. You come here, begging my father—"

"I didn't beg."

"*I don't care*! What possible reason could you have to want to go back after those vampires!"

"You saw it yourself!"

She literally needed a minute to understand what the hell I was talking about. "What're you...? Wait, the people in the cellar?"

"Yes, of course the people in the cellar."

"And why are they our problem?"

"Because they are, dammit! Because they're in trouble and we're the only ones who can save them!"

"That's ridiculous." She shook her head in frustration. "The only vampire in the world I'd like to off right now is Highgate, and instead I'm—"

"Highgate's dead."

That brought her to a halt. Hannah stared at me for a moment and then said, "You're kidding."

"No, I'm not kidding. I caught up with him at the New York Public Library and we had it out and I killed him. And if you don't believe me—"

"No, no, I believe you." She was clearly having trouble ditching the incredulity in her voice. "I just...I wasn't expecting it, that's all."

"Yeah, well, neither was he. And if you want to shout at me some more or talk about how useless I am or any of that other good stuff, then let's just hear it, okay? Just hit me with your best shot."

I stared at her. That's all. Just stared. I waited for another verbal lashing out, or for her to slap me again, or something. Anything.

For a moment that seemed to stretch forever, Hannah returned the stare. Her hand went up at one point and I braced myself to be slapped around again.

And then, slowly but deliberately, she lowered the hand to my cheek. She leaned forward and kissed me then. It was nothing especially extreme, little more than nuzzling of her lips against mine. Yet it felt good. Fulfilling. We parted and stared closely at each other, and the next kiss was deeper and filled with much more longing than I'd have thought possible.

Then, just like that, she pulled away from me and shook her head. "You're an idiot," she said, but there was no heat in the statement. "You're an idiot and you're dragging all of us into a fight that none of us needs. And the most irritating thing about the whole damned escapade is that I'm coming along for the ride when I should know better."

She crossed the room and dropped onto the bed, shaking her head as she did so. "Unbelievable," she muttered. She was silent for a few moments more and then added, as if it were something irrelevant and to be forgotten as soon as it was spoken: "Thanks for killing Highgate."

"No problem." I stared at her for a moment and then said, "Hannah...why? Why'd you make me like you?"

"Because I felt like it."

"Hannah, come on!"

"What do you want from me, Vince?" she said in exasperation. "Some kind of sexy back story? Some reason other than that it seemed like a good idea at the time? Because that's all it was. And if that's disappointing to you—if that doesn't fit in with what you think your transformation should have been—then that's too damned bad. Are we clear on this?"

"Hell no. Not in the least. Look, Hannah," and I tried to find the right words. "Hannah...Highgate said some stuff to me... about me...and the bottom line is that he was right. Because the

Body Man I was, the person I was, would have been obsessing about those poor bastards stuck in the cellar. I would immediately have mounted a rescue mission of some sort. I'm losing my attachment to humanity, and so are you, whether you want to admit it or not. And I'm not going to let that happen. You do what you want. But me, I—"

There was a sharp knock on the door and I heard Lawrence's voice from the other side, brisk and commanding. "All right, people," he said. "Ready when you are."

Quickly I opened the door. Lawrence was there, and Amanda. And Kubrick, standing there with his assault team, all of them dressed and ready to go out.

And Amber. She was standing a short distance away, looking just as she did that first night I'd encountered her. Apparently her arm had sufficiently recovered since she was now wearing it out of the sling. Her face was impassive; she was wearing the look of one who absolutely didn't give a damn about vampire assaults. All she cared about was…

Honestly? I didn't know what the hell she cared about right then. All I knew for sure was that it didn't matter. We had people to save.

"Okay, then," I said evenly. "Let's get it done. Hannah? You coming?"

She rolled her eyes and pulled her boots on. "I'm gonna regret this," she said.

"No, you won't—"

"Yes, I will. And I swear, Vince, if I wind up regretting, you'll know it because you're gonna regret it before I do. Understand?"

"Yes, ma'am," I said. And I actually think that, to some degree, I really did.

Twenty-two
My Hail Mary Pass

This time I rode my motorcycle all by my lonesome.

We rode down the Turnpike and took the exit at Newark, same as last time. I was riding in the lead, and there were two trucks filled with Body Men riding behind me. Every so often I would glance into the side mirror of the cycle. There I would see the image of a grim Lawrence Singer at the wheel. Kubrick was in the passenger seat. The driver of the second van wasn't visible to me, but I assumed it to be one of his henchmen. The sisters were both in the back of the lead van, that I knew.

I tried to imagine what that was like. There clearly wasn't a great deal of love between the two daughters. Obviously a good chunk of that hostility, if not all of it, was focused on me. I didn't know what was going on between the two of them, and more to the point, I didn't care overmuch.

The fact was that Amber was a great girl to be around.

But I wasn't in love with her.

Hannah, on the other hand, was as formidable a hunter as Amber had ever been, and even better, she was a vampire. She was just like me: a beloved child who was doing everything possible to keep a family unit intact. It was something that both of us knew was temporary. Sooner or later the fact that we weren't aging was going to put a permanent kibosh on the entire plan, and we'd have to go on the run unless we wanted to spend the rest of our lives wearing old age disguises.

At that moment, though, neither of the girls was of any prominent position to me. We were going up against a lot of vampires, and none of the people in my pack was truly aware of what the creatures were capable of doing, and what did and did not bother them.

My bag filled with my assorted vampire equipment was tucked solidly onto the back of my cycle. Everything was carefully and meticulously packed up. All was going to remain exactly where I required it to be until I had need of it. The main reason I needed the rest of the Body Men was to have some pure muscle behind me, especially if the Baron and his crew gave me any difficulties.

Once we got off the Turnpike, we quickly made our way through the streets once more. The entire time I was concerned that they might have relocated since we discovered them. After all, Duncan had done so with the Moveable Feast.

But even as I worried about such a thing happening, I dismissed it. The older generation of vampires tended to stay right where they were unless they were discovered by, say, an entire town. At this point just having a couple of vampires learning of their location wouldn't be sufficient to get them out of there. Having a host of vampire hunters descending upon them, on the other hand, would certainly prompt them to light out.

Either that or they would simply kill all the hunters.

Neither option seemed terribly appealing.

The streets were narrow and parked up with cars. The Body Men didn't care. They drove their oversize trucksters into whatever spaces they could find, jamming things up so that there was barely enough room for a single car to make it past at a time. This immediately resulted in cars honking in protest. Beyond being told with wide gestures to go around, they were ignored. Once again it became abundantly clear that Lawrence Singer's people had little care when it came to how people reacted to them.

I had dismounted from my cycle and gone to my bag of weapons. My actual stabbing stake was securely fashioned within my jacket. I had a short sword strapped to my waist. You could behead a vampire pretty quickly with one, and thanks to my vampiric strength, it was a rather handy little weapon to have around.

Most importantly, I had an oversized water gun strapped to my bag.

Theoretically it was a toy, but somehow the word "toy" didn't seem adequate to describe it. The thing was huge. It was a full-blown Super Soaker, accept no substitutes. I had swapped out the plastic water container it came equipped with for a much heavier duty water container; but it wasn't as if that was going to attract any attention, at least until it was too late. One of the men in Lawrence's group looked at me in silent confusion for a moment. Then his eyes widened in understanding. "Holy water."

"You got it," was all I said.

He smiled and gave a thumbs up. It was the first positive reinforcement I'd received from Lawrence's crew that evening. And it was quickly halted by an annoyed Kubrick slapping the guy on the shoulder and barking at him to pay attention, glaring at me the entire time that he did so.

Lawrence was emerging from his truck, and he had his phone to his ear. This immediately caused me to be apprehensive. "Who're you talking to?" I said, trying to sound casual. The last thing I wanted to do was make him suspicious.

He didn't appear to hear me. Instead he was just finishing giving specifics on the telephone as to what it was we were about to do. He was rattling off the total number of people he had on the scene, the estimated time until the break in; everything. The more he talked, the more apprehensive I became. Who the hell was he telling all this to?

"You okay? You look nervous." It was Amber, standing right behind me. I saw Hannah a distance off. She appeared to be trying to pay attention to the world around her and was chatting pleasantly with another one of the Body Men.

"Oh yeah. Yeah, I'm fine."

"Nice Super Soaker."

"Thanks. Say, uh...who's your dad talking to? Because he seems to be blabbing our entire attack plan to someone."

"Oh. The Echelon, most probably."

I wasn't much for interior body temperature, but what I did have ran cold in my veins. It was everything I could do to keep complete panic from my voice. "The Echelon, huh? Uh...why?"

"Standard procedure," she said with a shrug. "Echelon rules involving calling in an assault before we strike. That way, in case something should go wrong, they can send in back-up."

"That's, uh…that's a great rule," I said. "I don't remember it getting all that much publicity, though. In our Garrison, I mean. I'm just saying Garrison 13 doesn't have that rule."

"You very well might, but maybe Mr. Salk decides to ignore it. He could feel that it's unnecessary."

"You're probably right." Inside I was dying. Well…dying again. Lawrence Singer was busy giving advance notice to vampire central that we were about to stage a raid. We were going to be charging in with flashbangs, which are great if the person you're springing them on doesn't know you're coming. If, on the other hand, someone is providing a nice big heads up, then they're going to be ready. And the back-up weapons of holy water and such weren't going to do us any good for the reasons I've mentioned earlier. Yes, our bladed weapons and stakes would still be effective, but none of the prep stuff was going to work, and we might be overwhelmed before any of the other material was put to use. This had the potential to go very, very badly, and I had absolutely no way of warning them.

Well, that wasn't quite true. I could warn one of them. And I knew it wasn't going to go over especially well, but I had absolutely no choice.

Amber was about to bring up something else, something that—in all likelihood—had a great deal to do with our supposed marriage. Unfortunately, now was not the time. Before she could continue speaking, I said, "Excuse me a moment," and headed over to the one person she didn't want to see me talking to: her sister. Unfortunately I didn't really see any other option.

Hannah looked surprised as I approached her but kept her face carefully neutral. I said, "Pardon me," to the guy she'd been chatting with and pulled her over to one side. Very quickly, I told her who her dad was chatting with.

"Yeah? So?" she said.

I realized that I hadn't had the opportunity to bring her up to speed on what Highgate had told me about the Echelon. I did so now, in fast, low tones and her eyes widened as she listened.

"Well, shit," she said in a low voice.

"Yeah, you bet your ass 'shit.' We have to tell your father."

"Tell him what? That all the Garrisons are run by vampires? He won't believe it."

"He might..."

"He won't," she said firmly, with the air of someone who knew much more about these things than I did. "He's been born and raised as one of the Chevaliers. Not for a single minute is he going to buy into the notion that the bad guys are running the place."

"It doesn't matter what he buys. We've got to shut this down before—"

"I don't know if you've noticed," she said and pointed behind us, "but we don't have a 'before' at the moment."

Sure enough, the Lawrence Singer gang was moving in. They weren't going for subtle; the lot of them were converging upon the front door. Several of them had broken off and were heading around the back for the door that I had described was situated there, but they weren't being subtle in the execution of their raid. They were coming in front and back simultaneously, obviously anticipating getting the drop on a nest of vampires who had no idea they were coming (except they did know). Amanda Singer was right behind her husband and was gesturing in irritation for us to get over there as Singer and his crew converged on the front door.

This is not going to go well, I thought bleakly, but that didn't stop me from sprinting toward Lawrence as he drew within feet of the front door. As I ran, I put together an entire situation in my head that would explain why smashing in through the front door would be about the worst thing we could possibly do. It was rather involved but contained some of my best off-the-top-of-my-head explanations. The problem is that Singer never gave me a moment to say any of it.

"Take it down!" shouted Lawrence Singer, and before I could say or do anything else, the front door of the vampire club was kicked open. In flew the flashbangs, and the Body Men hesitated for a count of five to allow the exploding grenades to do their work.

For a few moments, I prayed that I was wrong. Maybe Highgate had been lying and vampires were not, in fact, running the Echelon. Maybe we would be able to make our assault without any problems at all. There was always that possibility and, for the moment, I had no choice but to see whether or not that was true, because Lawrence's guys weren't allowing for any other possibility.

We burst in through the main door into the front hallways. We saw no one. There were no vampires staggering around, no nothing. There was nothing but emptiness around us.

This did not deter Lawrence at all. "Second wave of flashbangs!" he shouted and his group spread out in front of him, throwing more of the grenades through doorways into connecting rooms. Everything moved with military efficiency; not for a moment was any of our progress slowed. Lawrence, his immediate family and several of his men moved forward while others broke off right and left into convenient areas. I hung slightly back, watching, waiting, praying.

And then, even as we headed forward, we suddenly heard screams from either side, through the doorways that the others had gone through.

Lawrence spun in response. The doors behind us slammed shut, closing us off from the entrance through which we'd just come. I cast a glance in Hannah's direction, a look of *I knew it, I freaking knew it,* and then the full lights suddenly came up all around us.

We were in a main foyer, and there had to be at least two-dozen vampires surrounding us. We were outnumbered more than two to one.

They were wearing gas masks and shields over their eyes. The flashbangs would have had no impact on them at all.

The vampires were all over the place: on the floor, on the stairway leading up to second level, and on the overhead balconies.

No one moved. Everyone was frozen as Lawrence realized just how screwed they were. There was nothing in his face, though, that indicated the realization.

Then one of the vampires slowly began a self-confident stride down the main stairs. Despite the fact that he was wearing a gas-mask, I knew exactly who it was: the Baron. No one else it could be. He walked with the easy, confident stride of someone who knew he was completely in control.

He hadn't noticed either Hannah or myself yet as he removed the gas mask in order to be able to speak clearly. His full focus was on Lawrence. Worse, he even greeted him by name. "Lawrence Singer, am I correct?"

Lawrence said nothing. At most he might have been prepared to give up his name, rank and serial number, but even there he was simply quiet, studying and sizing up the Baron.

The Baron was indifferent to his lack of reply. "How very impolite," he said. "You burst into my home, attempt to attack us, and now when I ask a simple question, you just glower at me. I don't really understand that. Ah…I wouldn't do that if I were you."

The preemptive commentary he had just provided us was directed at Kubrick, who was about to go for a crossbow that was slung at his hip. Kubrick's hands were poised over it, but upon receiving the warning from the Baron, he remained right where he was. Even then, Kubrick seemed hesitant, but a low word from Lawrence prevented him from making any further move.

"You are a very aggressive individual, Lawrence," the Baron continued then, as if Kubrick had been nothing more than a momentary distraction. "I am actually tempted to indoctrinate you into our wine cellar. I believe you will spend many happy months there. Well…not happy for *you,*" he said, and this drew chuckles from the other vampires. "But for us, certainly. As for the rest of you—"

Then he stopped.

He'd seen me.

Before he could say a word, I unslung my Super Soaker and aimed it straight at him. It only took me a second, faster than any human should have been able to do it. I prayed that, at that moment in time, Lawrence took no notice of my speed.

He started to say, "What are you doing here?" At least I think that's what he said; honestly, I'm guessing. The Baron got out simply "What are—?" and that's when I fired from the Super Soaker.

The liquid streaked across the distance between the two of us. The Baron was still so puzzled over what I was doing there that he put up no resistance whatsoever to what I fired from the Super Soaker.

It splashed over his face and upper clothing, and that was when the Baron began to shriek at the top of his lungs. He staggered back, screaming, clawing at his upper body, unable to get so much as a word out.

"Holy water for everybody!" I shouted and swung the Super Soaker wide of the Baron. I hit another vampire straight on and he had the exact same reaction the Baron had had: a fit of shrieking agony. More liquid spilled out, flying everywhere among the vampires and they all began shrieking from the contact.

"Get them!" shouted Lawrence and all hell broke loose.

Now, of course, it wasn't actually holy water. If you thought it was, then you haven't been paying attention. The liquid that was shredding the vampires' skin like sulfuric acid was no water blessed by a priest. It in fact *was* sulfuric acid. The container holding it was glass and I had lined the interior of the Super Soaker to be resistant to the acid that I was pumping through it.

My shots had to be precise. I couldn't allow puddles of sulfuric acid to bubble up on the floor so that our people could step on them and injure themselves. Everything had to be precise and any splashing had to be on the vampires. Fortunately enough, my aim was everything that could possibly have been asked of it.

The vampires had no idea what was happening. All they knew was that the supposedly harmless holy water was ripping their leader and others like them into shreds.

To the Body Men, this was simply business as usual. The fact that holy water had been introduced into the mix didn't mean a damned thing. These were vampires, and they were being hit with holy water that was giving them great injury. Who needed anything beyond that?

"*Kill them*!" shouted Lawrence. *"Kill them all!"* That was all the vampire hunters needed as they charged the vampires with their combinations of metal weapons and wood-crafted spikes.

Immediately the entire place was one vast melee. I had lost track of the Baron; still shrieking from the pain of the sulfuric acid, he had disappeared into a crowd of vampires who were themselves trying to make themselves scarce. They had no idea why holy water was suddenly injuring them; all they wanted to do at that point was put distance between themselves and their intended executioners. The Body Men were in their element, assailing vampires and chasing after them with a vicious gusto.

A voice spoke low and close to my ear. "The people downstairs?" It was Hannah. She was looking around, watching the chaos unleashed around us. It didn't seem to bother her particularly. Nothing ever did.

"Yes, exactly." I remembered every step of when we were brought up last time, so I was reasonably certain I knew which direction we had to go in.

And then Amber was right there. She had a crossbow cradled in her arm, just as she had that first time I encountered her. "Where are you guys going?" she asked immediately.

There was no time to fool around. "There's a place downstairs they have people strung up and they drink from them. You wanna come along?"

She seemed a bit surprised that I would give her that sort of straight answer. Her eyes narrowed. "How do you know?"

"Because we know, Amber, okay?" Hannah spoke up. "So *do* you wanna come? Or do you just wanna be a dick about it?"

Trust sisters to know exactly what to say to piss each other off. Amber didn't let the expression show on her face, but she was clearly annoyed by the challenge in Hannah's tone. "Where is it?" she asked.

"Good question." I started moving quickly in the direction that I was reasonably sure it was located. Hannah and Amber fell into step behind me. At one point a vampire, running for his life, placed himself exactly in our way. He saw us, saw me, roared, and came right at me. I ducked, sending him flying over me, and Hannah stabbed down hard with a stake. He was dead before he hit the floor. Good. One less thing for me to worry about.

We turned right, then left, and then I saw the door. I grabbed at it, yanked once. It held. I pulled a second time with greater ferocity and this time it tore open in my hand. Only belatedly did I suddenly think *Booby trap* but as it turned out I was just being paranoid. Everything was fine.

I charged into the wine cellar, the girls following me up. Amber gasped the moment we got down there. They were all right where I had left them: the human bodies just dangling there, breathing shallowly, doubtless tranqed up on something to keep them pliable. "Jesus," muttered Amber.

Once we were in the basement, we started freeing everyone. The freeing part was easy enough; simple bonds were keeping them in place. Once we pulled them down from where they were being held, however, the problem became more significant. They could barely stand; two of them couldn't at all.

"Wonderful," said Amber. Having overcome the initial shock of discovering the people there, now she was becoming frustrated with the actual difficulties of getting them out. "There's half a dozen people here."

"Two for each," I said. "Let's get—"

That was when I suddenly heard a click-clack sound from behind me, hidden in the further reaches of the basement. I whirled just in time to see the Baron. His clothing, his face, had the clear impact of being hit with holy water from a Super Soaker. I even thought I saw some steam continuing to rise from his skin.

What I did see, most definitely, was the flamethrower that the Baron was cradling in his arms.

I knew exactly where he had gotten it from: one of Lawrence's clean up crew. Somewhere in the house, perhaps even down here, one of Lawrence's crew was either dead or near dead. Either way, the Baron had gotten his hands on the man's equipment and had clearly just managed to suit up with it.

And I was what he was aiming at.

"Run!" I shouted at Amber and Hannah even as I did the dumbest possible thing I could have: I charged him.

I was correct in that I was his target. The Baron let out a deliriously happy roar as he unleashed a gout of flame at me. I leaped to the right and the flame sizzled past me. I crashed into a couple of cartons. Some human skin spilled out. Nice.

Flame was now roaring between me, Amber and Hannah, creating a vast curtain between us. The girls, seeing that we had run out of time, were hustling the people up the stairs. Some were still unfocused and unclear on what was happening; others were starting to come out of it a little faster. Either way, though, it was still hideously slow.

The Baron whirled to face me again and unleashed another blast of flame. I threw myself in the other direction and now the entire place was roaring with fire.

"This is all your fault!" the Baron was screaming. I was tempted to shout back that I wasn't the one using a flamethrower, but it hardly seemed to be the best time for snappy rejoinder, especially since I was aware of what he was talking about. He knew that I had brought the Body Men in, and they were wreaking havoc upstairs while I was busy helping with the escape of their drink sponsors. He swung the flamethrower around toward me. *"If not for you—!"*

I didn't wait for another shot. I leaped forward, somersaulting as the next blast of flame roared over my head. I came up within two feet of the Baron and swung. He ducked back, but I drove my right leg forward and connected. He gasped and doubled over, and an upward thrust from my left arm connected. His head snapped back and I came straight at him. I took a moment to grab the nozzle of his flamethrower and pulled as hard as I could. It ripped clear of the hose and I tossed it aside as I continued to pound on the Baron.

But even though he was still in pain, and was now unarmed, he was still fast. Incredibly fast. He brought his arms up and blocked my attack. Then he spun and slammed his foot into my gut. It sent me flying and I crashed to the ground a few feet away.

The entire place was going up in flames. Out the corner of my eye, I saw Amber pushing up the last of the victims. Hannah was already gone, doubtless having gone up ahead of her sister. It was just me and the Baron.

I started to scramble to my feet, but the Baron was already there. He struck two quick blows to the side of my head, sending me to my knees, and then drove another shot under my chin. My head snapped back and I went down. I tried to get up and something crashed into the side of my head. It was a piece of furniture, snapping as it collided with my skull.

I fell backwards onto the floor and tried to get up once more.

Nothing doing. My mind was going a mile a minute, but my body might as well have been dead already. I tried to bring my hands up to defend myself, but I couldn't convince them to move.

The Baron was just a few feet away, and he was still holding the exhaust from the flamethrower, even though it wasn't connected to anything. He started wailing away on me and I couldn't do a damned thing except take it.

"*You think this is over?*" He seemed oblivious to the fact that the basement was a cracking inferno around us. *"You couldn't be more wrong! I'm leaving behind your fried corpse and I'll—"*

A single blast exploded over the sound of the crackling flame. The Baron staggered, clutched at his shoulder, his eyes opening wide in surprise.

It was Hannah. She'd come back down the stairway and she had a gun in her hand. She fired once again at the Baron, and a third time.

He staggered from the repeated impact. Each bullet that struck caused screams of pain from him. I didn't know whether she was hitting him with wood or silver bullets; either way was going to cause him more damage than would standard bullets.

"Get away from him!" she shouted, keeping the gun level.

The Baron backed up and suddenly let out a horrific scream. He had stepped directly into a bank of flame and the unexpected contact caused him to go up. He screeched, slamming his arms at his own body, and Hannah made her way around as the Baron backed off. Suddenly we heard cracking from overhead. So did he. The Baron looked upward just in time to see a huge chunk of blazing ceiling come down upon him. The Baron only had enough time to let out a single terrified scream and then he vanished beneath a falling chunk of wood.

I barely noticed, because Hannah was busy reaching down and grabbing my hand. She pulled me to my feet and I had just enough time to say, "Thanks."

"Save it," she said, the air choking out around us. "We've got to—"

The obvious thing to say after "we've got to" was "get out of here," but we didn't have the opportunity. More of the ceiling was crashing down, including the entire area by the stairs. In the few seconds that it took Hannah to get me to my feet, we were surrounded on all sides.

Neither of us had much in the way of moisture in our bodies. If we went in any direction, we would be touched by flame and go up almost instantly.

"We have a problem," said Hannah in a low voice.

I was looking around and that was when I spotted the one thing that could be our salvation: the large coffin that I'd seen when we first arrived.

"C'*mon*!" I shouted, grabbing her by the wrist. The coffin didn't seem to be lighting up and I was beginning to wonder just what the hell it was made out of. I threw it open. Green cloth lined the interior and it fluttered a bit from the wind whistling in. "*Get in!*"

"Are you shitting me?" She did not, to put it mildly, seemed enthused.

I had no time for screwing around. I grabbed her by the waist, shouted, "Not arguing!" and practically threw her down into the coffin. She slammed into it heavily and I clambered atop her.

"*You're nuts!*"

"*You see another way out?*" I shouted at her and when no response immediately came, I continued, "*Then shut up!*"

And with that pronouncement, I slammed the top of the coffin down atop us.

Immediately the sound of burning diminished, but it was still hot as hell inside the coffin. A bit of smoke had filled it up when I closed the lid, but that didn't bother me particularly, nor was it going to bother Hannah.

That didn't deter her, however. "Get off me!" she said.

I did my best. I twisted my way around in the coffin so that we were pressed up against each other, rather than me lying atop her. As I squirmed around, I felt my body up against the wall of the coffin, trying to determine the heat on the other side. It didn't seem quite as bad as I was anticipating; the thickness of the coffin's wood was serving as protection. Unfortunately I couldn't predict how long it was going to last.

"Will you—?" Hannah was still trying to adjust herself around.

"*Knock it off*!" I snarled in her face. *"You think I like this? You think this is where I wanna be? I'm trying not to burn to death! And if you don't like that, then you can just get the hell outta here. Okay, pretty pretty princess?"*

Her mouth was still open, and then she closed it with an audible click. "Fine," she said.

"Fine," I replied.

We lay there in the coffin for a good, long time. The flames were licking at the outside, but they didn't seem determined enough to break through. Still, we couldn't count on anything.

But there was nowhere for us to go.

And so we continued to lie there. The heat appeared to be increasing, but it was difficult to determine by how much. Hannah had ceased yapping at me, which was good. I was certain that our time was limited, though.

"Why did you change me?" I said abruptly.

She stared at me in surprise. "You're kidding."

"We may die any minute." I sounded perfectly reasonable. "Might as well ask while we have the time."

"Go away."

"Love to. Can't."

We remained that way as the minutes ticked on. Hannah kept making an effort to look everywhere but at me. Then, frustrated, she said, "Don't you want to know where the other humans are?"

"I figured you and Amber got them upstairs to safety." Smoke was starting to waft through the coffin lid. Things were not looking good. "And then you came back down to try and help me. Which is, frankly, the part of all this I can't figure out. So which, once again, brings me around to asking why—?"

"Because you looked cute, okay?"

That stopped me cold. "Cute?"

"Yeah. You were cute." She sounded both exasperated and also chagrined. "Okay? I know you want there to be some long, involved story. There should be something huge involved. But the simple truth is that you looked cute, and sad, and lost, and I decided to make you mine. It was the first time I—" Her voice caught, but before I could ask her, she pushed her way through it. "It was the first time I'd ever converted anyone. First time.

Ever. Okay? And you were this hunter who was just going to get himself killed, and I changed you, and then I chickened out."

"Chickened out?"

"Yeah, I chickened out, okay? Would you stop saying the last word or two of everything I say?"

"Sorry."

She let out an exasperated breath. "And yes, I chickened out. I suddenly felt this great…I dunno…responsibility for you, and it scared the hell out of me, so I ditched you. Okay? I kicked you over to Duncan and figured he'd take care of you as well, if not better, than I would. All right? Happy?"

"I don't know if the word 'happy' is what I'd…" Then I saw the look in her face. "Yeah, fine. I'm happy."

"Good."

"Swell."

"Because—"

Suddenly we heard a thundering from all around us. Instinctively we threw our arms around each other as we heard whatever the hell remained around us crash in upon itself. The walls of the coffin shuddered under the impact as we held each other tightly. My eyes were closed and I was reasonably sure that Hannah's were closed as well.

The falling crash seemed to take forever, although it probably only lasted a few seconds. The entire time I expected the coffin to shatter under the impact, delivering us into the flames that would doubtlessly devour us in seconds. But it did not happen. Long after the crashing stopped, I continued to hold Hannah tightly. And then, slowly but definitively, the shaking stopped. Not only that, but the growing heat that I had felt from the outside of the coffin ceased as well. Whatever had been devouring us was slowly subsiding, eating itself instead.

Slowly I opened my eyes as I heard the last of the flame sizzling to a halt. Hannah's eyes were still closed; she opened hers seconds after I did. She looked around in the same puzzled manner that I had. "I don't believe it," she whispered.

"Me neither."

Minutes passed and there seemed to be no further indication of fire. Then, slowly, I pushed up against the lid.

Nothing happened. It didn't move in the slightest.

"Push harder," she said, which was completely unnecessary because I was already pushing as hard as I could. But I wasn't especially inclined to admit that, and so I pushed once more, making sure to scrunch my face up somewhat so that she could easily determine for herself that I was giving it everything I had and more besides.

None of it made the slightest difference. It still didn't budge.

That was when my cell phone went off.

We were both silent for a moment and then Hannah said drily, "You wanna get that?"

It wasn't an easy endeavor. I had to twist around somewhat to get my hand down to it and, the moment it was clutched in my palm, it slipped out. Fortunately Hannah managed to snag it and she brought it up to my face, snapping it open. "Yeah?" I said because I honestly wasn't sure what else I could possibly say.

"*Vince*!" It was Amber's voice. "*Oh, thank God. Are you and Hannah still down there?!*"

"Yup."

"*Where?*"

"There was a coffin down here. We managed to climb in before the whole place collapsed."

There was a pause and I could practically hear the thoughts running through her head. Then she apparently had the professionalism to focus her attention elsewhere. "*Good. Just stay put. We'll be down to get you as quickly as we can.*"

"What the hell happened, anyway?"

"*Fire from the basement that moved upstairs before we could stop it.*"

"How far upstairs?"

"*All the way.*"

It took me a few moments to fully wrap myself around that one. "Uhm...Amber...where are you, exactly?"

"*Outside where this place used to be. Don't worry: we have a crew at work. Utility outfits and everything. This isn't the first time we've had to deal with a building collapse.*"

"*Collapse?*" I promptly beat myself up mentally. Hannah was right; I *did* spend way too much time repeating the ends of other peoples' sentences. "The building collapsed?"

"Sections of it, yeah. But don't worry, it's under control."

"Terrific. Just swell."

"We're gonna get down there as fast as we can. Shouldn't be more than a couple of hours."

It had to be. If it took most of the night, Hannah and I were going to be coming out in broad daylight. As it was it was going to be difficult getting under cover again even if they got us out in just a few hours. It wasn't as if the daylight would kill us, but both of us would have problems that would be fairly obvious to a bunch of vampire hunters.

But there was no point in harping on that; certainly not to Amber, in any event. "Okay. Just hurry up, okay?"

"Hurrying."

I snapped shut the telephone and stared at Hannah. She just stared back at me, waiting to tell her what was happening. I filled her in as quickly as I could. When I was done, she still stared at me. Finally she said, "And if they crack us open and it's daylight?"

I tried to come up with a delicate way to address it and nothing came to mind.

"We're screwed," I said.

She took that in, considered it. Then she shrugged. "Okay, then."

I wasn't sure how to react to that. "How is that okay?"

"I took it into consideration."

I almost managed to laugh at that. "Really? I'd like to know your logic."

"Well," and she shrugged once more. "I figured if I was going to come back down here for you, it was making up…at least a little bit…for my walking out on you in the first place. And I figured we'd make it out, but if we didn't then, y'know…we'd find other stuff to do."

"And what kind of other stuff did—?"

She brought her arm around my neck and kissed me. It was deep and passionate and a hundred times better than anything I'd imagined in my head. Our tongues intertwined and I felt her fangs extending, as did my own.

Thus did we pass the time.

Twenty-three
My Understanding

They didn't reach us before morning. In point of fact, they didn't reach us until the following evening. By that point, Hannah and I had become…

…very familiar.

When we first heard the noises of rescuers coming, I checked my watch. I breathed a sigh of relief when I saw how much time had passed. I rousted Hannah, who was sound asleep by that point, and said to her the only two words that meant anything at that point: "Get dressed."

She did so as quickly as she could.

The phone had ceased ringing some hours earlier, having run out of power. Now, though, we could hear the shouts and excitement of voices as they drew closer to where we were. I kept looking at my wristwatch, assuring me that it had taken them a full day to get to us.

"Okay, look," I started to say.

"We say nothing. It didn't happen."

The brusque response from someone who was just finishing the elaborate endeavor of fastening her pants next to me caught me somewhat by surprise. "Excuse me…?"

"Nothing. Happened."

"Yeah, I love how you turned it into two individual sentences. But what do you mean nothing happened? Or nothing. Happened."

She smiled at me and stroked my face. "Honey, I am who I am."

"I don't think you know who you are."

"It was great."

"It. Meaning the thing that didn't happen."

"Yeah. That." She actually seemed a bit sheepish, which was nice to see. "It was great. And entertaining. And it made me feel better than I have in a long time." Then her face grew serious. "But I am who I am, and who I am isn't much for feeling better for a long time. Things are transitory, y'know? We're kidding ourselves if we think anything else."

"I still don't—"

She took my hand and squeezed it firmly, and there was genuine sadness in her voice. "Vince...we both know we're vampires. And our families are vampire hunters. Sooner or later, we know how this is going to end. So embarking upon a real relationship: it's absurd. It's ridiculous. If we try, it's just going to end badly, so better that we don't try. Y'know?"

"You're saying that we shouldn't try to have anything in our lives aside from just trying to exist because sooner or later our families are going to end us?"

She nodded. "Do you disagree?" she said quietly. "Do you?"

I lowered my gaze, unable to hold hers. "No. I guess I don't."

"Okay, then." She kissed me on the cheek and then we waited.

A few minutes later we heard our names being shouted and we responded immediately. Our shouts guided our rescuers to us and finally the top was broken away. We coughed violently, the fresh air rushing into our lungs. Lawrence was standing there, as was Amber and several other people. Just as Amber had said, they were attired in uniforms worn by crews involved in cleaning damaged areas. I didn't see anyone else around, but I could hear construction going on upstairs, over our heads. "Thank God," said Lawrence in a gravely voice. He looked like he'd been awake the entire time. Amber looked equally wasted, but they were clearly both relieved to be pulling us out of the rubble. "We thought sure you'd suffocated. We thought we'd find a couple of corpses."

"We had holes," I said. "In the coffin." It was complete nonsense. We hadn't thought about breathing at all because it wasn't really a priority.

"Thank God," he said again. Then: "Let's go."

The basement looked like a disaster area. I could now, for the first time, see why it was that the coffin had escaped the full impact of the firestorm. Concrete had fallen on top of us. There was debris melted all around us, huge smoked piles of rubble that had been transformed partway into briquettes. But the coffin itself had been spared, or at least mostly spared. There were huge streaks of black and brown on the wood; large chunks had been scorched. Yet it had held together, so that at least was something.

Lawrence and Amber urged us up the shattered stairs. Where there had been steps, there was now a ramp stretched down. It was shaky but enough for us to climb up anyway. "Come on," said Amber. She wasn't looking or sounding especially jealous, and that was a good thing. She needed to be professional. We all did.

The moment we got to the top of what had been the stairs, I saw where flames had devoured the upper sections of the building. "This way," said Lawrence, leading us toward what was obviously an exit somewhere in the rubble. We followed, not seeing any reason to argue over it.

"Here," said Amber. She tossed us jackets and hard hats. "Hurry up." Quickly we did as instructed and moments later we looked like we belonged to whatever crew was working its way through the place. As we made our way through the rubble, we encountered other workers in the rubble, clearing stuff away. There were holes in the wall and night's shadow was seeping through.

In short order we made it outside. The place was swarming with police, with construction workers, with everyone and anyone who could possibly have been involved with the clean-up. "Stand up straight" murmured Lawrence, and we immediately did so. A truck was waiting right there for us, and I saw Amanda in the back, gesturing for us to hurry the hell up. We did as we were instructed.

"We're aboard," Lawrence called and in short order the truck was easing its way through the rubble and destruction. Lawrence and Amber were seated up front; we were in a separate section in the back.

"Where's the rest of the crew?" I said.

"Gone," said Amanda. "We sent them on back. As soon as city officials and crews started showing up, Lawrence decided to minimize our on-set presence."

There was something in her voice that sounded different. It came across as formal, distant.

"Okay, well...that was pretty wise of him," I said slowly, "I guess."

"I guess," echoed Amanda. "They took your cycle back to the hotel. It'll be there waiting for you." She was pulling out a medical bag, opening it up with an official snap.

"We don't need the bag, Mom," Hannah assured her. "We're fine. Really."

"Yeah, we're fine. We were completely protected."

"Were you." Amanda continued to stare at us and then she snapped the medical bag closed once more. "Yes. Of course you were."

A long, uneasy silence then. Finally, unable to stand it, unsure of what was wrong but certain that I wasn't going to like it, I said tentatively, "Is something—?"

"Shut up," said Amanda.

It caught me off guard. I stopped talking.

Amanda closed her eyes in temporary pain. "Sorry," she said immediately. "It's not your fault. You're just trying to survive."

I immediately felt a deep chill down my spine. "I...I'm not sure what you're..."

"Stop it, Vincent." Amanda put up her hands as if she could physically make me stop talking. "Just stop it. And listen. Very carefully. Are you listening?"

I nodded. It was the only response that I could think of. I glanced at Hannah and she looked as confused as I did.

Apparently satisfied that she had my silence, Amanda took in the both of us and then said something that completely stunned me:

"You think a mother doesn't know her own daughter? Doesn't know who she is? *What* she is? I want you to answer me one question and one question only, Hannah: Have you killed anyone?" When a stunned Hannah didn't respond, Amanda continued as if the question had somehow been unclear. "Have you, in your pursuit of blood to drink, killed anyone?"

Hannah looked to me. I was stunned. I had nothing to say. Besides, it wasn't as if I had an answer. She looked back to her mother, who was waiting for an answer. "No," she said, her voice barely above a whisper.

"Are you sure—?"

"No...I mean, yes. I'm sure. Just, you know, drank from the volunteers who were—"

"Never mind, I don't need to know beyond that." She saw the astounded, stupid look in my face. "Come on, Vincent," she continued in vague annoyance. "Do you seriously think I don't know what my daughter is? Do you think I can't do the math and figure out that you would have run out of air inside that coffin long before we got to you?"

"There was a hole," I started to say. Then I saw the look in her eyes and silenced myself once more.

Hannah took a deep gulp.

"Are you going to tell Dad?" asked Hannah. Her voice was very small, like a child who had been caught out with her hand in the cookie jar.

"So he could drive a stake in your heart?" said Amanda. "If you had a daughter, would you do that to her? Would you?" and she addressed the question to me.

"My mother would with me," was all I said.

"Yes, I suspected as much," said Amanda ruefully. "Perhaps it's simply a mother/daughter thing. Or perhaps your mother is just more devoted to the cause than I am. All I know is that I'm not going to be responsible for the death of my little girl. Someone else was, and when I find him, I will gladly dispatch him. But that is something to be withheld for a different conversation, yes?" When Hannah nodded eagerly, Amanda folded her arms and looked from one of us to the other. "So here," she continued, "is what's going to be. You are going to inform the family that the two of you have fallen in love."

"What?" We spoke simultaneously and in shock, and it was Hannah who continued. "Mom, I hate to mention this, but I'm gay."

"No, you're not," said Amanda.

"No, I'm not," Hannah admitted. "But—"

"Your time in the coffin with Vincent turned you around. You can deal with that, can't you, Vincent." It was not a question.

"I…" I began to say, and I honestly didn't know what the next words out of my mouth were going to be.

It didn't matter. "Good," said Amanda as if the question had been settled.

"Wait! No…what about Amber?"

Amanda clearly had an answer ready. She had obviously thought this entire business through. "Amber," she said, "should be getting married after Hannah anyway. She is the younger daughter. It'll be difficult for her, but she'll adjust. I'm trying to save both my children so they can live out their lives."

"Are you kidding?" said a clearly appalled Hannah. "Amber's gonna kill me!"

"No, she won't, and you know she won't," said Amanda dismissively. "She won't be happy. She's spit, she'll snarl, she'll do everything a girl her age would do. Ultimately, though, the two of you are sisters, and that's how it's going to play out. She'll forgive you. Love happens. She'll be there when you get married…"

"Married?!" Once again the both of us were speaking as one.

"Yes, married," said Amanda with the clear intent that there was no room for negotiation on this. "You'll get married within the next twenty-four hours. You'll be very happy about it, and we will sell it to both your sister and your father. Hannah, you will stay here with your husband. And everyone will live happily ever after. Are we all clear on this? And," she continued before Hannah could speak, "if you have any protest to this, if you have any problems with it at all, then I'm going to tell the man driving this vehicle that you are both vampires and he's going to stop the vehicle and come back here and kill you both. Do we understand each other?"

Hannah's mouth was moving but no words were emerging. I did the only thing I could think of. I pointed at Hannah and said to her mother, "She turned me into one."

"How wonderful for the both of you." Amanda was clearly not impressed. "Again: do we have an understanding?"

Hannah and I looked at each other. There was nothing to say.

And then I thought about our time together in the coffin, and all the excuses that Hannah had made, and how she talked about how it all meant nothing.

And I smiled.

"Okay," I said.

Hannah flopped to the floor and rolled her eyes. Then her gaze rested on me for a long while.

And she smiled.

"Fine," she said.

I expected Amber to hit me right across the face.

She didn't.

Instead she kicked me as hard as she could.

We were in the lobby of the Plaza 25 hotel, seated in a pair of extremely nice red plush chairs. I thought that the surroundings might somehow quash whatever aggressive attitudes she might display. As it turned out, I could not have been more wrong.

I let out a startled gasp. It hurt like a son of a bitch; if there was one thing Amber Singer had not learned, it was how to pull her punches. I grabbed at the knee and held it, moaning softly. Being a vampire, it hadn't hurt me as much as it would have if I'd been a simple human. On the other hand, if I'd been human, then my future mother-in-law would not have been able to hold the prospect of being killed over my head.

"*That* was mature," I managed to get out.

She was clearly fuming as she got to her feet and started to storm across the lobby. Her fists were closed tightly and I could see her shoulders beginning to shake in what was sure to be a crying fit to end all crying fits.

And then, as she was almost to the large glass door at the far side of the lobby, she came to a stop. Her hands were still curled into fists. She stayed there for a long moment and then turned around and started heading back toward me. I moaned inwardly. Now what? Was she going to start wailing on my upper body as well? If she did, what was I supposed to do? Defend myself? A guy versus girl battle was going to get every person in the lobby on her side no matter what. Indeed, there were already a number of folks watching to see what the angry young woman was going to do next. The only option I was really going to have open to me was to sit there and take it. And why not, when you get down to it? I had just wounded her terribly. I'd spouted a nonsensical story about how I was now in love with her sister and I was going to marry her. It was absurd; I felt that Amber had to know that somehow. If she wanted to whomp away on me while we sat in the lobby of her parents' hotel, what the hell was I supposed to say or do about it? Nothing, that's what. I should just man up and take it in the way that I knew I had coming to me.

She walked right up to me, stood in front of me with her fists still shaking. If she had any reason to suspect I was a vampire, she would have killed me right there. Hell, I partly thought she was going to do it even though she thought I wasn't.

Say something. Say anything.

"Sorry." It was all I could think of. And I shrugged.

She stood over me and then she gently took either side of my head and kissed it on the top. I looked up in surprise.

"Be good to her," said Amber, and then she walked away from me.

I had no idea what to make of it, and decided that it would probably be best if I didn't make any attempt at all.

I knew at that moment that Hannah was upstairs, explaining to her father her sudden change in sexual persuasion. Although part of me thought that he would be appreciative of the shift, there was also the concern that he might come gunning for me anyway. So I decided that the best place to be would be elsewhere.

And I knew just the elsewhere to be at.

Minutes later I was crossing the bridge to Astoria and eventually I was rolling up to the hospital where I had left Molly. The entire time I knew that I couldn't be sure she was still there. But somehow it seemed worth it to check in on her. I had, after all, left her in not the greatest of positions.

As it so happened, she was in fact alive.

It was after hours, and the nurse at the front desk told me with a faint scold in her voice that yes, I could visit, but it would only be for a few minutes before they then threw me out. I assured her that would be more than enough time.

I looked in on Molly. She seemed to be sound asleep. I stood there for a couple of minutes and then started to turn away.

"Are you here to turn me?"

Molly's voice, all right, and naturally the one thing she would have asked of me. With a deep sigh, I turned to face her. She was staring at me hopefully.

"Do you want me to?" I asked.

Her jaw twitched as she lay there and stared at me. Then, somewhat to my surprise, she turned away. "I'm not sure," she said softly.

This caught me a bit by surprise. Curious, I said, "May I ask why not?"

"I dunno." She managed a shrug. "Stuff my parents said while they were here. About how much they love me and that kinda crap."

"People telling you they love you is never crap, Molly. It's a good thing. A terrific thing."

"I know." I saw that her eyes were tearing up. I took a tissue from a box nearby her bed and dried the moisture on her cheeks. "I know," I said again.

"I'm so sorry I betrayed you..."

"Don't worry about it. It all turned out."

Molly stared at me for a long moment. "I don't know whether I should want to be like you or not."

"No," I said flatly.

She seemed surprised. "Why not?"

"Because I'm dead, Molly," I said to her with all the patience I could summon. "I'm dead, and the vast, vast majority of the world is alive. And that means a lot. Being alive means everything. You're much too young to embrace the...existence that I have. You've barely started your life. Live what's in front of you," I told her gently. "Enjoy the company of the people who love you for what you are. Get strong. Get healthy. Have a lover, or lovers. Have a child, or children. Be and do whatever you want to be and do, and leave vampires in the shadows where they belong. Can you do that for me?"

More tears ran down her face and for several minutes I did

nothing but clean her cheeks. Finally I managed to get her to a point where she was calm again and then, very softly, she whispered, "Yeah. I can do that for you."

"Good." I embraced her then, held her tightly before releasing her. I got up from the chair I'd been sitting on and I started to head for the door.

"Vince," she said slowly. "If I'm very old, and I've done everything I want to do…can I maybe look you up then?"

I smiled. "Absolutely."

And then I was gone.

Twenty-four
My Mattress

The wedding was very simple. The Singer family was there, of course. Kubrick actually seemed happy for the first time since I'd encountered him because, for once, I was no longer a threat to his interests in Amber. This was, in fact, no big deal, because I was pretty damned sure that—with me off the table—Amber was free to pursue whomever she wanted, and that was *not* going to be Kubrick. The reason I was sure of this was because I overheard Amber and Hannah speaking before the wedding and when Hannah brought up Kubrick as a possible beau, Amber made some of the most sickening noises I'd ever heard a human being produce. Then, when she was done making those noises, the sisters laughed together. They laughed.

It sounded good to hear them laughing together. Whatever the hell else had gone on between them while they were growing up, it apparently had been finally set aside or resolved or something. Who was responsible for that? Yours truly.

The actual ceremony was performed by none other than Jeremiah Salk. No reason he shouldn't have since he was, among other things, a minister or reverend or some damned thing that you did on line to make it okay for you to perform a wedding ceremony. This, however, did not give me a warm feeling. All it did was remind me that Salk was somehow involved at a higher end of the spectrum than I normally inhabited. Sure, we'd trashed the club in Newark, but there were other clubs that operated on that kind of level. Whether Salk knew they were vampires or not, I had no idea. If he didn't know, then someone had to bring him up to speed. If he did know, then how much *more* did he know? There was simply no way to tell, and determining that bit of business was going to be extremely difficult for me, at least in the short run. In the long run, however, there was going to be far more than met the eye.

Amanda's eyes were closely upon Hannah and I as we stood up at the front of the convocation and said our vows. The edges of her mouth were in a small, upturned smile. Lawrence, he was still scowling. I didn't know what his deal was, but he still seemed suspicious of me for reasons he couldn't quite articulate. It might well have been involved with the fact that his gay eldest daughter had suddenly turned straight in order to be with this guy that he had grown distinctively unfond of.

Whatever. He'd come here to marry off a daughter and he wound up succeeding in that endeavor, so he had nothing left to complain about.

We had a nice dinner with the new in-laws and my mom and soon everyone was heading back to, or off to, where they were supposed to be. By the time 9 o'clock was rolling around, everyone was off doing their own thing. The only ones remaining in my house were Hannah, me, and of course my mom. And Mom had made arrangements to go stay over with Mrs. Rosen's family that evening. "You two should have the place to yourselves," she told us, and I didn't offer any real argument.

Then she added, "Oh! And hold on. I have something for you." She exited the living room and we heard her run upstairs. The thumping noise from her bedroom made it sound like she was crawling in or under something. Hannah, who had changed out of her wedding dress into a simple blouse and slacks, looked at me in confusion. I just shrugged.

A couple minutes later, Mom came back down the stairs. She was carrying what appeared to be a valise, and she placed it on the table between us. "Open it," she said.

I clicked the snaps on the old valise and opened it wide. Then I just gaped.

It was filled with money. Lots and lots of money.

"Your dowry," said Mom cheerfully.

"My..." I couldn't believe it.

Hannah, slightly more verbal than I—which was not an inconsiderable accomplishment considering the circumstances—was able to say, "You had it all the time?"

"Of course I did. It was tucked away securely in the mattress. I never trusted banks."

"*Screw the banks*!" I finally managed to find my voice. "You didn't tell *me*. You lied to my face, Mom!"

"Of course I did," she said yet again. "I didn't want you to know."

"Why the hell not!?"

"Because I love you, Vince," she said matter-of-factly, as if this was a simple fact that I should have known and that would explain everything. "But frankly, I saw this as an opportunity and didn't want to waste it. After all, how else am I ever going to be sure I have grandchildren?"

"Actually," said Hannah, who sounded utterly convinced, "that makes perfect sense to me."

"Thank you!" said Mom, and she embraced Hannah, which was the first time she'd ever actually held my wife close. "That's so kind of you to say."

That evening, Mom was off at the Rosens and Hannah and I were together in, of all places, my old bedroom. We stood there, staring at each other, each of us unsure of what move to make and who should be the first to make it. Or if any move should be made at all.

"I'm gonna leave, y'know," Hannah finally said to me.

"Yeah?"

"Yeah. Once my parents are gone from here, I'll be..." She indicated with her head the general direction she was going to be heading.

"Oh. Okay," I said, which was all I could think of to say.

"I'm gonna leave you the dowry. I mean, if you want to give me a few bucks for me being on the road, that's fine, but it's not a deal breaker."

"Good to hear."

"I mean, it's silly for me to stay around here. The only reason I came to New York was to be with my sister for her wedding and, well, I fouled that up pretty well."

"Yup. You did."

She bristled slightly. "Not that I didn't have help. I mean, you helped screw things up, too."

"Oh yeah. Big time."

"So we're…y'know…" She seemed to be having trouble focusing. "There's no reason to…"

"No reason at all."

We were silent.

Then four quick steps and she had come around the bed. She threw her arms about me and my lips merged into hers, and everything after that was something of a blur.

And as we dissolved into a blur of passion, all I could think was…

Grandchildren? Uh boy.

About the Author

Peter David is a prolific author whose career, and continued popularity, spans nearly two decades. He has worked in every conceivable media: Television, film, books (fiction, non-fiction and audio), short stories, and comic books, and acquired followings in all of them.

In the literary field, Peter has had over seventy novels published, including numerous appearances on the *New York Times* Bestsellers List. His novels include *Tigerheart, Darkness of the Light, Sir Apropos of Nothing* and the sequel *The Woad to Wuin, Knight Life, Howling Mad,* and the Psi-Man adventure series. He is the co-creator and author of the bestselling *Star Trek: New Frontier* series for Pocket Books, and has also written such Trek novels as *Q-Squared, The Siege, Q-in-Law, Vendetta, I,* Q (with John deLancie), *A Rock and a Hard Place* and *Imzadi*. He produced the three *Babylon 5* Centauri Prime novels, and has also had his short fiction published in such collections as *Shock Rock, Shock Rock II,* and *Otherwere,* as well as *Isaac Asimov's Science Fiction Magazine* and *The Magazine of Fantasy and Science Fiction*.

Peter's comic book resume includes an award-winning twelve-year run on *The Incredible Hulk,* and he has also worked on such varied and popular titles as *Supergirl, Young Justice, Soulsearchers and Company, Aquaman, Spider-Man, Spider-Man 2099, X-Factor, Star Trek, Wolverine, The Phantom, Sachs & Violens, The Dark Tower,* and many others. He has also written comic book related novels, such as *The Incredible Hulk: What Savage Beast,* and co-edited *The Ultimate Hulk* short story collection. Furthermore, his opinion column, "But I Digress . . . ," has been running in the industry trade newspaper *The Comic Buyers's Guide* for nearly a decade, and in that time has been the paper's consistently most popular feature and was also collected into a trade paperback edition.

Peter is also the writer for two popular video games: *Shadow Complex* and *Spider-Man: Edge of Time.*

Peter is the co-creator, with popular science fiction icon Bill Mumy (of *Lost in Space* and *Babylon 5* fame) of the Cable Ace Award-nominated science fiction series *Space Cases,* which ran for two seasons on Nickelodeon. He has written several scripts for the Hugo Award winning TV series *Babylon 5,* and the sequel series, *Crusade.* He has also written several films for Full Moon Entertainment and co-produced two of them, including two installments in the popular *Trancers* series, as well as the science fiction western spoof *Oblivion,* which won the Gold Award at the 1994 Houston International Film Festival for best Theatrical Feature Film, Fantasy/Horror category.

Peter's awards and citations include: the Haxtur Award 1996 (Spain), Best Comic script; OZCon 1995 award (Australia), Favorite International Writer; Comic Buyers Guide 1995 Fan Awards, Favorite writer; Wizard Fan Award Winner 1993; Golden Duck Award for Young Adult Series (Starfleet Academy), 1994; UK Comic Art Award, 1993; Will Eisner Comic Industry Award, 1993. He lives in New York with his wife, Kathleen, and his four children, Shana, Gwen, Ariel, and Caroline.

28323296R00140

Made in the USA
Lexington, KY
13 December 2013